Blood, Sweat, and Fears

HORROR INSPIRED BY THE 1970s

Blood, Sweat, and Fears

HORROR INSPIRED BY THE 1970s

EDITED BY
David T. Neal
& Christine M. Scott

N*P

NOSETOUCH PRESS

Chicago

Blood, Sweat, and Fears: Horror Inspired by the 1970s

ISBN-13: 978-1-944286-07-1

Published by Nosetouch Press
P.O. Box 11506
Chicago, Illinois 60611

www.nosetouchpress.com

For more information, contact Nosetouch Press:
info@nosetouchpress.com

Cover & Interior Design by Christine M. Scott
www.clevercrow.com

Table of Contents

Vivid Vinyl Visions

Banse itched to get home, liberate his fretless, four-string electric Ibanez bass guitar (which sported a groovy sunburst finish) from its case, and improvise several new, low-pitched rhythms. The air conditioning in the modest two-story suburban abode he'd inherited from his eccentric aunt four years earlier functioned, whereas the cooling system at Johnson Art Supplies had conked out half an hour into his Monday shift. The temperature outside had crept up to eighty degrees—quite odd for the tenth of April. Banse generally enjoyed his part-time gig, but the heat and an unusually high number of hostile customers conflated into an unpleasant, headache-inducing nightmare of a day. He longed to unwind in his favorite easy chair with a joint and then thump out an array of primal notes.

His boss, Marie Johnson, who at age twenty-four was five years younger than her clerk, approached and said, "You may as well knock off an hour early. I can close up. I doubt we'll get much more traffic. Thanks for taking the brunt of the verbal abuse from those assholes earlier."

Banse appreciated Marie's potty mouth.

He thanked his employer for the early furlough, walked out to the Wallace Falls town square lot in which his 1976 Ford Torino sat, climbed in, and revved the engine.

He piloted the vehicle to Argyle Avenue and parked outside his favorite record shop: Alley Cat's LPs. He'd been looking forward to this day since earlier in 1978, when he'd read in *Crawdaddy* magazine that his favorite band would release a blues album that spring. Banse intended to jam along after he'd listened to both sides a couple of times.

Inside, he made a beeline for the new releases section and flipped through an assortment of cardboard sleeves until he found what he sought: an LP titled *Dew Point* by Nadine and the Piglets.

En route to the cash register, he strode past two kids who both held copies of the fresh Jethro Tull album.

At the counter, a svelte bunny clad in a white satin shirt rang up Banse's single purchase: seven-ninety-nine plus tax. She was no older than twenty, and her waist-length hair smelled of patchouli. Banse handed her a ten-dollar bill and welcomed her to keep the change. She flashed a peace sign with her fingers.

As Banse headed for his car, a violin tune caught his ear. At the front of an alley, a vagrant fiddled out a breathtaking melody. Like a sailor drawn by the voice of a siren, Banse approached the fellow, counted out six quarters, and gently placed the coins within the open case that sat to the musician's right. He studied the man, who looked at least sixty, and wondered how such a gifted string player had ended up on the streets. The bum wore badly-stained corduroy pants, hole-riddled sneakers, and a loose-fitting, button-down shirt. The men nodded to each other almost simultaneously, and both smiled.

Banse listened for five minutes until the tune's denouement, all the while mentally composing a singular bass accompaniment. The fiddler played three final notes, then bowed.

"Like, that was beyond fab," stammered Banse. "I'm a bassist, and..."

"Bought yourself an album there, son?" The vagrant pointed the tip of his bow at the shrinkwrapped sleeve that Banse held.

"Yeah. Do you...have you ever recorded?"

The hobo cackled and said, "Wait right there, bass man." He lumbered toward a detritus-filled shopping cart six feet down the alley and pulled out a slick garbage bag.

Banse had forgotten all about rushing home to relax. He'd been entranced by this peculiar individual's prowess on the violin.

The older man shambled back with a cardboard sleeve in hand. He proffered it toward Banse, who accepted it. He could tell from the weight that a piece of vinyl sat within. Banse studied the cover: black-and-white artwork depicted a shirtless, muscular man with a unicorn's head, claws for feet, and a trumpet in hand. Banse wondered what sort of embouchure one could muster with horse lips. Over the artwork were nine letters in a jagged font: AMDUSCIAS. The back cover had only these words: SIDE A—past & SIDE B—future.

"So you're on this album?"

"Oh yes. Along with a dozen other violinists."

"A dozen?"

"Maybe more. The session seems so long ago in my memory."

"Is Amduscias the name of the band or the front man or something else?"

Ignoring the question, the fiddler said, "You may have that copy for a dime."

"Ten measly cents? I couldn't."

"As a bassist, you will appreciate the rhythms thereon." The man's scratchy voice sounded confident and truthful. Banse hesitated, recalled the euphoric rush he'd felt when the electrifying violin melody had reached his ears, fished a coin out of his pocket, and handed it over. The homeless man pocketed the dime and said, "Thanks. I'll use this at the payphone tonight." He waggled a finger at the two albums that Banse held and asked, "Which will you listen to first?"

"Yours. It's been a pleasure meeting you. What's your name?"

"The tune's supreme, and he who plays it is incidental."

Banse dropped the issue. Some men prefer to be anonymous. He waved farewell and trotted toward his Torino.

The sun set as he drove to Bagley Road.

Home. In the front den, Banse placed the two records next to his Panasonic Technics turntable. Floor-to-ceiling shelves filled one wall and housed Banse's extensive record collection. Some of the albums had belonged to his aunt, but most had arrived on a moving truck when Banse migrated from Hollywood, California to the unfamiliar landscape of suburban Northeast Ohio. Out west, Banse had gigged in an impoverished but gifted four-piece blues band that ultimately disintegrated when the drummer and the saxophonist (a couple) split to live on a commune near Portland. Around that time, Aunt Colleen had notified Banse that she intended to bequeath her home and worldly possessions to him. Banse had taken a day job as a coffee shop barista to make ends meet between then and the time the pancreatic cancer claimed his father's sister. She left him the abode and thirty-two thousand dollars. That was four years earlier.

In the kitchen, Banse quenched his thirst with an iced tea as he reflected on the totally radical violin line that the bum had played. If the Amduscias LP contained similar melodies, Banse would love to thump along. He'd taken to inventing rhythms unlike the actual bass guitar parts on extant recordings to stay sharp and keep his improvisational skills up to snuff. He had not performed in public since January (when his most recent band had opted to go on hiatus due to disagreements over whether or not to add a sixth member in the form of the keyboardist's girlfriend, a flute virtuoso).

In the library, which contained an array of books on ghosts and hauntings (subject matter that had fueled Aunt Colleen's imagination to no end), Banse sat and smoked half a joint and forced the memories of the unpleasant customers out of his conscious mind. His friend Walter, the guitarist from the recently suspended band, had scored two ounces of fine Blueberry weed and had traded half of it in exchange for Banse's spare acoustic bass. Walter was creating a solo project on a four-track recorder and intended to play all the parts himself.

Pleasantly buzzed, Banse returned to the den and powered up his Marantz 2325 receiver, the one connected to the JBL speakers. Two stereo systems dominated the room: the ancient equipment that Aunt Colleen had left behind and the newer gear Banse had installed with some of the wonga he'd inherited. Banse no longer used the old stuff and kept putting off selling the components.

Banse pulled the Amduscias LP from its outer sleeve. There was no inner paper layer to protect it, but the vinyl's surface looked remarkably unblemished for a record that had been stored outdoors in a garbage sack for God only knew how long. Banse placed it on the turntable. The needle found the groove.

Banse plopped down on the couch to the sound of a trumpet bleating four bars of staccato notes in the key of A, followed by eight more bars of the lone instrument producing a smooth melodic line that concluded with a soft D whole note. Banse perceived the timbre and performance as bordering on divine: flawless intonation, an intriguing lead melody that he could imagine accompanying on bass, and a simple but clever chord structure.

The trumpet continued to weave strings of notes that Banse swayed to, but now a violin joined it. Could it be the old man from the alley? He wasn't sure, but the caliber of the musicianship matched. However, the fellow had mentioned that multiple string players appeared on the recording. Indeed, a second violin joined in just then, followed two bars later by a third and then a fourth.

Banse couldn't categorize the style of this bizarre tune, which defied pigeonholing. A tin whistle sang what sounded a bit like an Irish reel, but that segued smoothly into a jazzy duel between the trumpet and an electric guitar that lasted twelve bars (with the violins adding counterpoint for the second half), and then the melodies ceased as three percussionists (one on bongo drums, one with a rattle, and one with a bass drum) created catchy and complex rhythms in 4/4 time.

Banse could resist no longer. He removed his instrument from its case, plugged in to the practice amp that he kept in one corner, and flipped the power switch.

He listened to another measure of the awesome drumming, then joined in.

He hadn't been so inspired since the day his high school girlfriend had promised she'd at long last sleep with him if he dazzled her with some fretboard fireworks. His fingers glided up and down the fretless neck, dancing and jumping from one note to another, producing a bluesy tone that had to this point been absent from the music's gestalt.

Banse had a sudden hunch that he could predict where the chord progression was heading next: it would follow the traditional twelve-bar blues structure for thirty-six measures.

Banse should have been more surprised when his prognostication proved accurate, but the evening had begun to take on a dreamlike quality in which subconscious logic trumped the normal governing rules of existence. A dozen violins now played on the record, nine of them in unison with one another and three warbling away with different melodies that somehow wove around Banse's bass line in the most pleasing possible way.

The trumpet returned, clear and solid and soaring over the strings. Banse reacted to it by simplifying his part gradually until he was only playing chord roots.

Banse tried to guess what would occur after the blues section, and he imagined this piece would come to a close and there'd be a moment of silence before the next selection. It would consist of just two chords, D and G, alternating: two bars of D, two bars of G, and on and on. It would be in 3/4 time.

The next tune commenced and fit the prediction completely, opening with a simple piano melody. Banse nodded and tried to rationalize the uncanny accuracy of his guess by figuring he was just in tune with what had been going through the composer's head even as part of his consciousness whispered, "Something unnatural's going on."

Instead of pursuing that train of thought, he focused on the music. From the left stereo speaker came the sound of the trumpet sustaining a D for six beats, then G for two measures, then back to D.

As Banse thumped his bass, a certainty welled up in his consciousness: *I'm guiding the music now. The record is somehow following my lead.*

He tested his hypothesis by jumping to C. The piano and trumpet did likewise, and now both began to wend melodies alongside a single violin (the latter instrument's voice came from the right stereo speaker). Banse got goose-flesh as he sensed sentient entities in the room with him.

He felt a sense of wonder rather than fear. What magic had the alley bum gifted unto him? He opted to speculate later and focus now on jamming with whatever or whoever had somehow manifested in his den.

He had once gone through a phase of studying the melodic bass guitar style of a fellow named Dave Pegg (mostly known as a member of Fairport Convention, though Banse's favorite bit of his work appeared on an Amory Kane album titled *Just to be There),* and Banse now shifted into such a style, using all four strings on his bass to produce a melody instead of simple rhythms.

The trumpet and the violin fell silent for a moment, and then the trumpet honked out just the root and fifth and third of the chord while the violin played in precise unison with the low notes. Banse burst out laughing, amazed and delighted even as he was baffled by what was happening.

That's when the vision began.

The edges of the framed painting over the fireplace mantel wavered and vanished out of reality. The painting itself (a wooded landscape dense with pine trees) lost all of its colors and became vague black-and-white outlines and shapes that began to pulse and wiggle.

Banse recognized the anomalous visuals as the onset of a psychedelic experience and wondered if he'd somehow been dosed, but he didn't let the butterflies in his tummy distract him; he kept playing a melodic bass line, moving his fingers to repeat the riff he'd just invented in a higher octave.

He stared at what had once been the painting and was astonished to see it morph into something that resembled the way a film looks when one wears 3-D specs. He saw a familiar bed with a plush monkey next to a pillow, and he recognized the purple drapes and matching linens at once: the room of his high school girlfriend, Nora, whose virginity he had claimed the summer after their junior year. The vision was now in bright, hyper-real colors, and Banse thumped away as he watched the teenaged version of Nora, nude, climb atop the bed. *This isn't how it happened,* Banse thought, and then gaped as a naked Thomas Smith joined Nora on the purple sheet. Thomas had been Nora's sophomore-year boyfriend, and she'd sworn up and down that he and she had never done more than reach second base.

Banse diverted his gaze to the fretboard as he played a particularly tricky couple of bars, then looked back and watched Thomas nibble on Nora's neck. He was dimly aware that an oboe and a cello now jammed along with the ear candy that radiated from the speakers.

Banse felt simultaneously nauseous and aroused as he watched Nora pleasure Thomas. *Side A,* he thought. *Past.*

The phone rang. The vision dissipated at once, and the music stopped though the turntable still spun. Banse set his bass in a guitar stand and staggered toward the receiver in the kitchen.

"Hello?"

"Where are you, dude? The game's about to start." It was Walter, and Banse suddenly remembered that he and his friend had arranged to watch ABC's Monday Night Baseball on Walter's Magnavox Console television unit, which dwarfed Banse's Zenith tabletop tube.

"I should have called. I'm not feeling too well. Probably mild food poisoning." Banse lied on autopilot as he visualized Nora in bed with that jerk Thomas.

"Great. Mild. Get your ass over here. I ordered a pizza."

"Sorry. Just not up for it."

"Your loss, dude. Howard Cosell's in rare form."

"I'll call you tomorrow. Maybe we can jam."

"Bye."

Banse hung up, started toward the den, turned and looked at the telephone, walked back, and unplugged it from the wall jack.

He returned to the other room and flipped the record to its B-side. *Let's see what the future holds,* he thought.

As he positioned the LP on the turntable, the phone rang. Again.

Incredulous, Banse returned to the kitchen and verified that he'd unplugged the damned thing. Maybe an extension elsewhere in the house somehow...No. Like the music and the technicolor visuals, this was some form of magic.

Banse picked up the receiver and cradled it on his shoulder. "Hello?"

"The Amduscias album only works once per day. It'll reset twenty-four hours from the moment you were interrupted." It was the scratchy voice of the vagrant fiddler.

"How..." Banse didn't bother to articulate his many questions beyond that one syllable. It didn't matter. Normal reality had gone utterly sideways and flown out the window.

"Enjoy the record, but use it wisely. I'll be in touch three days hence." Dial tone. Banse hung up.

He returned to the library to reflect on the surreal turn of events. To help him wrap his head around it all, a mere joint would not suffice. He loaded a bud into the bowl of his trusty purple glass bong, flicked his lighter, and inhaled.

Side A of the record somehow induced trippy visions of events he'd not been present for in reality. Tomorrow night, he'd investigate his hypothesis that the flipside worked the same way for happenings that hadn't yet occurred. He'd believed for over a decade that genuine magic existed in the universe (ever since his first experience with peyote the summer after high school graduation), but he felt disoriented and spooked by the magnitude and intensity of all that had just happened.

Perhaps it was a hallucination, he reasoned. There could have been something in the ink on the Amduscias record's sleeve, like the skin of a psychoactive toad. His gut told him that he'd glimpsed an actual moment from Nora's past, but he had to know for sure.

Back in the kitchen, he plugged in the phone and dialed information. He'd gleaned from the chatter of mutual friends that his ex-girlfriend now lived in Santa Monica. A friendly operator recited Nora's number, and Banse jotted it down. He pondered just how he'd phrase his delicate question, and then he placed the call.

"Hello?" Nora's mousy voice always made Banse smile. The timbre brought back many fond memories, and he was glad that their breakup had been amicable.

"Nora? It's Banse. I'm in Ohio now."

"Glen told me you were moving, yeah. How are you?"

"Honestly, I'm shaken to my core."

Her voice took on a focused and serious tone. "What's up, man?"

"I just need to know, honestly, if you slept with Thomas the year before you and I started going out."

Silence. Then: "Why dredge up ancient history?"

"I had a weird phone call," Banse lied. "It was Thomas. He was drunk and bragging and..."

"Cripes. Yes. I slept with him four times. I never told you because I just...I don't know..."

"It's fine. Like you said: ancient history."

"How's the Midwest?"

"Strangely pleasant. The air is so clean, and in the night sky I can see stars I never knew existed."

Nora chuckled. "Great. So, not to be rude, but my dinner's getting cold..."

"Sure. Sorry to trouble you. Thanks for confiding in me."

"Take care."

"Bye."

Banse hung up and ran his fingers through his hair. The vision had been accurate.

Three bong hits later, additional questions flooded Banse's consciousness. Who exactly was the alley bum? What did "Amduscias" mean? Why did the cover depict such a bizarre figure, and did the art hold any symbolic meanings? Most importantly, what images from the future would Banse perceive when he guided the B-side's music?

Banse planned to notify his boss in the morning that he was under the weather and would be unable to work his Tuesday shift. Might even need the whole week off. Nasty flu.

The public library, he thought. *Maybe I can find out something about Amduscias there.*

He wandered back to the den, considered listening to the blues album he'd purchased, and decided that for once silence might be more conducive to cognition. He shut down the stereo system, stretched out on the couch, and stared at the ceiling while striving to remain centered and sane despite the evening's events.

He fell asleep there and awoke half an hour after sunrise.

Tuesday.

Banse notified Miss Johnson via telephone that he'd been vomiting once per hour since midnight, and she advised him to keep away from the store until he'd recovered from whatever stomach bug ailed him.

Banse stopped by the record shop on his way to the library and walked the length of the alley between it and the toy store next door but found no trace of the vagrant.

At the library, Banse approached the reference area and wished he'd taken time to shave his neck stubble, for Janet (the coolest librarian in all of Ohio) sat behind the desk and beamed at him. She always radiated peaceful and soothing vibes. Banse wanted to puzzle out a way to seduce her one of these years. She asked, "How may I assist you today?"

Banse said, "I'm interested in finding out what this word means." He handed her an index card on which he'd printed AMDUSCIAS in magic marker.

Janet frowned and turned to the omnipresent dictionary to her left. "One moment." Banse had already checked his own dictionary to no avail, but Janet's contained like three times as many words, so he remained mute and glanced around as Janet flipped through the A section.

At one table, a scruffy college kid scrutinized a biology text. Old Missus Lee (who had owned a vegetarian grocery store before she and her husband had retired the previous year) browsed a set of encyclopedias. She took down the G tome. *Probably looking up groceries,* thought Banse, and he giggled. Janet made eye contact with him.

"Do you know if this word is archaic?"

Banse had to ask what "archaic" meant. With that issue clarified, Banse said, "All I know is that it's on the cover of a record album, but I don't know if it's the name of the band or one individual, or if it's the title of the project, or what." Janet nodded.

"I'll need some time for research. Shall I phone you when I have more information?"

"Please." Banse scribbled his name and phone number on a scrap of paper. He thanked the librarian for her trouble, then opted to head home to count down the hours until Amduscias "reset."

Banse's instinct was to get heavily stoned prior to the evening's experiments, but he set down the bong after merely half a bowl. *Have to pace myself,* he reasoned. He still had four hours to fill before the appointed time. He'd just decided to give the Nadine and the Piglets album a listen when the phone rang. He'd forgotten to unplug it after he'd called in sick.

"Hello?"

"Dude. I stopped by the art supply place to yammer with you, and your boss said you have the flu or some shit. Turned out worse than just mild food poisoning?"

"Yeah," Banse lied. "Can't keep any food down."

"Sorry. I'd hoped we could refine those two new songs tonight..."

"This feels like the sort of germs that take a few days to run their course."

"Hit me up when you're better. Need any chicken soup, or..."

"I'm all stocked up. Thanks."

"Bye."

"See ya."

Banse unplugged the phone.

In the den, Banse played side A of *Dew Point* and thoroughly enjoyed the four songs thereon. The album had an interesting structure: all eight pieces of music on it followed the traditional twelve-bar blues form, but each was in a different key. The first side featured vocals while side B consisted of four instrumentals.

Banse played side A again, this time while jamming along on his Ibanez. He'd long loved the blues. Playing the twelve-bar progression always relaxed him and reminded him of his early teens, when he'd first picked up a bass guitar (one with frets back then) and developed a love for the four strings. He'd always excelled in music class at school but had only ever dabbled on piano before he found the sort of instrument he wanted to be buried with.

Banse jammed with side B a couple of times, flexed his sore fingers, and checked the clock. He had time to scarf down some chow prior to showtime.

In the kitchen, he made two peanut butter and strawberry jam sandwiches. He'd found that sugar rushes helped him to think, at least in the short-term, and he needed some accelerated cognition right now as he pondered how he'd approach the "future" side of the Amduscias record. Could he will the vision to depict images germane to questions he had about his future, or would he just have to observe whatever the fates coughed up? Would he be able to guide or affect the vision by changing the music? How had the week gotten so weird so fast?

He brushed his teeth and recalled a bit of the "scientific method" his one high school teacher had been so passionate about. *Alter one variable at a time: that's the key. Play just whole notes at first. See if changing the pitch alone affects the vision. Yeah.*

Banse returned to the den and checked the clock on the east wall, then unplugged it and turned it so he couldn't see its face. The incident the night before had felt timeless and eternal in a psychedelic way, and he didn't want a reminder of external time in the room.

Banse exhaled. *Here we go.*

He fired up the stereo system, commenced side B, and picked up his bass.

Banse listened to ten seconds of silence and then imagined a clarinet and a mandolin entwined in the key of C minor in 6/8 time. Both timbres emerged from the stereo speakers. Banse thumped out a whole note, then another, then another. He kept his eyes on the painting, then willed a harp to join the session. Banse played another C, then tried an E flat whole note.

The colors within the painting began to melt and drain away, leaving black and white and some shades of grey.

Banse played a G note, then A flat and B flat. The outlines of the pine trees wavered. The visual took on that peculiar three-dimensional quality.

Banse opted to throw his scientific approach out the window and cut loose on the bass, thumping an array of rhythms. He added a viola and a tuba to the mix. The noise was like a progressive bluesy-jazz blend unlike any Banse had ever perceived.

What little remained of the painting's original shapes morphed into a clear view of the living room at the house's rear: there sat the TV on an end table in front of the thick black drapes that Banse usually kept drawn. Here was the sofa on which Banse and his most recent squeeze (a British bird named Charlotte who he'd met at the shopping mall's shoe store while he browsed for sneakers) had first kissed and later enjoyed assorted carnal pleasures together.

Banse simplified his bass line down to just roots and fifths as color seeped into the vision. He saw himself (clad in his bathrobe) sweeping open the drapes to reveal a wicked thunderstorm in full swing visible through the window. It seemed to be daytime in whatever future Banse was glimpsing, but dense dark clouds filled the sky and blocked the majority of the sunlight. Lightning flashed.

The Banse in the vision stepped closer to the pane as something impossible occurred out in the yard. The four maple trees (planted by Aunt Colleen long before Banse's birth) swayed back and forth, then tilted forward as if their trunks had grown rubbery.

It's not a literal future, thought Banse. *I'm meant to read meaning into this image as if it's from a dream.*

The trees looked like theater actors taking a bow on stage at the end of a particularly fine performance.

The Banse in the vision turned his head as if he'd heard something to his left. He approached the house's back door. Trepidation filled his face.

In reality, the doorbell rang. The vision dissipated as the music went mute. Banse cursed, set his bass down, and knew he'd have to wait another day to continue. He set his bass on its stand.

He flung open the front door. There stood Walter, as always clad in a too-tight tie-dyed shirt. He held a paper sack.

"Under the weather, huh?"

"I'm in the midst of some important research."

"Thought you might like some Chinese food. Hot mustard always clears my sinuses when I'm sick. It also works when I'm only pretending to be ill." Walter looked pissed.

"I'm not dodging you, but..."

"You missed an exciting ballgame last night. The Rangers demoralized the Yankees by scoring three runs in the bottom of the first inning."

"I really don't have time to..."

"Yeah. I see you're swamped playing with yourself. Enjoy a couple of egg rolls on me." Walter thrust the bag of take-out food into Banse's hands.

"I'll call you in a few days," Banse said as Walter retreated toward his car in the driveway.

"Whatever."

Banse closed the door. *I've got to document what's happened so far with the record,* he thought. *Give myself some notes to sift through to make sense of it all.*

He went upstairs to what had been Aunt Colleen's office, rooted around until he found a legal pad, considered using the typewriter instead, and concluded that he'd be better off jotting down his thoughts in cursive since his typing skills consisted of slow pecking.

Downstairs in the library room, Banse sat at a desk and toked on a spliff and organized his racing thoughts. He set down in writing all that had happened from hearing the bum's violin on through the vision of the trees bending.

Banse fetched a flashlight and went out back to inspect the maples. Their trunks remained solid and rigid and did not look at all capable of bowing.

Back in the kitchen, Banse swilled a mug of cold coffee and pondered what the second vision might have meant. Did the trees represent people? Was there a storm slated to hit the suburbs of Cleveland soon, or had the vision been a couple of years in the future? He opted to check the weather report.

In the living room, Banse tuned the television to WJKW just in time to catch the news. The meteorologist reported clear skies for the week ahead.

Banse shut off the tube and read through his handwritten notes. Why had the A-side revealed that Nora had lied to him? In the second vision, why did his bathrobe-clad self look afraid as he approached the back door? He mentally cursed Walter for interrupting.

Banse slept fitfully in his bedroom that night. He dreamed of the maple trees bending and lightning streaks filling the sky.

Wednesday.

That morning, Banse plugged the phone in on the chance that the librarian might call. He left a note on the stereo to remind himself to unplug the telephone prior to the next Amduscias experiment. He'd decided that he would once again jam with the B-side in the hope of learning more about the future.

Banse called information to get the number of Tower Records on the Sunset Strip in Los Angeles. He'd spent hours browsing and hanging out there when he'd lived in California, and he'd discovered that the staff collectively had an impressive awareness of pop culture (particularly music). Banse figured maybe someone there had heard of Amduscias.

He phoned the store and yammered with a young man who was unfamiliar with that particular record. The clerk put Banse on hold to consult with his colleagues. Two minutes later, he reported that no one on the payroll had ever heard of a band or an album by that name. Banse thanked him for his trouble and hung up.

Banse retreated to the library to take the edge off with four solid hits of weed. He'd decided it was time to change the bong water when the phone rang.

"Hello?"

"Dude. Did you catch *Saturday Night Live* this past weekend?" It was Walter.

"No."

"Some British guy did this thing with live cats where he stuffed them in his pants..."

"I have to be rude here: I need some solitude and time to think."

"Didn't mean to interrupt you, your Highness. Later."

Dial tone.

Banse filled the hours leading up to the album's "reset" by practicing a walking bass line, cooking and consuming a whole box of Kraft macaroni and cheese, and reading through his notes about his experiences with the magic LP. He vowed that tonight he'd be uninterrupted. He would remember to unplug the phone, and he'd taped a giant "DO NOT DISTURB" sign to his front door.

Night. Banse peered through the front bay window at the waxing crescent moon overhead, then closed the drapes and fired up the stereo. He picked up his bass.

This time Banse willed together an ensemble that included two steel drums, three piccolos, and an acoustic guitar. The painting pulsed and wavered as the colors faded from it. Banse stared as the shapes morphed into an image of himself. In the vision, he was naked and floating in a black void while seemingly grooving to some inner rhythm. With his eyes closed, the Banse in the vision swayed his head to music that the Banse in reality could not hear.

The power went out. The needle screeched across the record's surface as the turntable abruptly slowed and stopped. The vision vanished, and the room was silent aside from Banse swearing.

He stumbled toward a shelf on which he kept two flashlights. Just as he got there, the electricity came back on. Banse sighed and retreated to the library to get high and augment his notes.

The next morning, Banse concluded that the most recent vision was meant to encourage him to play bass in the buff. Though he'd held no instrument in the black void, he seemed to be inventing a string of low-end rhythms in his head. As Banse (clad in his bathrobe) swilled hot coffee in the kitchen, someone rang his doorbell.

On the porch stood Janet, the librarian. She wore a hippie skirt and a Cheap Trick tee-shirt. Banse looked her up and down, and she said, "I dress differently on my days off."

"Sorry. Please: come in."

In the front den, Janet handed over two sheets of photocopied paper and said, "I tried to phone you, but your line was out. I got your address from the criss-cross directory."

"What's this?"

"All the information I could find on the demon Amduscias."

Banse frowned. "Amduscias is a demon?"

"A duke of Hell. He's associated with invisible musical instruments, particularly the trumpet. Looks like a man with the head of a unicorn."

Banse felt a chill in his spine.

Janet continued, "I couldn't find any references to a band naming itself or an album after this demon, but my research was hardly exhaustive. If you like, I could…"

"That's fine. I'll read over what you found, and I'll stop by the reference desk if I have any additional questions."

Banse saw her out, bolted the front door, and burst out laughing. He always had a good chuckle when he was terrified. He'd been an atheist up until his peyote experience, after which he'd become a polytheist. He reckoned that if there are many gods there may also be evil entities as well. Probably quite a few morally ambiguous divine beings out there, too.

The unplugged kitchen phone rang.

Banse, numb, strode to it and picked up the receiver.

"Yes?"

"The Amduscias record will now function at any time," said the vagrant.

That's all Banse needed to hear. He hung up and headed for the den.

He stared at the artwork that depicted Amduscias on the record's cover. He wondered what would happen if he smashed the vinyl, though in his gut he knew he wouldn't. He was hooked now. The ability to glean the future and have visions of the past? Banse had been addicted to cocaine for six months out west, but this magic was a much stronger drug, and he knew he wouldn't be able to kick the habit now.

He picked up his bass and looked at the turntable, which had begun to spin of its own accord. An invisible entity pushed the power button on the receiver. Banse fetched his bass, eager and hungry for another vision. Another hit.

Banse thumped out a bluesy rhythm and willed three saxophones (an alto, a baritone, and a tenor) to join in. He added a banjo for a more bluegrass kind of vibe.

The vision this time showed the living room with the storm raging and the trees bent over. The real Banse watched his future self open the back door to reveal the homeless fiddler outside.

In the present, someone knocked on the back door. The vision vanished.

Banse set down his bass and grew aware of wind howling. *The weatherman said nothing about this,* thought Banse, and he smiled as his heart rate accelerated.

Outside, lightning flashed. Thunder rumbled.

Banse reached the living room and swept open the drapes. He gazed at the storm and was not at all surprised when the maple trees grew rubbery and bowed toward him.

Another knock at the back door.

Banse felt dread well up inside. Fear of the unknown. Despite being on the edge of a panic attack, Banse went to the door and opened it.

The vagrant stood outside. He held a sheet of parchment with tiny calligraphic text written on it in blood. A contract.

Banse stepped aside, and the "hobo" entered.

"My boss will see you now," said the scout.

Banse whispered, "I passed an audition?"

"Inventing fresh bass parts for eternity—doesn't that sound like your idea of Heaven?"

Amduscias stepped in through the open back door. Without needing to be told what to do, Banse pricked the palm of his hand on the demon's horn, dabbed his fingernail in the blood, and scrawled his name at the bottom of the parchment.

Banse found himself floating in a womb-like dark void. He felt totally relaxed and comfortable. He heard music in a key of his choice and, without actually holding an instrument, willed notes with the timbre of an electric bass guitar into existence. He heard the others, now, and sometimes he lead the tune and other times he followed. He understood that he was part of a much larger infernal orchestra, and while he was blessed to perceive just the instruments that were in tune with him, elsewhere in that black void the souls of the damned heard all the keys at once: a deafening and maddening cacophony.

Banse, for the first time in his existence, felt totally at peace.

The Bar Guest

It was 3:02 in the morning and Jozsef Pataki sat shivering in the big beige Caprice as it idled in the dark, parked forty feet down from the Thunderbird. The frigid February air pushed the car's exhaust down into a roiling plume of slumbering dragon's breath, the greasy grey blanket spreading out behind the car in slow motion.

Up ahead, on the corner just past the bar, the lights at the cross-street clicked over silently from green to red. Not that the changing lights mattered; there wasn't any traffic, neither vehicular nor pedestrian. There was no sign of life of any kind at this ungodly hour and in this ungodly chill.

Except me and Detective third grade Vincent O'Leary, Pataki thought; *one dumb mick and a loud-mouthed hunky who'd driven down to East Lib in the freezing dark to maybe—just maybe—bust a few low-life pushers.*

Sitting in the front seat, blowing on his hands to warm them, Pataki hunched down in his thick Shearling Coat and wrinkled his nose at the stench of Vince's car. He glanced down at the Chevy's overflowing ashtray, stuffed so full of Winston butts he wouldn't be surprised if the damn clunker didn't run on the stinky things.

Not that Pataki should judge, he smoked his fair share. But he always tried to keep the tray in his Chrysler butt-free. He chalked it up to his mother's obsessive cleaning habit; he remembered seeing her following behind his father, emptying the ashtray as soon as he stubbed out his Camel. Didn't matter if he lit another one right after, she'd just wipe it clean and put it right back in its place by the arm chair. His old man was sixteen years in the ground this coming June, done in by the long hours and dirty air from the mills. The pension he was due to receive got cancelled and his mother, who'd never worked outside the home a day in her life, had to take shifts at a local dress makers just to make ends meet. When they'd done the autopsy, his lungs had been black as sackcloth, so Pataki and his sister had brought suit against US Steel. But the company's defense team had the coroner in their pocket, and he chalked the death up to chronic cigarette use, so the ruling went in their favor.

And even though they'd all gone into debt putting him the ground and marking it with a slab of marble (Pataki still had six more payments to make on that gravestone), his mother still kept the glass trays out on the coffee and end tables, as a morbid tribute of sorts. A reminder of what bad habits can do.

Pataki knew he should quit and the stink of Vince's overflowing dish was another reminder that he should. And he would. Any day now.

Just above the ashtray was Vince's tape player, his latest 8-track cycling through its playlist. He'd bought it a week ago, had been playing it ever since and it was driving Pataki batshit. The songs were filtered through the Chevy's less than adequate speakers, and so everything sounded tinny and scratchy; and if he had to listen to some long hair whine about flying back to Memphis to find his Daisy Jane one more time, he was gonna rip the damn cartridge out of the socket, throw it into the street and stomp it to pieces.

He glanced out the window and across the street. There he saw Vince's shape standing in the shadows of the alley. The big Irishman was taking a leak on the side of the Pruitt building. Idiot should've relieved himself back at the stationhouse.

Pataki shook his head.

It was flipping freezing out; how Vince was able to water the bricks in this temperature was beyond him. But then again, his partner had been chugging Mother O'Leary's extra special Irish coffee all shift; which probably accounted for why the big Irishman had been standing legs spread and voiding himself for almost a full two and half minutes.

Pataki turned his eyes back down the street to the Thunderbird.

They'd parked on the opposite side of the street, to get a looksee at the place before heading inside, to scope if there were any lookouts; not that they'd done to grand a job at that. "I'll be damned if I's is gonna jog four blocks in this South Pole shite," was Vince's argument for parking closer than they both knew was prudent.

It was really cold and quiet, and with the icy wind that had been howling down from Canada all day. The streets weren't just empty; they were abandoned. No one was out and no one was going to be out.

The bar's cherry red and banana yellow neon sign, shaped in sweeping, stylized letters spelling out its name, shone bright and clear in the night. The frosty condensation on the windshield added a slight hazy glow to it and made it seem evilly eerie somehow—or maybe it was just that Pataki was in a black mood to begin with.

He hated this late night bullshit. He'd been asking for day shifts for weeks now; he was sick to death of the dark and ugly things that happened in it. But, if they were gonna crack this case, they had to work when the lean and desperate were doing things they shouldn't, and that meant late nights in questionable places.

Six and half months ago, a new strain of smack had started showing up on the streets, and it was some nasty shit. The boys down at the labs said it had been cut with some kind of back alley, manufactured hallucinogen; the kind of hippy-trippy shit Owsley had been cooking up in '66, only times ten. Precincts all across the city had had to deal with reports about people who had offed themselves while on the damn stuff and those junkies they'd hauled in high on the stuff, were raving about evil shadows that howled and unnatural things snarling in dark corners.

They were calling it Black Dog on the streets and on the Hill; and word was the name had gotten back to Plant and Page, and word was they were threatening to sue, citing libel and slander.

Pataki and Vince and every other detective in Zone 2 had been working overtime trying to find the source. The pressure was on to nail the sonofabitch who was bringing the stuff into the city. But for the last few weeks, they'd just hit a bunch of dead ends and greymeat addicts, dead in abandoned row houses and alleyways.

The night had started out looking grim, no new intel and no new leads; but then they'd gotten a call a half-hour ago, from Kenny BS, one of Vince's less-than-reliable informants. They needed to get down near the river right away.

There was a high dollar buy going down at 4023 Butler—the Thunderbird Café.

When Vince had told him about the tip, Pataki had doubted that it had anything to do with what they had been tracking, or that it was going to amount anything at all. The particular snitch who'd called it in had fed them lame information before and he was a paranoid, sketchy speed freak, so nothing he said (in Pataki's professional opinion) carried any real weight. He'd snorted when Vince had told him about it, and grumbled that Kenny Bullshit was just looking to get a tenner out of Vince so he could get a fix, that was all. The Thunderbird was too well-known, too out in the open for the traffickers of the ugly stuff that had been making the rounds on the Hill lately. It wasn't a junkie's flophouse, but a decent neighborhood bar. Why would a dealer risk doing a deal at this location on a weeknight?

If it had been a Friday or Saturday night, that might've given Kenny's tip a bit more validity—there'd be a big crowd milling about outside the entrance, spilling out onto the street. Easy to blend in then, get lost in a sea of faces. Make the deal, exchange the stuff for cash, and then disappear.

But it wasn't a Friday or Saturday. It was a frigging Tuesday.

And, it being a Tuesday, and it being after 3 am and given that all city bars normally shut down at one, the place should've been deader than dead. No crowds, nowhere to hide, there was way too much light on the street, too easily spotted from an apartment widow across the street. Vince had been excited about the tip, and waved off all of Pataki's reasons why they shouldn't follow up.

"Whaddya wanna do, Pats?" he'd cajoled. "Spend the night fillin' out paperwork, swillin' that Folger's instant crud? Or maybe, just maybe, catch a break on this thing? Whaddya got to lose?"

Pataki had relented, and so here they were, out in the dark and the cold, at three in the morning, looking down the street at what was supposed to be a closed and empty bar. No self-respecting dealer would arrange to do a buy at this hour, at this location out in the open. He'd told Vince that, four times from the station house to when they'd pulled alongside the curb on Butler Street not ten minutes ago. But what they'd seen when they pulled up...that made Pataki think that maybe he'd misjudged the whole situation.

The place should be dark, locked up for the night. Except, all the lights that should be off, weren't...which meant someone—or a few someones—were still inside.

The thought crossed Pataki's mind that he might've been too quick with his original assessment about Kenny Bullshit's tip. Maybe that jittery freak Kenny BS had given them something good after all.

Maybe there was something going down.

Pataki had wanted to check it out after they'd parked and given the area the once over, but Vince said he had to pee first.

Without his partner to back him up, Pataki had opted to stay in the car and wait. No sense in walking up solo and getting his head blown off. This new stuff the pushers had been spreading around made anyone who dealt with it more than a little trigger happy.

But in the short five minutes he'd been sitting here, in the dark and the flipping cold and in the nicotine-stench of the Caprice, Pataki had decided he regretted his choice.

The Chevy's heater was for shit and the stench of Vince's two-pack a day habit was giving him a headache. And now that damn longhair on the 8-track was telling Daisy to keep the oven warm. He was just about to say fuck it and open his door to escape the stink and the song, when Vince O'Leary's beefy knuckles rapped on the glass.

"Get the lead aht, Pats," the burly Irish detective's voice trembled in the cold. "We's got some low-life's to bust."

Pataki opened the door, and the frigid air ripped away any trace of warmth the interior had so weakly provided. He shivered as he stepped out onto the empty street. He raised himself to his full height and threw a glance at his partner. Vince stood with his fists jammed into his coat pockets, looking angry and cold. The air out here on the street wasn't any better than it had been in the Caprice; and he'd traded the gagging odor of stale ashes for the sulfurous odor of the mills down along the Mon. That distinctive steel smell was cloying and strong.

"We do this quick and by the book," Pataki said in a low voice. Vince shrugged indifferently, puffing on the ever-present Winston, grey smoke trickling from his nostrils.

"Don't we always?" Vince growled through another puff of cigarette smoke.

"But I'm tellin' you...if that sniveling little twerp Kenny Bullshitowitz has brought us down here fer nothin', next time I sees him I'm gonna shoot him on principle...Sendin' us out in this cold. Inconsiderate bastahd."

Pataki started down the street toward the Thunderbird and Vince followed a step behind. Off in the distance, the lights of the city glittered bright and sharp. From here on Butler, they could see down the hill toward downtown. There was life down there; car lights moving along the streets, lights in glass buildings, told Pataki that there were others up and about at this hour. But here on Butler Street, in the lower half of East Lib...

We might as well be on the moon, Pataki thought.

He and Vince were the only things moving and breathing.

Pataki had been in the Thunderbird a few times. Hell, every living soul in the city had, more than likely. The place was a landmark of sorts, part of the city's cultural mythology. The Thunderbird was one of those hole-in-the-wall beer and hard liquor joints. It had a small stage in the back and had live bands six nights a week. The quality and sound of which was your basic garage band rock and roll, or a few shades outside that—you wouldn't hear any pop or folk bands at the Thunderbird; no sir, just dissonant drums, gruff bass and raw guitars.

Stories had grown up around the bar, people told them over and over, expanding them or changing them as the need arose—who they met there, or who they saw play there. The only times police had ever been called to the bar were to roust some rowdy drunks. As far as Pataki could remember, nothing more violent that a frat brawl had ever taken place at the T-bird.

From where they'd parked, they hadn't really been able to see the entrance proper, but as they got closer, they could see the door to the bar was open. It wasn't flung wide, but just enough to let the night air in, and the inside light to spill out onto the sidewalk. Both men stopped.

This time of year, and in these temps, no bar was gonna leave a door cracked letting the cold in. And there wasn't any sound from within, no music, no voices; no one moving about, cleaning up or rifling through the till.

If a buy was going on, there should be voices. Laughter, negotiating, even an argument, some kind of talk. Something was off, something was wrong. Real wrong.

Pataki looked and Vince and nodded, and both policemen drew their service revolvers.

Pataki moved up to the door, Vince backing him

He poked his head around the open door, peered inside.

The lights were on, the Michelob, Rolling Rock and St. Paulie Girl signs over the bar were all ablaze, the mirrored wall behind them refracting the neon and adding sharp green and blue tones to the amber glow of the ceiling lights.

There were six dead people inside.

Pataki had seen death before, but not like this, and not with this much blood. It was more than Pataki was prepared for. He was a ten-year veteran, but his stomach was suddenly that of a first-day rookie. He turned away and vomited violently into the street.

"Jay-sus!" Vince barked, and then pushed past Pataki and to get a look into the bar.

Pataki's stomach kept heaving as he heard Vince's continued cursing behind him, and then the big man's pounding feet as he ran back up to the car. The detective finally managed to stand straight and wiped the sick from the edges of his mouth with a trembling hand. In his periphery, he could see Vince with the car radio in his hand, calling for backup and an ambulance.

Pataki watched as Vince gesticulated, as if that was supposed to convince the duty officer on the other end of the radio that Vince wasn't bullshitting him, and then he turned and forced himself to look back at the carnage.

His mind reeled as he stood gaping at the positions and condition of the bodies. He'd seen people murdered before, both here in the city and back in the jungle, but there was something terribly, terribly wrong with these corpses.

He'd seen all kinds of stab and gunshot wounds on victims and people that had gotten themselves dead, either on purpose, by accident or just through dumb luck.

Not one of the bodies inside the Thunderbird matched anything in Pataki's experience.

There were three near the front entry to the bar and three others further back, spaced out near the foot of the small stage that had been built for bands and live music acts.

Instinct told him to get inside, to find out what had happened, but at the moment, his feet refused to work. He stood rooted to the spot, trying to make sense of what he was seeing.

He couldn't tell if there were any more inside or if any were hidden behind the bar. There was no way of knowing how many people had been in the place when whatever had happened in here had gone down, but the evidence he could see told him that it hadn't happened long ago. Maybe minutes before he and Vince had pulled up, if that.

More than a couple of the chairs had been smashed; three or four of the two-top tables had been overturned, glass shattered, beer spilled. There was a cigarette still burning in an ashtray on the bar. A half bottle of Jack was dripping down into a puddle near the cash register.

The first body was a male, lying ten feet from the entrance, body pointed toward the back of the building. He had on work boots and jeans and a black long-sleeved turtle neck. Pataki guessed he was six feet or so, or would've been if he still had a head.

Farther back and seated at one of the tables was a dishwater-blonde female, looked to be about 5'5", 30–35 years of age. She had on boots, too, but these were the ankle-high, white fake leather, zippered-on-the-side type. She had on a pair of bedazzled bellbottoms and a deep blue halter top that showcased her ample endowments, which were slick with deep crimson that had gushed out after whoever had ripped out her neck, along with her lower jaw. Her deep green eyes, raccoon-ringed with too much mascara, were bulging and staring.

Just beyond the blonde and propped up against the bar was a third body, another male, and Pataki guessed he was the bartender, or at least a Thunderbird employee. The bar's logo on his ill-fitting T-shirt pegged him as such. He was a large guy, even put Vince's beer gut to shame and Pataki pegged him at least three hundred pounds, maybe more. He had thick arms, olive-toned skin and was as bushy as any hunky from Polish Hill. Black straggly hair and black straggly beard to match; the hair hung down past his shoulders, the beard to his round belly—which had been slashed wide open. The man's entrails splayed out over his gut and thighs like a scarlet and pink octopus. There was a sawed off double-barreled shotgun in one of the fat man's hands.

"Jay-sus, Mary and Joseph," Vince whispered close to him and Pataki grunted in surprise, spinning to face his partner. The big Mick was white as a sheet, and Pataki would bet good money that he looked just as pale and shocked because Vince laid a meaty hand on his shoulder.

"You ok, Pats?"

"Yeah, yeah; just caught me off-guard."

"What the foohk, Pats," Vince wheezed, his eyes bulging. "Oi mean seriously...what the ever-lovin' foohk..."

Pataki wiped his mouth again and spat out onto the sidewalk. The glob of spittle was phlegmy and orange-looking. His mouth was filled with an angry, metallic, acidy taste, and the distinctive tang of Thousand Island dressing. He knew that Rueben from Silvio's he'd scarfed down just before midnight was gonna come back and haunt him. He just didn't think he'd be tasting it twice. The damn thing had been in digesting perfectly well in his belly before he puked it all up.

"The uniform's on their way? They bringing a meatwagon?" he managed to ask.

Vince nodded and then swallowed.

"That one there ain't got no head, Pats. Where's the head?"

His skin was waxy and he was breathing heavy; given the cold and how out of shape he was, Pataki was thinking his partner might keel over from heart failure. And then, wondering if he looked that way himself, Pataki turned his gaze back toward the grim scene inside the bar.

He forced his eyes past the three grisly horrors at the front and tried to take in as many details as he could about the other three.

There was another female, a brunette with a Farrah-feathered 'do, jean jacket as bedazzled as the blonde's jeans, dark slacks and a pair of those ridiculous disco heels. Her wrists were decorated with what had to be ten types of jangly bracelets and it looked like she might have on the biggest pair of hoop earrings that Pataki had ever seen. They glittered shiny and gold through her dark brown hair.

She was face-down, one hand reaching toward the stage, a sad final gesture.

Pataki was kind of relieved he couldn't see her face. He couldn't really say why, he was just glad he didn't have to see if she'd died like the blonde—eyes open and scared shitless. She was lying in a pool of dark liquid which joined with the body next to her.

That one was laying in a fetal position, a black male, wearing a salmon-pink wide collar shirt and burnt orange flared slacks. His chin was tilted down and his arms were wrapped around his belly and to Pataki it looked like he'd just taken a really hard shot to the stomach... but like the fat bartender, this poor joker had been gutted. The man's hands and fingers were grabbing onto his intestines that had spilled out of him. Pataki guessed he'd been trying to push his guts back in and died in the middle of it.

The final body was bent backward over one of the tables, arms and legs splayed wide. This one was another black male, and had on a black leather coat, blue jeans and what looked like a new pair of brown ankle boots. They'd been polished to a high shine and the brass buckles caught the light, and twinkled in the dim glow of the neon over the bar. The man's upper torso looked odd, and when he realized why, Pataki could feel his stomach rebel and that awful impending rushing need to retch again. Pataki gritted his teeth and willed the sensation away.

It looked as though the man's neck and arms had been broken, they were all three bent back much too far, thrown back like a runner crossing the finish line—but it took a second look to understand why—the man's ribcage had been pried open and hollowed out. The rest of him, all the stuff that fit inside him, that had been ripped or torn away.

Who or what could do that to a man?

Pataki couldn't even begin to guess what exactly had gone down in there. Six people getting whacked at the same time, at various places in the bar? There had to have been more than one perp. Had to be.

Maybe they were still in there, hiding in the kitchen or stockroom. Pataki hated this part, the not knowing, the anticipation and fear-inducing tension of confronting a suspect. But that's what he'd signed up for, why he became a cop in the first place. To start to get a grip on what had happened, he was going to have to move inside.

The procedure for crime scene investigation were secondhand, but for some reason it was like trying to remember his ex's birthday...it was just gone from his mind. He shook his head to clear his thoughts. *Secure the scene, then look for evidence, ya moron,* he told himself. He gripped the gun tightly, looked at Vince and then stepped inside. "Pittsburgh PD! If anyone is in here and they ain't dead...get out here with your hands held high!"

His voice sounded loud in the enclosed space, and he surprised himself with how confident he sounded, considering his nerves were jangling with fear.

"You heard him!" Vince bellowed behind him. "Anyone in here still breathing better get his ass out here now, hands up!"

The two cops gave it a ten count and then lowered their firearms, but kept them out, just in case.

"Jaysus foohk," Vince muttered. "This ain't right, Pats."

Pataki's eyes scanned the room, dancing over the contents and gauging the space. It wasn't the largest bar, and given how most buildings on the block were built lengthwise to squeeze as much out of the real estate as possible, the room was longer than it was wide. The ceilings were fairly high, with several chandelier lamps and the building itself was several stories tall. Most likely there were apartments upstairs, personal living quarters or business offices. He could see the stairs that led to the upper floors tucked near the back, in a darkened alcove where a sign, one of those '30s art deco pieces, pointing to the location of the restrooms.

"Nothing is," Pataki, replied.

"What was that?" Vince asked.

"I was just agreeing with you. Nothing about this is right, everything about this is off; it's wrong, all wrong..."

"Ya think!? Jaysus, who does something like this? What does something like this? And what's that ghad-awful smell?"

Pataki opened his mouth to say he didn't know what Vince was talking about, but then it hit him, washed over him in a pungent wave. The stench of his own sick in his nostrils had probably kept it at bay at first, but now it assaulted him full force.

It was a wet hair kind of stink, rank and thick; swampy, grassy and muddy and stagnant.

Though the weekend had been a mix of snow and rain, the last two days had been free of precipitation. It had been a grey and overcast today, maybe a hint of a misting drizzle, but nothing that would cause anyone or anything to get soaked; and the streets and sidewalks had all been salted to keep from icing over. But it wasn't a wet street smell. It was a deeper odor, older...like something that had been dredged up out of a sink drain; old, soggy, something that had been festering for a long, long time.

Pataki looked down at the floor where they were standing, at the worn hardwood just inside the entrance with the rubber floor mat stamped with the Thunderbird logo. The area was caked with mud and foot prints, the regular traffic from the dozens who'd come and gone over the course of the bar's regular business hours. The door mat was covered with dirt and mud from where people had scraped their shoes before moving in to get a beer or something stronger. And the floor boards past that also had dried mud and shoe prints.

But, the stench wasn't coming from the mat or the muddy footprints. It permeated the entire bar and had a faint familiar tang to it. For a few frustrating seconds he couldn't place it, but then it clicked: it was a dirty water smell, the odor of the nearby Allegheny. The river was less than a mile away, and the water's edge sometimes smelled liked what he was smelling right now—but during the summer months. Here it was the middle of winter, freezing cold and the mud and soil at the water's edge would be hard and solid. That festering muddy aroma wouldn't be this strong. Anyone walking around down there this time of year wouldn't pick up a smell like this, let alone drag it with them all the way up to Butler Street.

Pataki forced his eyes to wander over the rest of the wooden slats of the bar's floor, near the bloody bodies, all around; looking for other prints or marks. Whoever had done this had to have stepped in the gore that had pooled around the bodies. The middle of the place looked like somebody had taken a 10 gallon tub of black cherry juice and just dumped it. There was a lake of the stuff. He looked all over the floor again, but there wasn't anything he could see. Nothing to suggest someone had fallen in the river and had made their way inside to—to do what? Dry off, strip naked and then kill six people? It was a ludicrous line of thinking and...

Vince pushed by him, stepping further into the bar.

"Don't...," Pataki started, causing Vince's head to turn back sharply. "Go slow...don't want to contaminate..."

"Wot am Oi, Pats? A rook?"

"It's not that...we just don't want..."

"We been ta-gether goin' on eight years, Pats. I knows the routine and I knows my job. Ya lahst yer lunch and the place is a bloody mess, I get it. I can hear yer noives rattlin' from here. It ain't natural what happened in here, but trust me...Oi ain't gonna mess it up for the lab boys."

Pataki opened his mouth, but closed it again in embarrassment. Vince was right. He was unsettled. But now that the initial reaction had passed, he wanted to get to the bottom of this. He needed to know what happened in here.

Both men had been partners long enough that just a look would let the other know what the other was thinking. Vince gave him a nod and a wink, then turned and took a step over to look behind the bar. It was a familiar gesture from the Irishman, one that let Pataki know that it was time to get to work. Pataki glanced down making sure he wasn't going to step in any of the gore and then moved toward the first body.

"No one behind the bar," Vince intoned. "Thank gawd. Six's bad enough as it is."

Pataki crouched down, reached into his coat and took a pen out of his suit jacket. He used it to move the body's booted left foot slightly. The pool of gore had spread out beneath it, at least eight inches to either side of the body.

"Till's intact, looks like. It' ain't been popped least-wise. So it don't look like this was done for the money," Vince said from behind the bar. Off in the distance, Pataki caught the thin wail of approaching sirens.

"This had to have happened between the time Kenny tipped us and when we parked, you reckon? I'm surprised no one upstairs, or in them row houses across the street didn't call it in...they had ta have heard somethin', screams or what not..."

"Maybe it happened too fast..." Pataki replied, not believing it himself.

"No one's that fast. And the damage done to them, that ain't quick work. There had to be screams, yelling something."

Pataki stood up and put the pen away. He glanced at the gruesome display before him once again, then back at his partner.

"Looks the bartender, if that's who he is, had enough time to grab the shotgun, but it don't smell like he got a shot off," Pataki noted. "That hog leg he's holding woulda spattered lead every which way..."

"Can't smell nuthin' except that wet dog," Vince sniffed. "But someone woulda heard that thing go off fer sure, but that guy...he never pulled the trigger. Who's ever done this, they weren't packin'. There ain't no shell casings or wall blasts, so it weren't guns that tore these poor basthads up. Had to be a knife; and a big foohkin' pig-sticker at that."

Both men looked at one another.

"Six people, all in one room, got themselves gutted by some knife-wieldin' psycho," Pataki said shaking his head.

"And one decapitated foohk, don't ferget him."

"One, two of them maybe; that I could understand," Pataki contin-ued. "But all six? Look at the arrangement of bodies..."

Pataki's eyes jumped from body to body, picturing how they had been before having their lives snuffed out.

"I bet my next paycheck they all got..."

The sound came from that alcove near the back, the one with the stairs leading up to the upper floors. A heavy thudding series of sounds, like someone stumbling on the steps.

Both men had their guns up and shouted at the same time.

"Freeze! Freeze! Pittsburgh PD!"

Pataki was ahead of Vince by a step as both of them moved to get a better view of the stairs. In the dim amber light that illuminated the narrow set of steps leading to the second floor, they saw another female, heavyset, grey-blonde hair, half-sitting, half-laying on the last three or four steps. There was blood on her face and she had one hand grasping onto the railing and trembling as she tried to get back to her feet.

"Stay down! Stay where you are!"

Pataki's voice boomed in the small space. Vince charged forward gun trained on the big woman, who looked at them with glazed eyes. Her mouth was opening and closing spasmodically, her breath wheezing from her lungs. Vince reached her as her eyelids began to flutter and her head to fall back.

Pataki could see the red leaking down the stairs now. She'd been hit, too.

He lowered his weapon and moved to help his partner.

Vince had knelt beside her and had put a hand behind her head, tilting it forward.

"Hey! Hey, lady, what was that? I didn't catch it? Did you see who did this? Who was it?"

"Was she saying something?" Pataki asked.

"Yeah, yeah," Vince breathed. "Real low, repeating herself. She's in shock."

The woman came awake suddenly, her eyes flying open and her body jerking. There was an awful sound coming from her throat, a half-choked half cry.

"Buh...buh...buh...!" Her arms were starting the flail and Vince almost fell over trying to keep her restrained. "Buh...guh...Buh...guh!" The hand she had been grasping the railing with came loose and scraped down the wall beneath it, her nails digging tracks into the stucco.

Pataki holstered his weapon and moved in and helped Vince steady her, both men taking a hold of her arms to keep her from harming herself. Her lower lip was covered in pinkish spittle and then a great glut of dark red blood jettison from her mouth and caught Pataki on the shoulder, staining his jacket deep crimson.

"Sonufabitch!" Pataki cried out.

"Buh...Buh...b-ar...b-ar..." the woman choked out, the strength leaving her as she collapsed back down on the steps. Pataki took a step back, a look of disgust on his face as her stared at the globs of red running down the front of his Shearling.

"She's saying bar," Vince looked up at Pataki, a quizzical look on his face and then started to turn back to the woman. "Least it sounds like 'bar'..."

Pataki made a move as to wipe his jacket, but then stopped, not wanting to get the blood on his hand. He looked back at the woman and Vince, but Vince's attention was focused on the stairs above her, into the dark near the top. Vince was frozen, his eyes wide and mouth open.

"B-b-ar...gist...," the woman huffed, as she tried to turn over on her side. Her entire back had been ripped open; the sweatshirt she was wearing was ruddy-brown and wet with blood. The steps beneath were soaked. "Bar...gist...bar...gist...."

Vince stood up suddenly, the last color in his face draining away completely. He stumbled back, gave Pataki a look of pure terror and then turned and bolted for the door.

Pataki looked after him, taken completely by surprise. His partner caromed off one of the bar tables, stumbled and fell to one knee and then he was up out the front door.

Pataki looked back at the woman and saw her go limp. Her eyes were open, and he saw the life leave her in a single shuddering breath. He looked at her, then at the wet red of her blood still dripping down the front of him. There was a sound near the top of the stairs. It sounded like a clack, like teeth snapping together.

Pataki leaned forward, looked up into the dark.

There was nothing there. Or was there? Suddenly a fear ran a fingernail down his spine and Pataki shivered violently.

He turned and darted out after Vince. Fuck it if there was still anybody left inside. There was something evil in here, something very, very wrong. Let the captain chew his ass about leaving a crime scene, he could give a shit. He wasn't gonna stay behind while some crazed lunatic with a knife...he was out onto the street and Vince was standing about ten feet away, his service weapon raised. Pataki ducked by instinct as Vince squeezed off a round. The bang was enormously loud in the quiet empty street and Pataki felt the round whiz by, three feet from his left ear, heard it spang off the concrete wall behind him.

"Whoa! Whoa! What the hell, Vince?!" Pataki's hoarse shout filling in the wake of the gunshot echoing off the buildings. The wail of the approaching sirens was getting louder and louder.

Vince was standing in the street, wide-eyed and shaking. Pataki trotted over to him, the big man's eyes were riveted on the front entryway of the Thunderbird.

"Vince, Vince," Pataki moved toward his friend and partner slowly, hands up. "Talk to me, Vince."

Vince's eyes looked like they are gooing to pop right out of his skull. His chest was rising up and down, and he was taking heaving, huge, gulping breaths. Pataki didn't think he'd seen anyone as scared as he saw this man before him. He was certain that heart attack that was surely part of Vince's future was only seconds away from triggering.

"Was it what she said?" Pataki offered.

Vince turned to him, dragging his eyes away from the entrance, started to raise the gun again but Pataki moved in quickly, forced the big man's hand and arm down.

"Get a grip, dammit." He hissed. "What the hell has got you so spooked?"

Vince's Adam's apple was bouncing up and down and he licked his lips. He was struggling to get it out; he started to say something, but then stopped. And started again. Pataki looked him in the eye, nodding encouragement.

"Barghest." The big man said at last, his voice small and rasping. "She said 'barghest.'"

"Bar guest? Yeah, so...one of the guest's is the killer, that's what she meant, right? Meaning that they're still in there...or close by. Come on man, we gotta do this. We gotta get..."

"No. Barghest. That's wot she said, Pats. Bhar-ghest."

O'Leary leaned into his brogue, drawing the word out, rolling the "r" and pronouncing the final syllable with an "eh" sound.

"It's in there, up the stairs. I saw it. Saw it comin' outta the corner of the wall..."

"What the hell is a bar-geest?" Pataki asked, confused.

His partner had lost it. Both of them had. The grisly scene had knocked them both off their legs and they needed to get back on track and figure out what the hell happened in there.

"Talk to me, Vince, I don't understand."

"My Grand Da, he was a country man," Vince muttered. "Worked for the distillery in Aberfeldy, big drinker my grand da. Notorious. He'd come home, late nights when me Da was supposed to be asleep, and sit in the big chair. My Da would tell me stories about how the old man would wake screaming, sayin' the black dogs were comin' for him."

"Black dogs?"

"Black dogs," Vince repeated, licking his lips. "Barghests. Devil dogs, moor hounds...evil beasts that would prey on those that could see what couldn't be seen. Mah Grand Da, he said he seen 'em. That they were comin' fer 'im 'cause he seen 'em. If they catch you lookin' at 'em, he'd ay...yer a dead mon."

"Vince, you ain't making any sense," Pataki sighed, exasperated. "What the hell are you..."

"They come for those that see what can't be seen, Pats! If you see where they come from, they hunt ya, hunt ya to death. Don't you get it!? You're drunk, you ain't seeing right. Blurred vision, things in the corner of your eyes, you know what I mean! Me Grand Da, he says them beasts was real, chasing him home nights cause he seen what he shouldn't see, into the places in between..."

Pataki couldn't make heads or tails of what his partner was babbling about.

"Them druggies in dhere! High as a kite on that shite, it let's ya see 'em...it's been huntin' 'em don't ya see? They musta seen one, called it to 'em, and it killed 'em all to keep its secret!"

Vince's lips were quivering, his whole body was trembling and Pataki was sure the big man was gonna burst a vessel in his brain, when Vince's eyes slid past Pataki, back toward the Thunderbird entrance.

Pataki started to turn to follow Vince's gaze when the big man let out a squeal, shoved him and then raised his revolver again, firing round after round.

The gun was deafening in the empty street, each blast resounding back and forth, drowning out all other noise. Pataki half-closed his eyes and threw up his hands to cover his ears. He was squinting his eyes, a defensive reflex and...he saw it.

Or thought he saw it.

A thin, gangrel thing, slitted yellow eyes, great big maw full of razors and jagged edges; mangy skin with blotchy fur patches, it was shadow-black and bony, a thing of pure terror. A greyhound-shaped mastiff five feet at the shoulder...

But it was the jaws of the thing that froze his mind with horror. Those teeth, stained red. The ones that had taken off the head of that poor fool in the bar, ripped out the throat of the blonde, gutted the disco pimp...those teeth and the thin black lips around them, trembling with rage and famished intent.

And then it was gone, a blink of the eye, an imagined thing.

Pataki forced his eyes open. It had been a blink, just a blink.

But there was nothing there.

And then something slammed into him, sent him sprawling, and he landed hard on the cold asphalt of Butler Street. The back of his head smacked hard against the street and he saw tiny sparks before his eyes.

He thought he heard Vince scream, but it was a faint sound, from far, far, far away.

When he opened his eyes next, the black and whites were there, lights flashing and there were dozens of people about. Uniforms and ambulance crews.

The entrance to the Thunderbird was cordoned off; they were just bringing the first body out. There was a crowd on the sidewalk opposite, news crew, too, with TV cameras and big lights.

Some EMT was bent over him, shining a light in his eyes, asking him questions. He had a blanket over him and there was something soft under his head.

He looked to his right and saw Vince's body in the street, covered by a cream-colored blanket.

"My partner..." he started, but the EMT told him to be still.

Pataki fought to sit up.

"What happened to Vince? Did that dog get him? Did anyone see it?"

The EMT looked at him confused.

"What dog?"

"The big black dog, the one...my partner..."

"Heart attack, Detective. He was stone cold by the time we got here. You had blacked out. We found you here, just like this. No one saw any dog."

"But that smell, you smell it don't you? That nasty wet smell?"

"No, Detective. I don't smell anything."

"It's gone," Pataki muttered. "It's gone. But I saw it. I saw it and it saw me."

The EMT looked at him with an odd expression.

"It saw me," Pataki whispered again.

✳

Disappeared

"Robert? Robert? Well it's about time you answered your telephone. I've been phoning you all day. She's gone, Robert. You have to go to Montana...Robert?"

"Yes, Mother, I'm here." He sighed. "What has Julie done this time, and why do I have to go to Montana?"

"Oh, Robert—it's not like all those other times. She's disappeared. Just plain disappeared." He could hear her sobbing between words.

"Mother, it's been a bad week for me—a really bad week..." he looked around his apartment. Bad was an understatement. Karen was gone. He was finished as a reporter. It was just a matter of time until his boss made it official. His head was reeling from last night's scotch and he'd regretted answering the phone as soon as he'd heard his mother's voice. He had thought—hoped—it might be Karen. Stupid of him.

"Robert—are you even listening to me? The police—the ones in Great Falls—they can't find her. You have to go—you have to find her—she's in trouble, Robert."

"Sure, Mother. I'm on the next flight." He hung up the phone and started up the stairs. Then, with a sigh, he retraced his steps, took the receiver off the hook and grabbed a bottle of Black Label before he slowly climbed up to bed. He was not going to Montana. There was no way he was going to Montana. He fucking hated Montana.

* * *

"Please put your tray tables and chairs to their upright and locked position. The captain has signaled we are preparing to land at Great Falls International Airport."

The stewardess moved up the cabin with a perky precision that was the best part of his day so far. She paused at his aisle. "Sir, I'm going to have to ask you..." she met his eyes and her tone lightened. Usually the problems where cranky old businessmen or overwhelmed moms with too many kids. This guy was fine—maybe 30, with dark, wavy hair, clear blue eyes and very well put together.

"You're going to have to ask me...what?" he smiled.

"Seat back to original position." She gave him her most dazzling smile, and added a wink for good measure. "We wouldn't want you to get into any trouble."

"I'm good at trouble, actually. Seems to follow me everywhere." He winked back as he straightened his chair and she reluctantly continued up the aisle. He watched her walk until she was out of sight, then closed his eyes. He was ten minutes from walking off the plane and into Great Falls. Walking into Julie's twisted life. Again. He much preferred to leave his baby sister's eclectic tastes alone.

But he had nothing left in San Francisco. Karen hadn't called. Not that night or in the week since. He couldn't leave his phone off the hook forever, and his mother had been particularly unrelenting. None of that had brought him here. He'd picked up a few tricks working at *The Chronicle* for the last ten years though, and what he'd dug up over the last few days had scared the shit out of him. Eight women had gone missing in Great Falls—seven if you didn't count Julie, because, really, that girl could be anywhere.

"Sir. Sir! We're deplaning—can I help you with your bag?" a gravelly voice brought him out of his thoughts. He looked around and realized that the plane was already half-empty.

"I'm cool." He said maneuvering out of his seat and pulling his bag from the overhead compartment. He was just to the hatch when he heard his name.

"Robert Wilson?" it was the blonde stewardess with all the right curves. "You dropped this, sir." She handed him a slip of paper. He looked down at the note.

Call Me! 438-5182
Christa

"Groovy." He smiled at her. "Maybe you can show me around Great Falls."

"Maybe I can." she winked again and turned to walk back to her station, using every curve to her advantage.

Maybe Montana wouldn't be so bad this time.

✳ ✳ ✳

"It's happened again, sir. J-318"
"El Paso?"
"Great Falls."
"Shit. Great Falls again? How many is that?"
"Eight, sir."
"Shit. Is it cleaned up?"
"Yes, sir. Of course, sir."
"Is it clear?"
"We think so. But eight is tricky."
"Eight is a fucking nightmare. Get Jenkins up here. Now."

✳ ✳ ✳

He took a minute to assess The Sherwood Apartments, which assured him in bright letters that Julie had found Modern Luxury Living. Seemed a bit drab to be calling itself luxurious but it was sure a step up from her last place. He watched his taxi pull off the curb and down the street. Part of him wanted to chase after it and get the hell back to San Francisco. Hell, part of him was screaming that this was not something he was going to be able to do on his own. The taxi turned left and out of sight. No choice now, unless he wanted to hoof it.

He walked through the front doors and took the elevator to the 4th floor, then followed the numbers down the hallway to the left until he reached 410. He knocked. What if Julie were home? How long had it been since he'd seen her? Two years? Three? It was Christmas, he remembered that. Just after dad died. And it was miserable. He swore to himself he wouldn't come back, ever.

"Hello? Julie? You in there?" he knocked louder. Silence.

He leaned down and checked underneath one of the two plants outside her door. Nothing. He turned to the other plant, lifting it carefully from its macramé home. "Bingo" he muttered to himself as he picked up the key "way to stay safe, Julie, leaving your key right here for anyone to find." Still, it was a relief to know he wouldn't have to break the lock.

He opened the door and was met with total silence.

"Julie?" he called loudly. He didn't want to interrupt anything, and he knew from experience that just because she didn't answer her door didn't mean she wasn't home. "It's me...Robert. Mother's worried about you—you really should call her now and then." He flicked on a lightswitch and waited. Nothing.

The place was nicer than he had expected—maybe Julie had pulled it together. The orange shag carpet looked pretty new and the couches were comfortable and modern. There was a circular coffee table covered in magazines and ash trays, and a color television under the bar. Not bad.

Robert set his bag down and walked around. Not a big place, but definitely comfortable. The kitchen had a full-size refrigerator and Julie had hung towels on the oven that matched the avocado color. Dishes were sitting in the rack, but they were dry. No dirty dishes in the sink or on the counters. Maybe he was in the wrong apartment. He checked the cabinets, and found them stocked—had Julie started cooking? It didn't seem possible. He opened the fridge to a wave of stench, poking around moldy vegetables and rotting leftovers. A week at least, he figured. The date on the milk was March 10. Okay—two weeks. He closed the refrigerator and opened a window, then moved into Julie's bedroom.

The bed was made and the curtains were drawn. He flipped the light on and walked over to the bureau, where Julie had arranged a bunch of framed photographs—one of her with two other girls, cocktails in one hand, cigarettes in the other. They were all laughing into the camera. The next was Julie with a man—no one Robert had seen before. Julie was looking at the camera, but the man was looking at her—like the photographer hadn't timed it just right. He turned the frame over, to where Julie had written Julie ♥ Darren 1974. So this was a new guy. There were two more pictures—one of their parents, one from years ago, of Julie with Grandma Doris.

He crossed the room and slid the door to her bedroom closet open. Her Samsonite lay on the floor. He slipped into the bathroom. Toothbrush, comb, makeup bag. She would never leave without her makeup bag—she couldn't have changed that much.

For the first time, Robert felt a chill run down his spine. Maybe Julie really was missing. He thought back to what Larry Jackson had told him on the telephone. There had been stories about seven women missing from the greater Great Falls area. Was Julie an eighth? He walked back into the bedroom, opened the frame and slipped the picture of Darren into his pocket. It was always the boyfriend.

*** *** ***

His mind raced as he dialed the number on his notepad. He scanned the notes he'd taken—seven stories had run over the last four months about women missing. No one had seemed to put it together. Had the police? Mother had insisted the police were doing all they could, but there was nothing to go on. Seven names, seven women, not from any particular neighborhood. All different ages. Two were housewives. One a college student.

"*Great Falls Tribune*. How may I direct your call?"

"Metro. Larry Jackson."

"One moment, please, while I connect you."

Robert glanced around Julie's living room as he waited. His fingers drummed the table top and his eyes fell on the mantel. Surprised, he pulled the phone across the room to see an old photo of him and Julie. How had he missed it earlier? He closed his eyes and thought back—it had been taken at the World's Fair in San Antonio. That had been a great trip—Julie just out of college, he just starting out as a hotshot young reporter in San Francisco. The whole world at their feet. How had things turned out this way? He sighed as he remembered how that trip had ended—with Julie running off with those damn hippies. Couldn't miss a chance to see the Dead. She could party with Robert anytime. That was the first time she'd run off, and here he was, ten years later, chasing after her again. He actually hoped—prayed—it was something as ridiculously stupid as a Grateful Dead concert.

"This is Jackson."

The echo from the receiver pulled Robert from the past.

"Hello. Robert Wilson here. We talked on the telephone several days ago about my sister Julie. About all the—"

"Yeah, yeah, I remember ya. What can I do ya for?"

"I'm here in Great Falls. I was hoping I could come down and take a look at the articles you were telling me about?"

"I already told you, there's not much information. But I did some diggin' after I talked to you. I'm not sure if it's anything" he lowered his voice "but I found more. A couple girls in surrounding areas. A couple guys here in Great Falls. Twelve people. None of the stories are connected. All through different precincts."

"Any chance I could get a look at those files? Just a quick look," he persisted. "One journalist to another."

"I can show ya the articles, but I don't know if I can get all the files. Not one was written by the same guy. I got a weird vibe when I went to my editor about it."

Robert jotted down the address for the *Tribune* and hung up the phone. He had a very bad feeling about this.

✳ ✳ ✳

"I thought you said ten?" Robert asked suspiciously.

"There were. Or at least I thought there were. I went to the microfiche. Checked Fort Benton and Conrad—didn't even have time to look at Helena—that's where the real story might be...I've put some calls out to some fellows I know at other newspapers...We might be on to something here."

Robert nodded. Larry wanted the story—probably his ticket out of Great Falls. If he broke the story, he could land himself a job in New York or Chicago. That didn't sound half bad. A new start in a big city.

Robert was reading through the articles and at the notes Larry had scrawled on some of them. Some of the articles had files attached where Larry had managed to pull the source material. Something was wrong here. Robert had been a newspaper man for a long time. These articles—so brief, so little information. It was almost as if they had been...censored.

Larry and Robert pored over the files trying to find connections. Did these people know each other? Go to the same bar? Have a mutual friend? Robert felt that they were missing something.

"Mr. Jackson, Mr. Franklin would like to see you in his office," a secretary interrupted, straightening up and throwing a smile when she saw Robert.

"Thanks, Nancy. I'll be there in a few minutes," Larry mumbled without looking up.

"Sir, he wants to see you now," Nancy sounded apologetic.

"Go ahead," Robert nodded, "I'll keep looking."

Visibly annoyed, Larry got up and headed next door to his editor's office, not bothering to close the workroom door behind him.

"...big story in Helena...next flight...not a request..." Franklin's voice boomed through the office.

Robert glanced at the doorway and back to the files. He couldn't make out everything that was being said, but he had dealt with enough editors to know that Franklin was pulling the plug on any story he and Jackson might find here. He quietly gathered up the articles and the files, casually tucking the stack under his left arm. As he headed for the main entrance, he heard footsteps trailing him.

"Sir, excuse me, sir," it was Nancy, calling after him. He increased his pace, making his way out the exit and into pedestrian traffic. Something was going on here and he was going to figure out what. He was going to find Julie.

✹ ✹ ✹

"Jenkins—what the hell is going on?"

"It's certainly nothing we anticipated, sir. The initial results were quite promising—amazing even. We had every reason to believe we'd found the optimal combination."

"Optimal combination? Optimal combination? I have fourteen dead bodies in Montana. So I don't think your combination was what most people would call optimal. Do you have any fucking idea of how hard this is to manage?"

"We're at a critical juncture. We think we're close. Montana's bad— I get it. But look at New Mexico and North Carolina. We're confident there's a viable combination here—we just need two, perhaps three more trials. We can determine a more diverse geographic sampling, if you feel unable to cloak us in an acceptable capacity."

"Who the fuck do you think you're talking to here? Do you know how hard it is to make bodies disappear? And why the hell is Montana so fucked up? Your report is so vague it borders on insubordination."

"Perhaps. But we're close. And when we hit it, we're gonna change the world."

✹ ✹ ✹

Robert's pulse was racing as he hailed a cab on the main drive. Thank God one had been right there, before Nancy, or somebody worse, could chase him down.

"Where to, mister?"

Where to? He needed to think—needed to figure out his next move. "Sherwood Apartments—on North Elm—I don't remember the exact address."

"Yeah, yeah—I know that place. It's nice."

Robert was already scanning the articles, looking for anything that might lead him in a direction, anything at all. A blur out of the corner of his eye....

"Did you see that?"

"What's that, mister?"

"A car—a Chrysler—just behind us—I could've sworn..."

"I ain't seen nothing like that mister."

Robert looked out again—looked in every direction. There was nothing. *Oh, God, not this again. There is nothing out there,* he mentally scolded himself. *No one is following you.*

"Ya want me to circle back?"

"Yes—No—no, of course not. Sherwood Apartments."

"You okay, mister? You don't look too good."

"Just drive."

※ ※ ※

At Julie's he laid out the articles and the files on the coffee table and considered a plan. Of the fourteen articles Larry had pulled, four had files attached. Robert jotted down the addresses on his notepad. Where would Julie keep maps? Why would Julie keep maps? He stood up and walked into the kitchen anyway—that's where he would keep them if he didn't have an office. He started opening drawers. Utensils. Towels. Tupperware. Maps. He stopped, stunned. She had maps. Neatly folded. Found the one for Metropolitan Great Falls. Three of the articles had addresses within the city. He'd work his way out to each. Someone had to know something. There had to be a connection.

※ ※ ※

Robert figured the bus had dropped him about half a mile from 34492 Valley Oaks Way. He walked quickly as he followed Julie's map and the street signs. Damn. There it was. He knew it even before he could see the numbers on the porch. The grass was overgrown and weeds were taking over the roses. There were three damp Sunday papers on the porch, one of them was starting to molder and break apart. The place felt totally deserted, but he knocked anyway. Linda Porter lived here. Had lived here. No one answered. He tried the neighbors, both sides and across the street. No answered doors. Either no one was home, or no one wanted to talk. Strike one.

421 Plumas Ave. A twenty minute bus ride. He looked out the window of the bus and watched as the neighborhoods changed. The lawns looked a little greener, the cars a little newer. He turned to look

out the opposite window—was that man in the next row looking at him? He had quickly turned away and was now reading a newspaper. Had Robert seen him before? The bus stopped abruptly. This was his stop. He exited from the rear and ducked behind the back of the bus, waiting to see if the man followed him.

No one else got off the bus. He straightened up and told himself to pull it together.

✴ ✴ ✴

"No one's going to answer that door." a conspiratorial voice came from behind him. Robert turned to see an elderly woman in a purple muumuu, holding a cigarette, ashes dangling. "Friends of theirs, are you dear?"

Robert paused. "An old friend of Mindy's—just happened to be in the neighborhood—thought I'd come by and say hello."

"You haven't heard then? Saddest story I've ever seen. Your friend Mindy went missing—off with another man, is what we all think. Truth be told, and don't take this as anything against your friend, I mean a girl can do what a girl wants to do, but more than once I happened to notice gentlemen friends, shall we say, when James wasn't home. So off she goes one day, gone for good. But James, he can't believe it. Gathers us all together, ranting that she's gone missing. Poor man lost it, I'm afraid. Calling the police at all hours to come out, telling stories about how Mindy would never leave, wanted all the neighbors to help call hospitals and search the woods out yonder. Poor man."

Robert found himself nodding as she talked. Just another bored housewife. Another shimmied husband. Never thought their own girls would leave.

"...and then one night they just came and took him away."

"What? They what? Who did? They took him away where?"

"Well, how would I know that? They took him in an ambulance. To get help, I suppose."

"When was this?"

"A couple weeks back—sorry there. young man, but I don't think you'll be able to say hello to your friend for quite some time...."

✴ ✴ ✴

"Well, of course we were worried about Patty at first, but it turned out to be nothing. Not nothing, exactly—she ran off and got married!

Isn't that wonderful? Except of course that her father and I were sitting right here watching All in the Family while our baby got married." Mrs. Monroe sniffed loudly but produced a broad smile. "We're just so relieved she's happy. And okay."

"So you've seen her then? She and her new husband are back now?"

"Well, no. She sent a postcard. From some tropical-sounding island. It had a beautiful sunset on it—the postcard she sent, that is."

"Postcard? May I see the postcard? Did she telephone you as well?" Mrs. Monroe's eyes narrowed. "Who did you say you were with? Why are you asking me all these questions? The police think everything is just fine."

"I'm with the *Tribune...*" Robert lied easily, "following up on a story, maybe."

"Well, there's no story here. And I'd like to get back to my show now." She stood and motioned toward the front door.

"Of course—I don't want to keep you from your show. I'm so relieved to hear that Patty's all right." He paused. "But may I use your bathroom before I go? It was a long ride out here."

Her face softened. "Of course—it's the second door on the right, down the hall there."

He gave her a winning smile and headed toward the bathroom, as Mrs. Monroe walked to the television to put her show on. Robert closed the door to the bathroom and then backtracked to the first door on the right—one that was obviously Patty's. A tie-dyed rug and lava lamp didn't seem like Mom and Dad's style. Was there a diary? A calendar? Something that would show that Patty was really planning to run away with her boyfriend? He looked quickly through her nightstand drawer—nothing—and was about to hurry back out to the bathroom when his heart caught in his throat. There on her bureau —a framed photo, identical to the one in Julie's apartment. Patty was one of Julie's best friends.

※ ※ ※

He was almost running, now, back to the bus stop. He hadn't heard Mrs. Monroe ask him if he was all right. Hadn't heard the door close behind him as he ran outside to get air. His head was spinning. Could this be a coincidence? He had to get back to Julie's. He pulled the framed photo from his jacket pocket and looked for anything that might give him an idea as to when or where it was taken. Nothing. A branch cracked behind him and he spun around. Just shadows. He couldn't shake the feeling that someone was behind him. He turned onto the next street, then made a quick left into a dead-end alley. He slow-counted to 10 and then jumped out into the street. No one was there.

It was happening again. Just like it had in San Francisco. He stifled a sob, and ran, full out, to the bus stop.

✳ ✳ ✳

Julie ❤ Patty ❤ Susan 1973. It was written on the back of the picture, the one framed on Julie's bureau. It was a copy of the same picture he had taken from Patty's room. He looked carefully at the surroundings. Not much to tell it apart from any other lounge...except....

He'd had time to calm himself down on the bus ride. Time to make a plan. Something was going on here. And where in the hell was Julie. Every time he came back here, he had a flicker of hope that she'd just be curled up on the sofa, scolding him for worrying. Telling him to give her space.

He picked up the telephone receiver and dialed the number on the scrap of paper.

"Hello?"

"Hey there—is this the beautiful Christa from Flight 219 from San Francisco?"

"Robert? Groovy—I didn't think you'd call. It's already almost 3:00. I'm only in town for two nights before my next flight out. And who wants to waste two nights, you know?" she giggled and he could hear ice clinking. He got the idea that Christa didn't waste too many nights.

"That's just what I was thinking...dancing? Drinks? There's this lounge my sister told me about—I'd love to check it out—I don't remember the name of the place, but there's a lit-up Johnny Cash poster over the bar..."

"Ooh—the Man in Black—I love that place, they have the best music, and you should see me on the dance floor..."

"Baby, I can't wait to see you on the dance floor."

"Pick me up at 7?"

"Uh, actually I don't have a car here...."

"Okay" she giggled. "Then I'll be the guy on our date."

✳ ✳ ✳

When he opened the door he almost reconsidered his entire plan. Christa was standing on the porch step, and she was without doubt the foxiest chick he had ever seen. She was wearing a slinky black top, tight in all the right places, emphasizing every curve and tied together in a tight knot at her waist. She had her hands on the hips of her white Saddleback Dittos, a coy smile on her face. She could tell by how Robert was looking at her that he was impressed.

"A little better than my stewardess uniform?"

"Yes...yes!" Robert laughed. "Although you would look beautiful in anything."

"Ooh, baby, that's nice." She ran her fingers down his chest and he leaned down for an easy kiss.

"Have a drink here, first?" He raised his eyebrows in question.

This could all just be so easy.

But then Julie's face flashed in his mind.

He pulled away, eyes smiling down at Christa. "On second thought, let's go—I can't wait to see you on that dance floor."

※ ※ ※

"Ooh—Donna....Donna! It's my friend Donna—come on," Christa pulled him toward the back of the lounge, where she plopped Robert down on a velvet cushion and settled easily onto his lap.

The evening careened on, Christa with her Golden Cadillacs, Robert with his Black Label. Christa was as intoxicating on the dance floor as his drink, and he knew if he didn't follow up on Julie's photo soon, he would have to come back tomorrow. Just as he was considering that that was a perfectly good plan, as Christa's fingers tightened around his waist, her breath hot on his chest, Robert saw him. The man from the bus this morning. The man with the newspaper.

"I'll get us more drinks." He whispered into Christa's ear. "Don't go anywhere."

"Why don't we skip more drinks and go back to my place?" she purred back at him.

"Mmmm" Robert turned his head to watch the man move toward the bar. "One more drink" he said distractedly as he shifted out of Christa's grasp.

He made his way to the bar, weaving in and out of the crowd, trying to find the man, following the direction he'd been going. Where could he have gone? He glanced around the bar, turned back to check the dance floor. Nothing. But he'd been here. Robert was sure it was the same guy. Wasn't it? He planted himself on a barstool and looked around again. Nothing.

"What are you drinking tonight, sir?" It was the bartender.

"Cadillac and a Black Label." He fished a $5 bill from his wallet, tried to focus. "And maybe a question?" He pulled the picture of Julie out as the bartender came back with his drinks. "You know these girls?"

"Those crazy girls? Of course! You should see 'em out on the floor" he gave a good-natured smile. "Patty used to work here, best cocktail waitress in Great Falls. The other two would come in here all the time on weekends, meet up with her, dance, party, you know. Not so much lately though." He lowered his voice, so Robert could barely hear him over the music and chatter. "Had a falling out, I think. That one there" he pointed to the one that must be Susan "she came in here looking for that one" he pointed at Julie "and that one" he pointed to Julie again "told her to stay the hell away from her. Young girls these days—they're so dramatic." He paused, considering. "Also, that one" pointing to Susan this time "she was in here earlier tonight—haven't seen her for a couple hours, though."

"Robert, what are you doing? I thought you were getting us drinks." Christa had worked her way over to the bar and was walking her fingers suggestively down Robert's chest. "You didn't forget about me, did you?" she pouted.

"How could I forget the most beautiful woman here?" he smoothly handed her the drink and leaned in for a long, slow kiss. Julie could wait one more day.

"Let's forget the drinks, okay?" He breathed into her ear. "I can't wait to get you all to myself."

Christa licked her lips and let Robert lead her out of the bar. She didn't notice that he was searching the place with his eyes as they headed for the door.

✳ ✳ ✳

Robert opened his eyes to sunlight streaming in through the bedroom window. He gently scooted from under Christa's arm and carefully climbed out of the bed, trying to make as few waves in the water mattress as possible. He smiled to himself at her quiet snoring, then winced as he stood up, regretting the last drink they'd had last night. He needed water. And aspirin.

He found a glass in the dish rack and wandered into the bathroom to look for aspirin. Second shelf of the medicine cabinet—bingo, Bayer. He helped himself to two—no, three, and gulped them down with water from the tap.

"You aren't leaving already?" her voice was sleepy as she leaned against the door, her nightie barely covering her.

"Good morning to you too, foxy lady." He put his arms around her and drew her into a kiss. "Yes, I have some things I have to do today. A reporter's work is never done." He kissed her again, more slowly, and whispered in her ear "but I'd love to see you again. Tonight if you're free."

Christa smiled up at him. "I fly out tomorrow night, but tonight I'm all yours." She paused coyly. "What did you have in mind?" she asked as she ran her hands down his naked back, then rested them playfully on his jeans.

"How about a repeat of last night? Same bar, same drinks, same everything?" He gave her a wink.

Christa giggled. "That place is pretty groovy. Okay, how about I pick you up at 6?"

"How 'bout you loan me your car for the day, so I can be the guy tonight and pick you up? And so I can get back here sooner." He added, pulling her close.

"You sure you have to leave right now?"

"Well, it is awfully early..." he noted as he guided her back to the bedroom, slipping her nightie off on the way.

✳ ✳ ✳

Robert opened the door to Julie's place, part of him still hoping that she had returned last night, that everything was fine, normal. But everything was just as he had left it. He sat down and glanced at the articles and files he'd left on the coffee table. Read through each of them one more time, slowly, looking for anything he might have missed. Anything that might connect the stories. He made a list of the names from the articles, but since there were no files, there was no easy way to contact the people that might be able to help him.

Frustrated, he walked into the kitchen and dug through the map drawer for the phone book. He'd have to do some good old-fashioned journalism. There were ten other people missing, and he intended to find out what the hell was going on. He sat back down and starting matching names to possible numbers from the phone book. He wrote down several possible numbers for some of the more common names, and made a few guesses when only initials were listed in the phone book. When he was finished he had ten names and fifteen numbers. It was a place to start.

"I'm sorry. The number you have dialed has been disconnected. If you feel you have reached this message in error, please try—" Robert hung up, and crossed the number off his list.

He dialed another number. Counted the rings. When he got to twenty, he hung up. Made a note on his list.

He dialed the next number on his list.

"Hello?"

"Good morning, ma'am. Am I speaking with" he checked his notes "Lisa White?"

A pause. "Yes."

"My name is Robert Wilson. I'm calling from *The San Francisco Chronicle*," he lied.

"*The San Francisco Chronicle?*" she asked suspiciously.

"Yes, ma'am. I heard about the recent disappearance of your husband, and I was wondering if I might have a few moments of your time?"

"How did you hear about his disappearance? The police don't seem to care and the *Tribune* only ran a few lines about him missing."

"Yes, ma'am. You see, I'm visiting my sister here in Great Falls and happened to see the article about your husband. I don't know why, but I sensed there might be more to the story, so I thought I'd call. I'd be happy to come out to your place if you have a few minutes today. I promise not to take up too much of your time. Would that be all right?"

"Well..." she trailed off.

"I think a follow-up story could help you." he decided on a tack he felt she couldn't refuse, "it could encourage the police to take another look at the matter."

"Really? You think so?" Robert almost felt bad at getting her hopes up. "Well, okay then, if you think it might help. If you can make it by 10, I have a couple hours before the Arts Luncheon. I wouldn't normally go out, what with Kenny missing, but it's been planned for a long time. And I promised I'd be there. And I'm driving my friend Betsy." She sounded guilty. Interesting.

Robert promised he wouldn't stay long and hung up the phone, a million thoughts swirling through his mind.

✳ ✳ ✳

Lisa White was not what Robert had expected. She was young, and she was beautiful. She reminded him of Farrah Fawcett, with all that gorgeous blonde hair and those big blue eyes. Her makeup was flawless, her nails manicured. Her low-cut dress left little to the imagination. There was no way a man in his right mind would have left her behind.

"Thank you for seeing me on such short notice," Robert smiled as he followed her into her home. "I hope the story I write will help bring Kenneth home."

"Kenny," she said with a smile. "He goes by Kenny. Hates the name Kenneth, actually. Only his father called him that."

"Sorry," Robert opened his notepad and pen. "Kenny." He jotted down the name on his pad and looked up "So, Mrs. White, what can you tell me about Kenny and his disappearance?"

"Call me Lisa. Everyone does." She sat down on a chair in the family room and gestured for Robert to do the same. She looked at him for a moment, sizing him up, and sighed.

"It's not unusual for my husband to be gone for a couple of days at a time. He works for the government and sometimes his assignments require him to be away. He can never tell me where he's going, or what he's doing, but he always comes back. And he's never been gone this long before." She looked at Robert with big, worried eyes. "Something's wrong."

He jotted a few more notes on his notepad before asking, "I know this may sound patronizing, but I have to ask: have you tried calling his work? Asked them to put you in touch with him?"

She gave him a withering look. "Yes, I called his work. Of course I called his work. But the number I have is disconnected. I've tried it a dozen times." a tear rolled down her cheek. "And then I went to the police. At first they were interested; they took my statement and asked for his picture. I thought they were going to help me. But when I called the next day to see if they had found anything, they told me that he probably just ran off. They said that it happens all the time and there wasn't much they could do." She looked miserable.

"Is it possible that they're right? That he ran off?" Robert asked delicately.

"No," Lisa was suddenly defiant, tears now streaming down her cheeks. "He was actually planning on quitting his job to find something more 9 to 5. We were talking about starting a family. This was going to be his last assignment."

Robert nodded sympathetically. He couldn't imagine anyone leaving Lisa White—unless she was lying.

"Lisa, if the police refused to look into your husband's situation, how did the *Tribune* find out about it?"

"My friend Martha's husband works for the paper. I asked him to run a story about Kenny and he did as a favor." She looked at Robert and added, "Got in trouble for writing it."

"What do you mean he got in trouble? From his editor?" Robert asked, puzzled. He'd been a reporter for over ten years and sure, he'd been in trouble over some of the things he'd written, but that was sensational stuff. Stories that brought scrutiny to government officials and big businesses. Never stories about missing persons.

"One of the managing partners of the *Tribune*, actually. That's like his boss's boss. So it was a big deal. Told him to leave the story alone. Didn't offer any explanations. Martha wasn't even supposed to tell me."

"Well, Lisa, no one's told me I have to leave this alone." Robert stood up and headed for the door. "I really appreciate your time today. If I have any more questions, would you mind if I telephoned you?"

"So you're really going to try to find out what happened to Kenny? Of course you can call. Anything to help find Kenny."

"One last thing" he paused at the door. "Do you have a picture of your husband that I could have? It might help to run a picture of Kenny with the article I'm writing. Maybe someone has seen him."

Lisa nodded and walked to the sideboard cabinet in the dining room. She opened the middle draw and rummaged for a moment before pulling a snapshot out. She traced her finger over the picture before bringing it over to Robert.

"Here you go," she said with half a smile. "And thanks for your help. I know Kenny, and I know something is wrong."

"I hope I can find something out. And I hope everything's okay. Maybe Kenny just got caught up in an assignment," Robert said reaching for the snapshot.

Robert looked down at the photo and gasped, his knees going weak.

"Is everything okay? Do you know my Kenny?"

"Yes. No. I'm fine" Robert stammered trying to compose himself. "I'm sorry. I still get choked up over stories like this. Thank you again for your hospitality."

He took a deep breath and forced a smile. He walked out to Christa's car, forcing himself to relax and walk at a normal pace, knowing Lisa was watching him from the doorway. He unlocked the car with shaking hands, then turned to give Lisa a reassuring wave. She waved back and disappeared into the house. Once he had slipped into the driver's seat, he took out the photo and looked at it one more time. He did know Kenny. Only his name wasn't Kenny...it was Darren.

※ ※ ※

"Agent Kenneth White is dead in Great Falls. We just got the report." He handed over a file.

"Shit. What happened?" he asked, opening the file.

"Same as the others, but this time it's one of ours. And word is Kenny was good. He should have seen the signs. Should have been able to defend himself."

"We're absolutely sure?"

"Yes."

"Does Jenkins know?"

"Yes sir, he's getting a copy of the same file right now." He paused. "Sir, there's more."

"More?

"Yes, sir. There's a reporter from San Francisco sniffing around."

"We tracking him?"

"Yes, sir, of course. But he's investigating. He's tracking the missings. Maybe starting to put things together."

"Well let's find a reason to get him back to San Francisco and out of our business."

The agent cleared his throat.

"What—what else? Jesus Christ, just spit it out."

"He does live in San Francisco, sir. But it turns out he is our business. Turns out he was in San Antonio."

※ ※ ※

It was almost six by the time he found a parking spot outside Christa's apartment. He grabbed his notebook and jogged toward the entrance. He hoped Christa wasn't annoyed with him for being gone all day. He'd had a quick shower at Julie's place, but his heart just didn't seem to be into another night out. It had been a long day—the time just seemed to vanish—and he was worried about Julie. "Shit." He muttered, realizing he'd left the bottle of gin in the car. He couldn't exactly show up empty-handed, after being gone all day. He turned back toward the car, just in time to see the tail of a blue Chrysler turning the corner. He sprinted, full speed, trying to get to the corner in time to catch the license number. He was not crazy. Deep down, he really believed that. Had to believe it.

But there was nothing there. He stood at the corner, panting. No car. No taillights. Nothing.

He walked back to the car, grabbed the bottle, headed up the stairs. His head was starting to throb. He needed a drink. He walked down the hallway to Christa's, and let himself in easily. Silly of her to not lock the door. He tried for a light tone, wanting to diffuse any anger Christa might be feeling. "Hey, foxy lady. Sorry I've been gone so long. Hope you haven't missed me too much." His words were met with silence.

The apartment was small, and it only took Robert a minute to realize that Christa wasn't there. He walked around again, looking for a note. She'd probably had a chance to go out with friends, and wanted him to meet her somewhere. They'd already decided to go back to the Man in Black so it was no big deal if she went ahead. He felt bad, though—hoped she wasn't sore at him. It had been a long day, and he was tired, but he sure wouldn't mind if tonight ended the same as last night. And this morning. He smiled at the memories.

He checked the fridge, the notepad by the phone, the nightstand, the coffee table. No note. Huh. He walked around more carefully, looking everywhere he could think of. Nothing. Maybe she was mad at him. He sat down on the couch and picked up his notepad off the coffee table. He did a double-take, putting his notebook back down and looking again at the coffee table. It was a simple wooden table, with a couple of magazines and an ashtray cluttered on top. A pretty common table, he imagined, simple and stylish.

But the coffee table that had been there this morning had been glass.

✳ ✳ ✳

He'd called of course, but the police wouldn't even talk to him. There was nothing unusual about a girlfriend not being home, or forgetting to leave a note. He'd seen her only this morning. He could hear how ridiculous he sounded on the phone, trying to explain that something was wrong. He'd called United and had at least been able to verify that Christa's shift hadn't changed. She'd told him that sometimes her flights got switched and she had to leave earlier than planned. But not this time. Her scheduled flight out was still 8:30 tomorrow night. A flight to New York. He knew how much she was looking forward to it, had a sister who lived there. The irony was not lost on him.

He drove back to the lounge, mostly because he couldn't think of anything else to do. He spent a fair amount of the drive convincing himself that Christa would be there, with Donna or some other group of friends, curled up on the velvet cushions, laughing her way through Golden Cadillacs as she waited for him. He was surprised at how much he wanted that to be true. Only a week ago he had thought his world was ruined; ruined when Karen had walked out. Maybe he'd found something—someone—even better. Someone who could understand him and accept him.

Christa was not at the lounge.

He circled the place once, then planted himself on a barstool. Then changed his mind, found the pay phone and called Christa's. Maybe he should have waited longer at her place. He'd waited until 6:30 and then left her a note, figuring she could catch a ride with her friends. But maybe he should go back for her. He hated to think she was stuck at her apartment, having to call a cab to get to the lounge.

He sat back down at the bar, wrestling with what to do, motioning for the bartender. It was the same one as last night.

"Black Label?"

Robert nodded, impressed that he remembered. He must serve hundreds of drinks every night.

"No lovely lady with you tonight?" he commented as he served up the drink.

"The night is still young." Robert forced a smile.

The bartender paused, considered, then motioned his head to the left. Robert followed his gaze, his eyes widening as he spotted the woman sitting quietly by the fire pit. It was Susan. The third girl in Julie's picture.

* * *

"Can I buy you a drink?"

Susan looked up and smiled politely, but Robert could see the stress in her eyes, in the way she held herself.

"No. No, thank you. I'm waiting for someone."

Robert pulled a chair close to Susan's. "At least let me introduce myself. I'm Robert Wilson. I'm Julie's brother."

"Oh my God—has she been with you? I've been so worried about her. I come in here almost every night, I've been going by her apartment, but she's never there. The agency says she hasn't called for a work assignment for weeks."

"Look, lady. I don't know what game you're playing, but I know Julie told you to stay away from her. What were you doing? Threatening her? She steal your guy? Why are you trying so hard to find her?"

The stunned look on Susan's face was all Robert needed to know he'd guessed wrong. So much for investigative intuition.

"What? No," she stammered. "No, it's nothing like that. Julie—she's the best friend I ever had." She paused. "Does this mean you don't know where she is either?"

"Yeah." Robert felt utterly defeated. "Yeah, that's what it means."

Susan looked at Robert, sizing him up. Then she seemed to make a decision. "Julie did tell me to stay away from her, but not in the way you're thinking. She told me to stay away because she wanted to keep me safe. It all sounded so crazy—she sounded so crazy—she said I wouldn't be safe if I was around her. Ever since she started seeing that new guy—that Darren guy—she was so worried all the time." Once Susan had started talking, the words rolled out on top of each other. Like she'd been waiting for someone to talk to. "He was so controlling. He never wanted Julie out of his sight. He was totally obsessed with her. And now I haven't seen her since that night, and I just don't know what to think. I feel like all my friends are disappearing, and there's nothing I can do about it, and I just end up sitting her all alone every night hoping they'll just show up again, like magic, you know?"

Robert thought about all the times he'd walked into Julie's apartment, just hoping she would be there and things would be normal again.

"Yeah, I know what you mean." He looked at her. "I really do."

The music had started playing and Robert noticed that a crowd had formed on the dance floor, and at the bar. He looked around, guiltily, for Christa.

"Can you excuse me for just one minute?"

"Sure. Yeah. Of course." Susan turned back to the fire and took a large swig of her drink.

Robert circled the bar and wandered through the crowd, looking for any sign of Christa, or her friends that they'd hung out with the night before. No luck. Damn.

He circled back to Susan. He wanted to find out as much about Julie as he could. He felt bad it had been so long since he'd seen her. Here was someone who could tell him Julie's favorite spots—places she might go if she was in trouble.

"Can we get out of here? It's too loud to talk."

"What?" Susan looked startled. "I don't think—"

"Don't worry—I'm not hitting on you," Robert tried for his best big-brother smile. "I just want to talk about Julie."

"I don't know—I don't even know you, really."

Robert pulled out the picture of the three girls and handed it to Susan. "Help me. For Julie. I really am her brother, and I really intend to find her."

"Okay. Let's go."

※ ※ ※

Robert let himself into Julie's apartment and held the door open for Susan to follow him in.

"Can I get you a drink? I've got some Black Label, and I think there's some wine."

"No thanks, I'm fine." She moved to the couch and pulled a pack of cigarettes from her purse. "Got a light, though?"

"A light?" Robert was having trouble focusing. "A light. Yeah, sure." He grabbed a lighter from the kitchen counter and headed back toward...toward Susan, to...to light her cigarette...he started back to the living room....

※ ※ ※

"No, Robert—STOP!" She jumped on his back and tried to pull him off Susan. "Robert, stop, stop, please." She ran to the kitchen, grabbed a glass of water and threw it in his face.

He looked around the room, confused. Everything was out of focus. His eyes narrowed as he looked across the room and saw "Julie? Julie, is that you?" He saw that she was leaning down looking at something. She was crying. "No, no, not Susan." She was holding something. Someone? "I wanted to keep you safe. Why didn't you stay away?" She looked up at Robert. She was so thin, her eyes sunken, her face pale. "Oh Robert. It's not your fault."

"What? What happened? What's wrong with Susan?" He looked down at Susan's rumpled body with dawning horror.

"Robert." Julie stood up and looked him in the eye. "Don't you understand? Darren tried to help me—told me things I wasn't supposed to know. Things about what happened to us in San Antonio. About how they changed the way our brains work. Except things went wrong—things they didn't expect. Things they can't control. He thought he could help me. And now he's gone, too. Just like Patty. And Karen. And Christa. And now Susan." Tears streamed down her face. "Don't you see, Robert? It's us. It's been us all along."

* * *

Jenkins took a deep breath as he opened the door. Things hadn't progressed as quickly as he had hoped, and he dreaded this meeting. They were going to pull the plug. He just knew it. But he knew he was close. It was all this crap that was happening in Montana. No one cared about the successes. Or the potential. He wondered if he could somehow get his data out, maybe find some interest in the public sector.

"Jenkins! Jenkins come in! Great to have you here." He had never seen his boss is such a jovial mood. Hadn't even realized he could smile. This was not what he had expected.

"Is this about New Mexico? Because I feel like we're really close there. Really close to a big breakthrough. With just a bit more time...."

"Oh, yeah, yeah, New Mexico is fine. Well, frankly, we don't give a shit about New Mexico. But congratulations! You're gonna be moving up to a new lab on the fourth floor. Everyone's excited about your research—you're gonna have an unlimited budget, and all the help you need."

Jenkins kept his face neutral. "But not because of New Mexico." It came out as more of a question than he meant it to.

"No, no—it's not New Mexico they care about upstairs. It's Montana they're interested in."

A Stranger Passing Through

So a man walks into a bar and he says to the bartender...

But this was rural Minnesota, the visitor was no more human than I was, and afterwards, no one was laughing.

1974. A no-horse town, with a single bar off the dirt road that passed for a main street. I'd gone into the bar for a quiet beer and had settled down nicely enough, so I was none too pleased when I smelled one of my own kind on the dry night air.

I tensed, and a few minutes later the door flapped open. There he was, a tall heap of dust and flapping leather. He'd chosen the long-rider look—even had the broad-brimmed hat and the stained red kerchief round his neck.

Some farmer snorted a kind of laugh, muttered to his companion, a bleach-blonde lady of the night. The guy behind the bar, a big man with tattoos down his arms, glanced at the "we don't want no trouble here" shotgun on the rack behind him.

"Help you, Mistuh?" he asked.

The visitor smiled, but he was looking straight at me.

"Just here for pleasure, friend."

This guy had been around a while. The clothes hanging off him weren't part of some retro look; they were old, and his tall leather boots were worn enough for him to have ridden with the original bushwhackers. They'd always said the South would rise again, and in this case they might have been right.

I was tired of trouble, and pretty tired of people in general.

So I turned away.

There were four other patrons in that night. The shotgun never came down from its rack, the farmer never reached the door. I didn't want to see what happened to the blonde.

It isn't romantic, it isn't cool and gothic like in the stories. It's just meat in motion. Like watching men at work in the slaughterhouses, not even looking into the cows' big, dark eyes as they press the bolt-guns home.

The tinny jukebox got damaged somewhere along the line, and all I could hear was Cash's "Ring of Fire" playing over and over again. The music drowned out the rattle in their throats, and the drumming of their heels in the sawdust. It fit.

I went down, down, down and the flames went higher...

When he was almost done, he offered me one of them, a thickset man who wasn't quite dead. I could see the blackened skin where the traveller had touched him.

I sipped my beer, and pulled my hat further down to hide my own big dark eyes. *No thanks, you mad bastard.*

And then he was gone. He was the walk-away type, one of those who fed and then left, unconcerned as to what might be found the next day. The sort who drew FBI, marshals and those people with rubber gloves who poked around in the remains.

Some of my kind are too deranged to realise that they need to clean up after themselves. This one was different. He was old-style, so far gone that he no longer feared being followed or cared what came after him. The worst sort to mess with.

My beer no longer tasted so good. I stepped around the bodies and through the rear door of the building. A small fenced yard, a chain where a dog might once have been, and a heap of rusty butane cylinders. Two still had gas in them, the fullest one hooked up to a hose. I followed the hose to a squalid back room and a stove. That would do.

It only took a minute to drag the bartender's body to the stove, like he'd been in back all along. I opened up every valve I could find, threw a lit match and ran. You'd be surprised how fast I can run. There was a crump behind me as the butane caught, and then the bar was a shower of timber and body parts, a brief prairie flower of orange and yellow.

The big sky went dark again, and I sat on a boulder, watching the flames die down from a couple of miles away. The long-rider might no longer care, but I'd been seen passing through town, and I had plenty of reasons for not being noticed. I reckoned that the gas explosion would take care of any minor traces, and mask the feeding in the process.

Time to move on again.

* * *

I blame the movies. If you think that the overblown "doomed romance" stuff of today is bad, you should have been there in the seventies. Not just Hammer Horror, flapping capes and fainting maidens.
This was the era of masterpieces like *Three on a Meathook,* after
all. The titles were bad and the pictures were worse. An adolescent
introduction to the dark side, and if you were really keen, grainy underground horror films and pretend-snuff. Mix that up with frustrated,
too-late-for-the-bus hippies, and plenty of drugs. It was a nasty brew,
as pointless as it was tasteless. Orange and purple wallpaper spattered with blood.

The scene in London back then was destructive, even self-de-
structive, as far as my kind were concerned. The city was riddled
with predators, clever enough to cover up their tracks but not clever
enough to move on. What we were called doesn't matter much. The
older ones (I'm talking centuries here) liked to be known as *Edimmu,*
which made them sound interesting. They weren't, in general. Those
of us who could still think clearly used the term "Returned," as in discarded, thrown from the grave and left to fend for ourselves.

I'd been there, at the spiked-drink and groupie parties. It fascinated
and disgusted me at the same time, like staring at speeding cars and
waiting for the bloody, buckled mess that would follow. Some dark
attraction had brought the worst of the Returned into the same twisted circles. All those who weren't catatonic or utterly insane, orbiting
around each other and making the whole thing worse.

I didn't take part, of course. I was the guard at Buchenwald who
never pulled the trigger, never actually held the syringe. I only watched
the long shuffling lines, not looking at the faces. So that made it alright.

Until that one night in Chelsea, when I tried to burn the uniform...

1973, a hot summer. There'd been a grubby white screen pulled
down to cover most of the lounge wall. It was an improvement on the
décor. I remember the whirring of the projector as Christopher Lee
flapped his way through another painful plot. That was high kitsch,
the Returned showing vampire films to drugged-up teenagers. Maybe
some of us wanted to be like that, instead of facing up to the reality
of what we'd become. We wanted to be Christopher Lee, but there
were no vampires.

Only us, too restless to stay in our graves, and never knowing why.

I'd ended up there by accident, drifting from one place to another
without purpose. The film was halfway through, and the seven or
eight groupies, all around sixteen, seventeen years old, were well
baked, Quaaludes going down nicely with each glass of Blue Nun.

"Feeding tonight?" asked the host. He stood between the projector and screen, an enormous Peter Cushing flickering over his fat body. He was half-watching the film, half-watching a blonde teenage boy whose jeans had miraculously come undone in the last few minutes. The host liked to play with his food.

I shook my head, ready to leave. His swollen pink tongue flickered in and out, like a lizard I'd seen in Regent's Park zoo the week before. But the lizard was what it should be. He wasn't. He should have been re-buried and weighted down long before this.

I thought of the forty, fifty years that some of those doped-up teenagers might have had left to them. For a brief moment I saw their families, their achievements to come, the joys and losses...

Something turned inside me. I was fast enough, even back then, fast enough to do the unthinkable.

It took less than a minute. The kids didn't even notice, their eyes fixed on the screen or the ceiling, depending on how many 'ludes they'd been fed. First I broke his legs, then his arms. He thrashed on the carpet, shrieking and mouthing off. There were a lot of rude words, but I wasn't interested. I dragged him down the fire escape, and looked around, sniffing the midnight air.

The canal towpath was rough cobbles, cracking the Returned's skull as I hauled him along.

"You...can have them all." He was pale, too long since his last feed. I imagine he'd been counting on that night.

"I don't want them. And I don't want you, either."

He sank quickly, finding his way down between discarded boots, kettles and the general detritus of our great navigational heritage. His type are collapsed lungs and flattened arteries, however well-stuffed they were when alive. Floating is not a common skill in the breed. This one was broken, damaged and deprived of true life. He would mend, but not quickly. He would surface, eventually, but it would be hard work.

I found a telephone box and rang for an ambulance. Concerned neighbour, overdose, dear oh dear. They promised to get straight there. The kids would live, though they might have a lot to explain.

That was the first time I'd attacked another Returned without provocation. And I was feeling something new. It wasn't a mission. I wasn't planning to turn on my own kind in some kind of comic-book scenario. Maybe it was just the idea that I didn't have to put up with them all the time.

I'm not sure I even cared that much about the doped-up kids. It was more the waste, the pointlessness. That was how I reasoned it. I kept out of circulation for a while, and heard nothing that worried me. So I tried an experiment. I went to another, bigger party in Greenwich... And that was my mistake.

When the news of what I'd done in Greenwich sidled its way across the London scene, the threats began. There weren't that many Returned in the city, don't get the wrong idea, but some of those not-many liked the idea of a challenge. And I was a new diversion, a chance to hunt one of their own for a change.

The attacks began a few days later. An Edimmu caught me in Highgate and nearly tore my arms out of their sockets. Something else, darker and more dangerous, shadowed me across London for five days, leaving me drained and confused. It was getting too much.

I booked a long-haul flight to the US of A. Speed had allowed me to survive, but at the cost of having to feed more often, and keeping my eyes open constantly. Every shadow might be another chancer, wondering if he could bring down the Returned who'd crossed the boundary. There was talk of money, lots of it, and an open invite to certain events.

I had become a competition for dangerous retards, eager to pay me back for what I'd done...

※ ※ ※

That was how I'd ended up in Minnesota, but that night with the long-rider had left a sour taste in my mouth. So I sought the cities instead, on the grounds that at least they weren't London.

I reached New York in the autumn of '74. I didn't really know what America had become. The last time I'd been there was around the time James Garfield was assassinated. It didn't look like much had improved. Nixon had fallen, and some potato-head named Ford had immediately pardoned him. The streets of New York were not exactly awash with optimism.

The Big Apple was brighter, poorer and more drugged-up than London. Harder drugs, harder people, in a city on the edge of bankruptcy. The Kray Twins, had they not already been banged up in dear old Blighty, would have messed themselves if they'd met some of the cases I came across.

And if they'd ended up in the Manhattan House of Detention, or The Tombs, as it was apparently known, they'd have messed themselves twice for good measure. Which would have added to the ambience of the place, I suppose, given its reputation as a hellhole.

It was because of The Tombs that Seamus Connors came into my life. Or unlife, if you prefer.

I'd known that Seamus was in the States, even had an inkling that he was in New York, but I hadn't intended to look him up. He'd been six months old and puking on his grandfather's shoulder when I'd seen him last.

But when I read in the *New York Times* that Padraig Connors's grandson had been arrested and slammed into The Tombs, I stirred. Old habits, old memories.

Padraig had been an old Fenian from Listowel, a big, bushy-eyebrowed man with a taste for the potcheen. He'd go to any rally, getting himself beaten black and blue by the authorities on a dozen occasions, and he wrote enough seditious material to fill Dublin Public Library, but he wouldn't hold a gun. He drank, spat and slept his way through the good women of County Kerry, but he stuck to his principles. I'd known him well, and I'd liked him.

I hired a lawyer, an expensive one. It didn't take long to find out the details. It appeared that Seamus had royally annoyed someone from one of the Italian families. A man called Carmine 'The Cigar' Galante, in fact. I had no experience of the Mafia, and no real interest in them, so I went ahead without worrying.

The case was dubious, to say the least. There were a lot of convenient statements which suggested Seamus was involved in fraudulent accounting for the Teamsters. Who that gang were, I didn't care. I did care that Seamus had been shoved into The Tombs for refusing to testify against his own boss, a man Carmine Galante wanted taking down. It was depressingly simple.

I paid off an alcoholic deputy commissioner, a judge with a gambling habit and an overworked assistant District Attorney. Seamus was out in a week.

"What happened?" I asked him as we drove away from Manhattan in his clapped-out Chevrolet.

"Mob, City Hall. All the clichés." He frowned, a thin man in his mid-twenties with sandy hair. "Like a bad crime novel, and worse. This city is falling apart. Beame says he's going to turn it 'round, but the mayor ain't the problem. It's the slime under his feet that wants washing away."

"So you didn't do anything?"

"I was set up. Teamsters, farm unions, three or four different Sicilian operations. Whoever you work for, someone is out to bribe you, get you arrested, or just have you shot in a backstreet."

I grunted enough to seem understanding. Seamus was the earnest type, who really had thought he was doing the right thing by the union. I stopped listening, and concentrated on driving on the wrong side of the road. Mostly.

"You look...pretty much how Granda described you." He was hesitant. When he said Granda you heard the Irish in him.

"I age well."

"You sure do."

I ignored the question under the statement. Not a lot more was said until we reached his apartment, a brownstone already emptying of its white inhabitants. The nice people were fleeing to the new suburbs, leaving cockroaches and crime for the poor and the black folk to deal with.

His place was spacious, graceful and falling apart. The ceiling had enough stains to make it art.

"The plumbing's shot," he said, noticing my gaze. "One day a bathtub's gonna fall on my head. Coffee?"

"No, thanks."

I can drink it, but what's the point? I don't like the taste that much, and I have to bring up the liquid later. Where's it going to go? My kidneys stopped doing anything useful too long ago to remember.

He fixed himself a cup, and sat back in the one armchair. I was comfy just standing, looking round.

"You didn't have to do that. Get me out, I mean," he said at last.

"Consider it your Granda's gift. Or an old favour repaid, however you like to see it."

"Well, thanks." He looked almost shy. "I have something stashed away, a few hundred..."

I waved my hand dismissively, and I think he was relieved. He was trying not to show it though, which was manners.

"You got somewhere to stay?"

I shrugged. "Not especially."

That was the start of it. I stayed there in the crumbling brownstone as his guest. He showed me around. We saw a few ballgames, admired the new World Trade Center towers and reminisced about his grandfather. We didn't speak about Seamus's father, though we both knew that he was still alive. There were bombs going off in Britain that probably had his name on them. Seamus's mother had fled to

America with her ten-year-old son, leaving Wolf as far behind her as she could.

Wolf Connors was IRA. Not the Free Ireland kind, though. More the psychopathic, bludgeoning murderer who enjoyed his trade more than he cared about Eire. He didn't hate the English; he just liked killing, and having an excuse for it. He once shot a Garda for looking at him, as easily as he would have raised his pistol to a soldier or a barking dog. I'd known Returned I liked better than Seamus's father.

The son, on the other hand, was almost another Padraig, which is what had got him locked in The Tombs. His Granda would have been proud of him for that.

Every night I ate dinner with Seamus and brought it up again somewhere discreet. Every eight or nine days I paid good green dollars at the back of some hospital, visiting those who were already on their way out. Intensive care was my restaurant, a way of pretending that I had any conscience at all. Or maybe it was no more than another habit.

Seamus had plans, if he could pull them off. There was an accountancy position in a Seattle company which was still open, now that the charges had been dropped. He may have been naive, but he knew his job inside out.

We were sipping imported Irish whiskey one evening, listening to the police sirens outside, when I slid an envelope out of my jacket.

"That reminds me. I borrowed some money from your Granda, many years back. To tell the truth, I'd forgotten about it until all this came up. As the old bugger's no longer with us, maybe you could use it."

He opened the envelope, read the amount written on the cheque.

"Granda never had this sort of money."

"I've had it for a long time. Guess the interest must have added up."

He didn't believe me, but I wasn't budging. I stared at him until he had to look away. After a long silence, he smiled awkwardly and poured us both another whiskey.

"He came over to see ma and me, just before she died. First time he'd flown, and he was shaking like I'd never seen. Granda, the big man, scared half to death by a flight across the Pond." He sipped his drink slowly. "He said that you'd turn up one day. Like as not."

"He was usually right. Stubborn, drunk and trouble to be with. But right."

We drank a toast to Padraig, and the cheque stayed with Seamus.

* * *

I'd sorted things out and paid my dues to old Padraig in the process, but I'd forgotten that this was New York, the Sicilian hunting ground. Two days later, while Seamus was out shopping for groceries, we had a visitor.

Whoever it was, they wouldn't stop pressing the bell. After five minutes, I went down to the hallway, opened the front door.

It was a nice Italian man. Oiled, crinkly hair, a fine Mediterranean tint to his eyes, his skin, and neatly-pared fingernails. I imagine that his mother loved him very much.

He smiled. Beautiful teeth.

"I got business with Connors."

"He's not here." I stood easy, balanced, but this guy was only a messenger. He had no problem telling me what was up. It seemed that if The Tombs weren't good enough for Seamus, his "friends" in the Bonanno Family had more imaginative suggestions as to where he might stay. I'll spare you the clichés he used. I think he might have tried to reinforce his message with a beating, but there were too many people on the street that day.

I thanked him for his kind words, and slammed the door. I could have walked away right then. After all, I'd done my bit for Seamus. Couldn't shelter a man from everything....

I thought it over, said nothing when he got back later that afternoon. He could leave New York that night, if I made it sound important enough, but who knew what friends this Carmine Galante had in Seattle? I certainly didn't.

I decided that I wanted things to stay clean. Padraig would never have left a fight half-finished.

The next day I made a few enquiries, and paid a visit to one of the guys who'd helped manoeuvre Seamus into prison in the first place. A runner for the Bonannos, easily found in a Brooklyn bar where the minnows spent their free time. I encouraged him into a back alley, using dollar bills like candy, and asked him exactly what plans they had for Seamus. He didn't want to discuss the matter. I'd heard of this Omerta, the code of silence that was supposed to govern the Sicilians. I wasn't impressed, and after a few minutes, neither was my new friend.

Persuaded by a broken rib or two, he told me about a little Italian restaurant in Brooklyn. He would set up a meeting with his *Sotto*

Capo, some sort of underboss. That seemed high enough up the chain for what I wanted. I let him stagger off to find some bandages, and went back to sightseeing.

✳ ✳ ✳

The attack came the day before I was supposed to meet the *Sotto Capo*. I don't think it was a coincidence.

I'd spent my time keeping in the shade. I was finding it a bit too bright on the streets. Shopping, reading the papers under coffee shop awnings, a visit to the museums to see what they'd gotten wrong. I slipped into the Bronx Museum of Art, which had been set up in the County Courthouse. I was curious. Did they have courtrooms full of contemporary paintings, with the browsers listening in to the judge's summing-up? Sadly, no. The art was in the public rotunda, not that I got that far.

The stranger came at me while I was bringing up beer in an ornate restroom. I'd had a couple at lunchtime, and could feel them swilling around inside me. I locked the cubicle door, bent forward, and....

Wood splintered. Someone cracked my head against the toilet pan. It would have stunned a living person—or maybe killed them. I twisted 'round, and received a fist in my face, then another. My back was arched over the porcelain, hard enough to hurt.

"This'll take some time," said a hoarse voice. "I hope."

I glimpsed a lean face, kicked out at it, missed. I thought at first he was like me, but he wasn't. One whiff of him told me that he was high, cocaine-spiked and more. Angel Dust was part of the mix, I was sure of that. His skin was red and dry, his pupils wide.

He slammed me back again, almost breaking my spine, and hit me hard in the belly, once, twice. Grabbing a piece of the splintered door, I lashed out at his head, made contact, and slid between his legs.

A museum guard, or maybe an officer from the courts, looked in to see what the noise was. My attacker turned and snarled at the guy, so I rammed my boot into his crotch, giving the guard long enough to take out his gun. Whatever happened I knew that I could take being shot better than this youngster. I'd had the practice.

"What the fuck..." The guard was solid, salt-and-pepper hair, plenty of years on the streets. He would shoot rather than throw himself into a violent fight like this.

My attacker snarled again, unsure, which gave me time to slide towards the wash-stands.

"He's got a knife!" I yelled, looking suitably scared and victim-like.

I was clean, respectable-looking in a suit, polished shoes. I'd checked myself in the mirror that morning and I knew that I could be any New York professional out on a lunchtime stroll. The other guy was frayed jeans and sneakers, grubby overcoat. Prejudice can be a useful thing. The guard took sides, settling his muzzle in the direction of the scruff.

My attacker didn't like the odds. If he turned back to me, he'd be shot. If he took out the guard, I'd have him....

He ran. The guard grunted into his radio, flat-footed over to me.

"You OK, buddy?"

I eased myself up, grabbing a wash-basin for support. I didn't have to pretend that I was having trouble standing. Those vertebrae would take days to come quite right, and I was in for some uncomfortable nights.

"Goddamn junkie," I gasped in my best American accent. "Didn't get anything, thanks to you."

There was more, a twenty for the guard, the suggestion of a crime report waved away, but eventually I managed to leave the Courthouse, creaking as I went. Common sense dripped its way into my mind, but I had Seamus to think of. So I would make that meeting. I would not be in a good mood.

※ ※ ※

I found the place easily. Gino's Family Ristorante. My informant had left me with no doubts as to which family liked it most. It was a Bonanno favourite, apparently. The main room was empty, so I ordered food, and waited. The ravioli was very good, wild mushroom and garlic, served with a strong Sicilian red.

I was less impressed by being shot in the chest during the tiramisu.

The impact nearly threw me off my chair, and the pain, although it was brief, ruined the meal. I straightened up. The shooter had come in through the kitchen doors, another man behind him, sharp-suited and tall. The restaurant's single waitress, a big, soft-eyed woman, was pressed against the wall, knuckles at her lips.

"He's gotta be wearin' a vest," said the shooter, looking puzzled.

I frowned. I was guessing that his companion was the *Sotto Capo*. A classical Sicilian mobster with dark, wavy hair and olive skin. He tapped the shooter on the shoulder.

"Finish it, Louie."

A dull impact, a sharp pain in my belly. I was annoyed now. In a second I was at the shooter's side, ripping the gun out of his hands and throwing it into the remains of the tiramisu.

"Figlio di puttanta!" The *Sotto Capo* stepped back, eying the half-open kitchen doors.

I took the shooter's arm, my eyes still on his boss.

"I'm assuming that you work directly for Carmine Galante. I hear that you chaps like vendettas and retribution, that kind of thing. So I'll make my point."

It didn't take long to rip the fingers from the man's gun hand, one by one. All I had to do was snap the joints at the big knuckle and pull hard. Little finger, gone. Ring finger, gone....

Blood sprayed the tiled floor. The waitress screamed, and so did the gunman. Italian eyes were not smiling. From the smell, the shooter had pissed himself.

"I can do this for quite a long time," I said, glancing at the boss's own right hand.

There are times when I get stupid, even after more than a century. I had seen his side-glance, but had assumed that he was looking for an escape route. He wasn't.

The kid from the Museum of Art was in the kitchen doorway. He looked worse than before, bloodshot eyes dancing wildly in their sockets, but this time they'd given him a handgun. Two more bullets hit me, one on the shoulder, one somewhere near the kidneys. That one really hurt.

"Go down, you fucker!" he shrieked.

I let go of the other henchman, or whatever he was, and left him to sink to his knees and count his remaining fingers.

Pain is pain. A few more bullet holes and even I would be in trouble. The boss-man was eyeing the gun on the floor, even the waitress might be armed.

So I broke one of my own rules. I remembered Minnesota, and the bad old times in London, and I became like the other mad, pointless members of my own kind for the first time since Greenwich....

It didn't feel good, but it was necessary. In films, the monster laughs maniacally, or howls at the moon. The bad guy pauses, to let his victim know that the end is coming. It's a spine-chill moment, a punctuation mark between life and the coming darkness.

In reality, we just kill.

I closed the distance between me and the kid, threw the gun away so hard it stuck in the wall panel, and ripped his shirt from his back.

The girl screamed again as I slammed my open hand against the junkie's pockmarked chest, and I fed.

I lost any pretence of being human. I was Edimmu, no better than the rest, with the desperate hunger of the dead.

As his sallow skin crumpled under my fingers, he managed one gasp, and I drew him into me, fed from every last pathetic cell of his body. He didn't cry out after that, because there was no air in his lungs, no beat to his ruined heart. No life. When I was finished, I threw his dead husk to the floor.

The waitress had passed out, the other gunman was whimpering as he tried to wrap a napkin around his mutilated hand. Part of me wanted to slaughter both of them as well. The junkie hadn't had much to give.

The *Sotto Capo* was standing there, waiting to be next. His wet lips moved in a prayer; his eyes were closed. I wanted more, but I needed a messenger who might make sense.

I was in front of him, and then I was behind him, stroking his neck.

"Tell Mr. Galante," I said. "Seamus Connors is leaving town in a few days. He won't ever hear from the Bonanno Family again."

The *Sotto Capo* nodded.

"*Si.*"

"If Connors is followed or threatened, I'll find you. Do you understand?"

"*Si.*"

His fear filled the air, mixing with the tang of his mate's urine. I could smell that he was convinced. The ache inside had left me. I managed to walk out the door with some semblance of normality, grabbing an expensive camel hair coat from the rack. There were a lot of holes in my suit which some bright spark on the street might just notice.

The ravioli really had been good, but I wasn't going to pay for the service.

❋ ❋ ❋

I didn't mention my afternoon's business to Seamus. My wounds had closed by dinnertime, and I'd slipped on a fresh outfit. He showed me photographs, views out over Seattle bay. Gateway to the Pacific, said the accompanying leaflet.

"Looks decent," I said.

He grinned. "I get a relocation package. The guys at the *Washington Post* put in a word for me, after I gave them some extra material from the account books. They're feeling generous after Watergate." His grin turned more anxious. "Do you think I've put myself at risk again? Some of the records might sort of connect to the mob."

He was clearly a slow learner for a bright guy.

"I don't think they're interested in you anymore," I said. I wasn't going to explain any more than that.

He was safe enough, but I wasn't. Maybe I'd living in the last century for too long, somewhere inside my dead brain. These were the 1970s, after all, and the world was going global. Word of my encounter with the *Sotto Capo* might do the job for Seamus, but I'd got myself noticed.

There would be others of my kind somewhere in New York. And a loose word, a muttered report in clubs or bars—these could easily make their way across the Atlantic. Jets and phones carried half-truths, whispers, which might be picked up back in London. Greenwich would not have been forgotten.

So I thought again of the Midwest and the big, open spaces, where the only good use for the land is to stand and stare at that sky. Where there are plenty of small towns, where there are no mobs, no Returned and nothing much ever happens.

But not Minnesota.

※

Shadows of the Past

He wore his light grey suit. True, it was a good six years old and maybe considered out of fashion, but it was still his favorite. Given what he was about to through, he could at least wear his favorite suit for the occasion.

Everything had started with a letter. Just a routine security interview, the letter had said. After thirty years, it was a part of his life that he had grown accustomed to, like visits to the doctor's office. Not always a pleasant experience but a fact of life nonetheless.

"Good morning, Mr. Fendelman," the man thirty years his junior said as he got up from the table he was sitting at. Fendelman smiled and extended his hand. The young man took his hand and shook it.

"Same to you, Agent..."

"Glover."

"Good name."

"It's served me," Glover replied with a smile as he withdrew his hand. He pointed to the table he'd been sitting at and offered Fendelman the chair across from his. Table and chairs alike were neither expensive nor ornate; merely functional. Fendelman expected no less out of a government office.

Sitting down, Fendelman looked the agent up and down. He was in his early thirties, perhaps, certainly born after the war at any rate. Dark hair that was a bit on the longer side of an acceptable crew cut and intelligent blue eyes that looked at him as the two men sat at their respective ends of the table.

"May I ask, Agent Glover, why I'm here? I am meant to be retiring in a few more weeks, am I not?"

"That is the case," Glover conceded with a nod. "I've merely been asked to go over some old ground."

"Old ground, you say?" Fendelman stroked his thin grey beard as he spoke. He looked at the younger man thoughtfully that showed curiosity more than anything else.

"That is correct, sir. Specifically from before you came to the United States after World War II."

"You mean my time in Germany?" Fendelman raised an eyebrow. Glover nodded.

"That's right. In particular some of the details regarding the construction of the V-2 rocket."

Fendelman laughed. Glover looked at him confused. Fendelman sighed and shook his head before offering an explanation.

"That was more than thirty years ago, Agent Glover. We have come a very long way since then. Take the Saturn V for example—"

"I'm well aware of NASA," Glover interrupted in as polite a fashion as possible. "I understand you yourself worked on the Saturn V rocket."

"*Ja,*" Fendelman's background bled through for a moment. "I was in charge of various things at various points. All under the late Werner Von Braun, of course."

"Of course, Mr. Fendelman. You were even awarded the NASA Distinguished Service Medal for your work."

"Just so." Fendelman spoke like a proud father. "That was just before the first Apollo landing back in 1969."

"As I read in your file. All of which is very impressive, but..." Glover's voice trailed off. He glanced down at the table. Silence fell over the room around them as the younger man suddenly seemed uncomfortable, reluctant even.

"But what?" Fendelman asked with a raised eyebrow. Glover looked up at him and took a deep breath.

"What I have to ask you about is serious, Mr. Fendelman. As I said, it regards your time in Germany during the war and the construction of the V-2's."

"Are you not speaking of technical matters?" Fendelman inquired. Glover shook his head to indicate in the negative.

"I'm afraid it involves how they were constructed. To be more exact, by whom and to what extent you as a member of the rocket team were aware of the matter."

"What was the phrase they said about President Nixon? 'What did he know and when did he know it?' Is that what you mean?"

Fendelman's tone was almost playful, certainly meant to be disarming. It seemed to have something of the desired effect on the serious young man in front of him who smiled and gave a short laugh. He nodded and said he was looking for answers along those lines.

"If you mean: was I aware that the rockets were being built by prisoners that the answer is that I did know."

"Were you aware of the conditions under which they were being constructed?" Glover asked as he opened up a small notebook on the table. Fendelman shook his head.

"Nein," Fendelman replied as Glover wrote in the notebook. "I cannot say that I was aware."

"Do you recall ever visiting the underground factory at Mittelwerk connected to the concentration camp at Dora?"

Fendelman shook his head.

"If I had, I would have been aware of the conditions, not that I could have done much about things, of course."

Glover stopped writing. He lifted his gaze up off the notebook to look at Fendelman. He sat the ink pen he was using down and folded his hands together, leaning forward as he did so.

"Why do you say that?"

"For a very simple reason..." Fendelman replied before his voice trailed off. Glover raised an eyebrow of his own and Fendelman continued, sensing the young man wanted more. So he obliged.

"It would have done no good."

"It would have done no good?" Glover repeated. Fendelman nodded and continued.

"It was a terrible time, you know? Von Braun was arrested and imprisoned twice for not being seen to be contributing enough to the war effort. Did you know that?

Glover nodded that he did.

"He may have been aware. If he or I, or any of us, had raised objections to how the prisoners were being treated, we, too, would have been imprisoned. Or shot, perhaps."

"Is that so?" Glover's tone was one of skepticism. Fendelman nodded and took that as his cue to continue.

"Not only was Von Braun arrested, but the thugs," he said with disgrace in his voice. "The thugs guarding us in those final days were actually ordered to kill us so that we couldn't be captured."

"Good thing we got to you before they could," Glover found himself agreeing. Fendelman gave a thin smile and nodded in agreement.

"If I may," Glover interjected, "I do want to ask if you recall who it was that first suggested the use of slave labor for the V-2's?"

"Someone in the SS, I would assume."

"So not someone from the team such as yourself?"

"I would not imagine that to be the case, Mister Glover. I am certain that it was not me."

"Alright," Glover said apparently satisfied. "I ask because some new information has come to light in recent months."

Glover turned around and lifted a dark brown briefcase up from beneath the table. He opened it up and took from within a folder that he sat on the table between them. It had the FBI seal on the front, Fendelman noted as Glover closed the briefcase lid before opened the folder.

On top of a stack of papers was a photograph. It was black and white, clearly decades old, and revealed a group of men in what appeared to be black uniforms. It was what was on each of their left arms that caught Fendelman's attention even before he had it pointed it out to him: swastika armbands.

"You recognize the uniforms these men are wearing?"

"I do. They are SS uniforms."

"That's their leader, Himmler, in the middle." Glover pointed at the man in the middle who had his face tilted up, his eyes hidden behind the light reflected on his eyeglasses. Fendelman nodded and Glover's hand moved along the photograph to another man in the group. This figure was clean-shaven, fairly young and had a serious expression on his face. Glover tapped his finger on the photograph and looked up at the older man.

"Is this you in 1944?" Glover was matter of fact in the tone of his questioning. Fendelman said nothing at first, just leaned forward a little, but more to get a closer look at the image.

"That fact that I was in the SS technically has not been hidden, I should have thought."

"The files, including an affidavit you signed when the team was transferred to here in Huntsville, said you were mainly administrative but did do some technical work on the V-2 program. I saw nothing in the files about your being a member of the SS."

"Agent Glover," Fendelman replied with a heavy sigh as he leaned back from looking at the photograph with his head slightly titled to one side as he looked across the table. "Are you going to blame me for an oversight made decades ago? One undoubtedly made by one of your predecessors?"

"Were you in the SS?" Glover persisted. Fendelman nodded slowly, his eyes closed.

"I was required to be in the SS due to my work. It is not something of which I am proud of. I did have that uniform and I wore it for official functions, but I hated it. Never quite fit correctly and itched like hell."

"Still," Glover replied in the same matter of fact tone he had used earlier, "your membership in the SS meant you could have been tried and imprisoned after the war."

"Yet I was never prosecuted. Why is that, I wonder?"

"Not yet, sir." Glover's tone didn't change as he spoke. He slid the photograph to one side with his finger to reveal one of the papers that had lain underneath. It was a typed document, though, whether it was the combination of eyesight or the document's font, Fendelman could not read it.

"We have testimony from a number of survivors who worked at the facility. They reported that not only were you involved in picking prisoners for tasks but that you were seen both beating prisoners and ordering executions. In fact, we have an eyewitness who identified you from the same photograph I showed you as the man who beat him for standing on a piece of equipment."

"It was decades ago. I am certain this is a case of mistaken identity."

"Then you are not denying you visited the Mittelwerk facility?"

"I may well have. I do not recall..."

"Do you deny beating prisoners or ordering executions?"

Fendelman said something in German that Glover didn't understand. Fendelman saw the look of confusion on the agent's face. He closed his eyes and nodded before translating.

"Of course I do."

The two men bounced back and forth for the better part of two hours. Fendelman was polite and tried to be helpful. Or rather, as helpful as he wanted to be, Glover thought. Glover finally closed up the folder and looked at the man across from him.

"I would like to interview you again. Would that be alright with you?"

"That would be convenient," Fendelman agreed as he stood up. "When would you like to speak to me again?"

"Today is Thursday, so how about on Monday?"

"Agreed."

"That will allow you time to collect your thoughts. After all, it was a long time ago, as you said."

"I will see you Monday." Fendelman extended his hand again as he left. Glover looked at it hesitatingly for a moment before accepting it.

The younger man offered a hollow smile before removing his hand and allowing Fendelman to leave without another word.

* * *

After spending the evening brooding about the interview, Fendelman felt ambivalent about them the next morning. As he had said over and over again, it had been a long time ago. In fact, he hadn't thought much about those days in years. Not since that dumb song about Von Braun had come out. It seemed odd that after these years he was being forced to talk about it once again.

Once out of the bed, he went to the bathroom connected to the bedroom and turned the shower on. He let the water warm up as he stripped out of his pajamas. He caught a glimpse of himself in the mirror above the sink and looked at himself, seeing the grey hair on his scalp and in his beard. He stroked his beard, as if to ask his reflection where all the years had gone.

Then he saw it. Or something, just there in the corner of the mirror. The hint of a shape, a figure perhaps. He turned his attention to it, fearing a burglar. Yet the moment he tried to focus on it, it was gone. He was briefly reminded of 'the observer effect', the notion that looking upon something caused it to change.

He went to look further but the sound of the water running through the shower head changed, going from a steady rushing stream to what sounded like an artillery barrage. Fendelman walked away from the sink and pulled the shower curtain open. The water was coming out of the head in fits rather than all at once. Muttering under his breath, he turned the handle to lower the water pressure for a few moments before turning it up again. The shower head emitted water normally and Fendelman stepped inside, pulling the curtain closed behind him.

The water was a bit too warm, causing him to turn the handle to the right a bit. The water took a few moments to catch up, but once it did, Fendelman closed his eyes and stood under the running water. He let it pour onto him, feeling as it hit and dripped it way onto and down his skin. He found himself relaxing, his breathing becoming deeper with each new cycle of inhalation and exhalation. He smiled and opened his eyes, only for the smile to drop off his face.

He blinked his eyes repeatedly. The water pouring out was not the usual, clear color. Instead it was an almost scarlet red. Looking down, Fendelman realized that the shower had not drained either and the water now angle deep around his feet and so clouded that he could not see his feet beneath the red water.

Realization hit and he took an instant, instinctive step back. The water traveled like a wave up and down the length of the tub, washing around him. Fighting back a sickening feeling, he took a step forward through the still running water and turned the handle to the off position. He felt the water hitting his face again as he turned the handle and he closed his eyes, hearing and feeling the flowing water come to a sudden halt.

Without even parting the shower curtain, Fendelman stepped onto the rug, red water dripping onto the cold floor and the white rug next to the shower. He grabbed the towel off the holder next to him and hurriedly dried off. He almost scrubbed his body with the towel, as if trying to get the unclean feeling off of his skin.

Then he stopped. He looked at his hands and noted there were red droplets all over them. Just as suddenly as he'd stopped, he started to dry again and he stepped off the rug and walked quickly out of the bathroom.

He traversed the house at a speed that was surprising for a man of his age. He found the phone in the kitchen and, after wrapping the towel around his waist, he pulled the Huntsville area phone book out of a kitchen drawer. Skimming through it, he dialed the number of the first plumber he could find.

An hour and a half later and now dressed, Fendelman watched as the plumber named Phillips looked at the tub of blood-red water. The plumber turned the faucet on and off, stuck something into the drain and repeated this for a few minutes before looking up. Catching Fendelman's gaze, he shook his head and ran a hand through his blonde hair.

"Well, it isn't blood," the plumber said with a southern twang to his voice. "Though I can see why you would describe the color that way."

"Would you tell me what it is, then?"

"Sure," he answered as he stood up. "I'll need to get under the house to look at the pipes to be certain, though."

"Certain of what?"

"That this is nothing more than rusting pips. Happens all the time with iron and metal piping. They rust over time, like any other piece of metal and the rust comes off in the water."

"I see," Fendelman said, almost relieved.

"Yeah." Phillips' tone was almost uncaring. He stepped by Fendelman, who followed him out of the bedroom and into the hall. "It means that probably all the piping has gone bad and that it will need to be replaced."

"Is that expensive?"

"Can be." Phillips nodded.

The two men walked through the house and out the front door. They stepped off the porch and walked around the side of the house in silence. Then the plumber slowed down and looked off into the distance, a confused expression on his face.

"There is one strange thing about this, though."

"What is that, Mister Phillips?"

"The water color."

"What about it?" Fendelman's tone was impatient. Phillips shook his head and started walking again, only replying to Fendelman over his shoulder.

"It's normally brown or orange with rusty pipes. It sure as hell isn't blood red."

Fendelman absorbed the words for a moment. *That is odd,* he thought to himself. Though just because this one plumber hadn't seen it didn't mean it wasn't possible. He smiled before he followed in Phillips' footsteps to show him where the door was that led to the crawl space under the house so he could check the pipes.

✳ ✳ ✳

Once Phillips left, Fendelman called his secretary out at the Marshall Space Flight Center to say he wasn't coming in to work. It had been noon by the time the plumber had finally left and he looked at a clock. At that point, it seemed futile to go.

A few years earlier, the thought would have been foreign to him, especially at the height of Apollo. With Apollo over and the new Space Shuttle not yet flying, he felt superfluous at times. Maybe that was why he had listened to Amelia when she had suggested he consider retiring at last. Wasn't like he wasn't pushing retirement age as this point.

He went into his study and sat down behind the desk. He looked around the room and took in the silence of the house around him. Amelia was gone to visit her aunt, Will was with his new wife up north and Patrica was off at university. He suddenly felt very alone as he looked around the room, at the bookcases with all of the books he had acquired since he had come to the U.S. decades earlier. The thought made him smile and he closed his eyes.

When he opened his eyes again, he wasn't in his study. The room—or rather the space—he found himself in was vast. He judged that from the sound of footsteps and movements that seemed to echo off of walls he couldn't see. He was still seated, though in an uncomfortable position that made his back ache. He reached around in the dimness for something that he could grip to pull himself up but he found nothing. Finally he put his hands to the ground and pushed himself up slowly.

"You!" A man yelled out from somewhere in the distance angrily. "What do you think you're doing?"

The echoing effect of the space made it difficult for him to figure out where the voice had come from. Searching for the sound, he was struck by something. The man had not called out in English. He had called out to him in German.

"Where are you?" He called out in German, seeking the man. Fendelman felt unable to move and stayed where he stood. The air had taken on a stale quality suddenly as he took a deeper breath He tasted chalk-like dust on his tongue as well as an ugly taste he could only describe as metallic. He spit foul-tasting saliva onto the dark ground he was unable to see.

"Where am I?" He asked aloud. He turned first right and then left, searching for either the man or the source of the noises that were going on around him. He felt for the eyeglasses that he had left in his shirt pocket and found neither glasses nor a pocket. Instead of his shirt, he felt soft material and what seemed like a patch that had been sewn onto whatever shirt he was now wearing.

He looked down and saw a flash of bright light. It was followed by a sharp pain to the back of his head that caused him to cry out as he fell onto the ground. He hit with a thud and he groaned, feeling unable to either move or take in his surroundings.

"Please..." He said before his voice trailed off. He felt a movement of air on his left side followed by yet more sharp, sudden pain that this time afflicted his left arm. He cried out again as he was sent off balance by the impact which rolled him onto his right side in a single fierce and painful move.

"Get up!" It was the same voice he'd heard before. "Get up, you lazy bastard!"

Fendelman opened his eyes. He gasped and cried out before realizing he was in his study. He tried to smile but pain overwhelmed him. His head hurt, as did his left arm somewhere around the elbow. He forced himself to stand up only to have to sit down again as the study spun around him.

Sitting there, he wasn't sure what had happened to him. He reached first for his head, rubbing his right hand over the back of it where the pain seemed to originate from. He flinched as his hand went over a sensitive area and he found what felt like a large bump protruding from a spot near the spot where skull and neck meet.

Feeling sick and with the room seeming to spin, his eyes kept opening and closing. For a moment he thought he glimpsed someone in the doorway of the study. He called out for Amelia before sense caught up with him. He closed his eyes and when he opened them again, the figure was gone.

If anyone had been there at all, Fendelman thought to himself as he closed his eyes again. Fighting off nausea, he leaned forward a bit in the chair and reached now for his left arm. He struggled to move the fingers on his left hand and his arm didn't seem to want to move. Feeling stiff and hurting, he unbuttoned the cuff of his shirt's left sleeve and slowly rolled it up. He grimaced with pain as he pushed it up past his elbow where he finally looked.

The area around his elbow had turned into a sickly series of colors. Blue, purple and black now had taken over from his usual paler complexion. Fendelman stared at it in disbelief, slowly and painfully rolling his arm over to see the elbow itself better. He could only sit there and look at it, wondering what had happened to it.

✳ ✳ ✳

Despite the grogginess and the pain in his left arm, Fendelman managed to get out to his car. It was a struggle to drive up first to Whiteburg and then down the length of that road until he reached Governor's Drive. He had been forced to grip the wheel with his left hand at times and every bump in the road had been like a new injury to him. He'd kept his grip on the wheel, though, his teeth firmly clenched the entire drive.

It had taken an agonizing few minutes, but he arrived at his doctor's office. Thursday afternoon was normally not a busy time at Doctor McIntee's office. Hannah, his nurse, had seen him come through the door with his left sleeve rolled up and holding out his arm. She had rushed from behind the desk towards him.

"What happened, Mr. Fendelman?" She had asked as she ran the short distance to him. Fendelman had been honest and said he didn't know.

"I dozed off at my desk," he told her as he she looked at his elbow. "I woke up with this and a bump on my head."

"Were you attacked? A burglar perhaps?" Fendelman shook his head no. "Let me get the doctor. Sit down until he gets out here."

Having used so much of his energy just to get here, Fendelman took the offered seat. He slumped down into yet another uncomfortable chair and closed his eyes as his head fell back. He grimaced as it made soft contact with the wall, inhaling through clenched teeth. His teeth barely parted for him to exhale and he leaned forward again.

Where was I? What happened to me?

The more he thought about it, the more familiar his surroundings had been. Now, even the unseen man's voice and words seemed familiar as they echoed around his mind.

Don't be foolish, Magnus! He told himself. *You didn't go anywhere. You were sitting in your study, remember?*

Hearing footsteps, Fendelman opened his eyes again and turned toward the back of the office. Doctor McIntee had come out of his office and was racing down the small hallway with Hannah trailing behind him. McIntee looked at him worriedly.

"Hannah says you came in looking like someone had beat you," he said shakily. "I hate to say it, but it looks like someone beat you."

Fendelman said nothing, just looked at the two of them as they came to a stop next to him. Before he knew it, Doctor McIntee was flashing a small light in his eyes and asking him to follow the movement of his fingers.

"Well, you're still responsive which is good. You might have a concussion, though, and I won't know about the elbow until I get you back there."

The next little while had been a bit of a blur. Fendelman remembered ending up in the exam room and vaguely recalled being helped into it by Doctor McIntee and Hannah. He laid down and felt groggy as they went about him and checked on him. He had tried to go to sleep, but they had always brought him back around just as he was drifting off onto the edges of consciousness.

He closed his eyes again and they stayed closed for a few moments. He opened them again to find the room had gone black. Forcing himself to sit up, he realized he was neither lying on the exam room table nor in the room itself. He took a breath and realized from the taste in his mouth where he was.

"Where am I?" He yelled out. His voice echoed back at him from the distance over the sounds of footsteps and movements in the dark around him. He could make shapes out around him and he blinked again and again trying to make sense of it all.

"You!" It was the same man who had yelled out before.

Remembering which way he had been been struck from before, he turned to face the man he was sure was about to attack him. He stood up as straight as he could and peered into the darkness and saw the shape of a man, the darkness making the details indefinable, approaching him.

"You!" He shouted at the approaching figure. "Where am I?"

The figure continued at him and details began to make themselves apparent. The man wore dark clothing, a uniform of some kind from the looks of it, that almost blended in with the surroundings. The man's skin complexion was white. He had shouted in German.

"Herr Fendelman!"

Fendelman closed his eyes and opened them a moment later. The bright fluorescent light in the exam room ceiling almost blinded him and he lifted his right hand up to shield his eyes. He saw two figures standing over him. One was Hannah, a look of concern on her face. The other figure wasn't clear at first as Fendelman's eyes adjusted. For a moment it was someone he didn't recognize, yet somehow felt familiar. The next it was Dr. McIntee, who had appeared next to her and Fendelman turned to look at them.

"Are you okay?" It was Hannah who had asked the question. Fendelman nodded and he felt his hand suddenly become heavy and he lowered it down towards his face.

"I was afraid you'd become unconscious," Hannah explained.

"I might have, for a moment," Fendelman replied. Dr. McIntee moved Fendelman's hand and quickly shined a light into both of his eyes. He clicked the light back off and took a step back.

"Your arm isn't broken, just bruised. You've almost certainly got a concussion, though. I've called up to the hospital and they're sending an ambulance over for you."

"Ambulance?" Fendelman shook his head. Dr. McIntee had expected this and offered an apologetic smile.

"It's just overnight so they can keep an eye on you. With you having a concussion, I can't very well send you home. It's a thousand wonders you made it here at all in your condition. Which leads me to ask something, if I may?"

Fendelman nodded.

"What happened to you? Do I need to call the police?"

"*Nein,*" he said as he shook his head again. "I was asleep and woke up like this. I only wish I knew what had happened."

"Sleepwalking?" Dr. McIntee offered. "I've heard of people walking into things. I had a young girl in here the other week who had sprained her wrist after falling down some stairs."

"*Ja.* It must be." Fendelman offered a smile back at the doctor.

"Though you woke up in the same place where you had fallen asleep, right?"

Fendelman nodded. For a moment, the doctor looked back at him with a look of confusion. The smile, though, was back soon enough and McIntee shrugged.

"Sleepwalking still seems the most likely answer."

With that both doctor and nurse walked away. Fendelman laid there and held a hand up to his face.

Sleepwalking. That was the only answer.

✳ ✳ ✳

The evening in Huntsville Hospital passed without incident. Another doctor and a couple of nurses had kept their eye on him as he lay in a bed. Despite the headaches and occasional nausea, he found himself bored and wishing for either company or something to take his mind off of things.

His thoughts turned to the FBI man, Glover. Fendelman wondered what he must make of events, as he was certain that they were keeping track of his movements. What would they think of the man they were interviewing calling a plumber out over blood-colored water and then having to go into a hospital with injuries that might appear odd? Would they think he was crazy? Or a man having bad luck? Or did Glover and the FBI already think something worse of him?

Fendelman grappled with those questions himself as he laid there until the lights were turned off. He slept a dreamless sleep that, after his previous ordeals, he was thankful for when he awoke the next morning. The doctor, a man whose name he had never learned, had pronounced him fit, though asked that he take things easy over the next few days. Fendelman had agreed and the doctor seemed satisfied.

As he checked out of the hospital, his left arm still tender and aching, he had used the payphone in the hospital's lobby to make a quick phone call to a colleague. It had been rather embarrassing to ask someone to move him a short distance back down to Dr. McIntee's office, but his car had been left there from the previous day. Thankfully, Gus Gorman had been home and willing to pick him up.

Gorman was one of the new generation coming into Marshall for the Space Shuttle. Tall and thin, looking at him when he pulled up outside the hospital, Fendelman noted that Gorman and Glover were quite alike in terms of basic physical appearance: tall, dark-haired, thin, and in their thirties. Though Gorman's hair was a bit longer and he sprouted a mustache that seemed oddly popular, ridiculously so. Getting into the car, Fendelman reminded himself of the old American expression about not looking a gift horse in the mouth.

"Thank you for coming to get me," Fendelman said as he closed the car door. Gorman smiled and put the car into gear.

"No problem. Glad I could be of help."

The car pulled out of the hospital and moved in the direction of Governor's Drive. Gorman glanced over at Fendelman, who sat silently staring out the passenger side window. Gorman cleared his throat and the older man looked at him.

"I tried to come in to see you yesterday, but Jill said you had called in. Something about a plumbing problem?"

"*Ja,*" Fendelman replied. He quickly laid out what had happened and what the plumber had told him. Gorman had given him a strange look and a "hmm" in reply.

"This was all after your talk with that FBI guy on Thursday?"

Fendelman glared at him.

"How did you know about that?"

Gorman looked at him defensively. Fendelman immediately felt bad and gave a sigh. Gorman didn't relax though, his eyes darting between the street in front of him and his passenger.

"We all heard you were being interviewed. I just thought it was one of those routine security things." Gorman said before falling silent as they reached Governor's. They sat for just a moment before the traffic light changed and the car completed the turn down towards McIntee's office.

"Did anyone think anything else?" Fendelman asked. Gorman shook his head and finally smiled.

"Should they have?" His tone was friendly. Fendelman returned the smile and turned his attention back out the window.

"No."

"So it was just a routine thing?" Gorman asked. Fendelman looked back at him and gave a quick nod.

"What's the saying? 'More or less' I think?"

"That's right," Gorman asked as the car braked. Fendelman looked out the windshield in front of him and saw they were approaching the office. His car was the only one in the lot, its white exterior standing out against the brick building it was parked next to.

"What are you going to do when you retire?" Gorman asked rather suddenly. Fendelman didn't turn to look at him.

"I'm thinking of writing. It's something I've always wanted to do."

"That was something that Von Braun was good at, after all." Gorman noted as he turned the car turned into the parking lot. "A novel or something?" He added as he parked next to Fendelman's own car.

"Or a memoir. Tell the story of how we came here and everything we did."

"Even before?"

"Perhaps." Fendelman opened the car door and swung a leg out the door. He had barely gotten a foot on the ground before Gorman spoke again.

"I always wondered what it must have been like during the war. To have been on the wrong side."

Fendelman turned.

"The wrong side?"

"Yeah. I mean you guys were fighting with the Nazis after all. They did some pretty horrendous—"

"We," Fendelman interrupted angrily. He turned in his seat to face Gorman. "We were engineers, scientists. You think we wanted to kill people? It was the last thing we wanted, young man."

"I'm sorry—" Gorman tried to speak but got only those words out before Fendelman cut him off again.

"We worked for the Army. They wanted weapons. We gave them what they wanted. Same thing when we got here. It was the only way to make progress."

"I didn't mean to offend," Gorman offered. Fendelman sighed and rubbed his eyes, suddenly feeling tired. He looked at the distressed younger man and smiled.

"I sometimes feel like we will never repay the wages of sin. That no matter how well our rockets did, how many Saturn rockets lifted off, no matter how many men walked on the Moon, we're still the enemy."

"You were good people in a bad time," Gorman offered. "You did what you had to do."

"*Ja.*" Fendelman turned to get out of the car. "We did what we had to..." he muttered before climbing out and closing the door. He gave Gorman a wave goodbye and watched as the younger man reversed the car and drove away.

Gorman was a good man. He understood how things were and how they had been, even if he was too young to have been there. If only more people like Glover thought like he did.

Fendelman smiled at the thought as he walked the short distance to his car. He reached into the right pocket of his trousers and extracted his keys. He worked his thumb around the ring holding the keys together, feeling the coolness of the metal. He stopped to rub a spot on his left arm between his arm and elbow that was itching before unlocking the door and climbing into the car.

✳ ✳ ✳

Since the plumber had advised him not to use the water, Fendelman had been forced to eat a TV dinner and drink one of Amelia's sodas when he got home. While neither was exactly what he wanted, it was an improvement over the hospital food he had eaten the previous evening. He had turned on the television and flipped it to the local CBS station, not so much to watch it but to fill the house with some noise.

He had left the television on even when he had walked back into his study. The room had been just as he left it the previous afternoon with even the light still on. That wouldn't help the utility bill when it arrived, but he would deal with that when it came in.

He sat back down in his chair and looked around the room. His attention was drawn to the three framed photographs that he kept on the right side of the desk. Two of them were the obligatory photos of Amelia from before they got married, looking half her age when he had met her as a widower living in what was then this small town, as well as a photo of the children. It wasn't either of those pictures that he looked at, though.

His attention focused on the third picture. It had been taken shortly after they had arrived at Fort Bliss, the rocket team's original home after they had been put to work for the Americans. They had all been gathered, about one hundred of them, and had a group photo taken. Years after the event, Von Braun had given copies of it to those still working on Saturn. In a way, it showed how far they had come from those early days. There was Von Braun in the front row, near the middle, with his right hand in a trouser pocket, while Fendelman was standing just down from him in a suit that looked white now. Had it been white?

Fendelman smiled. He picked it up, the coolness of the frame and the glass holding the picture coming as a surprise given it was spring outside. He sat the picture back down after a moment and leaned back in his chair. He thought back to his conversation with Gorman in the car. Maybe he should write. There was, of course, the possibility that no one would ever read it, but it would be something. A way of speaking for himself at least.

He reached down to the desk drawer to open it when he felt a bit of an itch on his left arm. He wondered how long it had itched before he had noticed it, remembering how it was when the children had gotten chickenpox. While sense told him not to scratch, instinct meant that he could not resist the urge. He tried to compromise by rubbing the area on the underside of his arm not with his fingertips or fingernails but with the top of his hand instead.

The old adage though proved true. The itch would not go away but instead remained. He would rub and rub until aggravation finally got the better of him. He pushed the chair back and stood up, walking out of the study and into the hallway towards the bathroom in the hallway. Maybe one of the children still had an ointment or something in there he could to elevate this sudden itch.

He unbuttoned the sleeve as he walked. Reaching the bathroom, he stopped only long enough to flip the light switch, before he walked over to the sink. He quickly rolled the sleeve back, trying his best to ignore his still protesting left elbow. He rolled his arm to look at the troublesome spot.

As expected, there was a rash. Yet the rash was an odd one. He had expected a patch of maybe red or pink. This was a darker color, a blue or maybe a black, it was hard to tell which. Gritting his teeth, Fendelman bent his elbow and lifted his arm up closer to his face.

Yes it was a darker color. Weirdly, he saw something familiar in the rash. If he hadn't known better he would have thought the rash looked like a series of numbers. He could make out a one at the start, a seven and a three elsewhere. In fact it looked like....

Fendelman laughed and slowly lowered his arm. He opened up the cabinet above the sink, stepping back slightly to avoid the door. Finding the ointment he was looking for, he quickly squeezed some onto his arm and dropped the squeeze tube onto the counter. He rubbed his fingers over the spot, going back and forth over it. The ointment smeared back and forth but showed no signs of drying.

Which each wipe back and forth, the apparent numbers became more distinct. He stopped rubbing and yet again bent his elbow upwards. He looked at the rash and read it: 140673.

Fendelman gave out an almost primal growl and stopped rubbing. His right hand felt sticky and he looked at it in disgust. Using his left hand, he turned the hot water handle, forgetting for a moment about the water. It was only as he watched the water pour onto his hand that he remembered and he gave out yet another growl. He withdrew his hand and shook his head, sending red water droplets into the cabinet and onto the pale yellow paint on the bathroom wall next to him. He turned the water handle off and angrily ripped the towel off its handle, taking it with him as he left the bathroom.

He threw the towel down on the floor by his desk as he walked back into the study. He rolled his sleeve back down and struggled to button it back closed as he sat down. His attention again turned to the photographs on the desk. He picked the group picture up again and held it in his right hand.

"Time," he muttered. He looked at the photograph for the longest time and then set it back down again. He once again reached into the still-open drawer and pulled out a few sheets of paper. Finding an ink pen on the desk, he took the cap off of it and started to write.

✳ ✳ ✳

By the time Fendelman decided to go to bed, he had written only about four pages. It wasn't much, he knew. Mainly about their arrival at Fort Bliss years earlier. That had seemed a good starting place and the beginning of the story. He would write more, of course, but felt tired at present and craved nothing more than a good's night sleep. At least it would be in his bed this time.

He changed into his pajamas, still folded up where he had left them the previous day. They were blue-and-white-striped and he suddenly felt uncomfortable in them. He had a troubling feeling, that twisting and churning in his stomach that made it difficult for him to lie still in bed. Probably the hospital food I ate or I undercooked the TV dinner. He would be fine in the morning, he decided.

He awoke in darkness. He reached over for the lamp on the night stand but he felt nothing but air, instead. He rolled over and stuck his face not into his pillow but onto solid, hard ground. He opened his eyes and recognized his surroundings. It was where he had had been before, when he had been dreaming or whatever had happened.

It was happening again.

He got to his feet and looked down. He wasn't in his pajamas, anymore, but another pair, ones that had to have belonged to someone else. They were grey and black with the stripes going vertically, quite different from the ones he had worn when going to sleep. Neither did they fit well as they were quite baggy and hung off of his body.

"You!" It was the same man who had yelled out before. Fendelman turned as he had previously and started walking towards where the voice had come from. He became aware again of the noises around him and figures that he couldn't quite make out. As he had expected, he saw a figure approaching him. He stood tall and pointed towards the advancing figure.

"Are you in charge here?"

"What?" The figure called back with a question of its own.

"Are you in charge here?" Fendelman repeated. The figure came closer and more detail became apparent. Fendelman felt his arm lower and he took a step back. He recognized the uniform of the figure approaching him and looked at it in disbelief.

"You're SS?"

"Are you blind?" The figure, revealed to be that of a man in early thirties perhaps. He wore the black uniform of an SS officer. Fendelman shook his head and took a step back.

"Something's wrong!" His voice bounced back at him off the walls. He was in one of the tunnels at Mittelwerk, he knew that. How he wasn't sure nor did he understand why he was wearing a prisoner's uniform.

A sudden thought occurred to him. He rolled up the left sleeve and there he found what he had hoped would not be there. The rash, the apparent numbers, were there in all their morbid glory.

"The only thing wrong is that you are not working!"

This was a different man's voice. It sounded familiar somehow and he turned towards where the voice had originated. He felt a shiver go up his spine and he took a step back involuntary. For he recognized the face of the other uniformed man standing a few feet from him.

"How did he make it here from Auschwitz?" It was Fendelman, thirty years younger and several pounds lighter, standing there looking at him disapprovingly. The younger Fendelman, dressed in his full SS uniform, shook his head at his older self.

"Get him out of here. They need one more outside, anyway."

"Yes, sir." The younger SS officer grabbed him and began to pull him away. Fendelman struggled, unable to break the younger man's grip. He looked pleadingly at his younger self, mumbling sounds that would not form into words. The younger Fendelman just shook his head and walked away.

All of it seemed familiar. *When was this? Sometime in '44 or maybe '45,* he thought. Well it had to be. Had he ordered someone to be dragged off? He couldn't, wouldn't recall. He desperately searched his thoughts, those memories he had locked away so long ago and not thought of again.

What had happened? What was happening?

The tunnel gradually gave way from darkness to daylight. It came at the edge of vision and gradually grew brighter and brighter. It was a spring day, complete with a cloudless blue sky. Yet all Fendelman could focus on was the drab and greyness around him: the prisoners, the dark colors of the guards and SS officers, the trucks and everything it seemed around him. It was a platform that he was led to a platform by the SS officer.

"Here's the last one!" The officer called up to some men already standing up on the platform, one of them in his shirtsleeves. Two of the men grabbed him and lifted him up onto the platform, dragging him along. Fendelman realized where he was being led.

Four other prisoners had already been lined up. This wasn't just a platform: it was a gallows. The other four men had ropes around their necks and Fendelman quickly found a fifth around his. His attempt to raise his hands up led to the man in shirtsleeves delivering a quick punch to his stomach, causing him to nearly double over.

"Ready?" One of the men called down to someone. There was a *"Jawohl"* called back and Fendelman heard the sound of footsteps running on the platform. He managed to lift his head up and catch a brief glimpse of his younger self walking out of the tunnel and toward a car. He opened his mouth to speak and felt the platform beneath him give way. He felt a rubbing against his neck and a scream work its way from his lungs to his mouth.

Fendelman sat up in his bed, gasping for air. His body was covered in sweat and he tossed the covers off of him. He reached for the lamp and this time found it. He flipped it on, the dim light turning the dark room a pale yellow. He swung his legs out of the bed and stepped on the soft carpet.

He hurriedly walked to the bathroom, flipping on the light switch. He turned the sink on and cupped his hands, splashing water on his face. Yet again, he had forgotten about the color and only remembered when he opened his head and saw red water pouring out of the faucet.

Fendelman took a horrified step back. He looked up into the mirror and saw the red water dripping off of his face and onto his pajama shirt. He stepped forward and pulled this towel off of its rack, hurriedly wiping his face with it. He then struggled with his hands, his left arm aching at the elbow.

He used the towel to turn the faucet off and he realized he was still panting. He glanced over at the tub, the red water still in it. Phillips had been unable to make it drain and the water seemed to be there, mocking him.

He rolled up his left sleeve. The rash was still there, the apparent numbers all too visible. Fendelman rolled his sleeve back down and walked out of the bathroom.

He looked at the bed. Though still tired, he didn't feel like going back to sleep. Instead, he walked out of his bedroom and into the hallway. He walked to his study, reaching in where he flipped the light on. He walked through the illuminated room and sat down, once again at his desk.

The four pages he had written were still there. He picked them up, looking over his words and memories. They were true, he knew that, but it wasn't the beginning. He sat the pages aside and reached down to open the desk drawer again. He pulled out some blank paper, picked up his ink pen and began to write again.

❋ ❋ ❋

Glover scarcely recognized the man who came in for the second interview on Monday morning. Fendelman seemed to have aged years over the weekend. Not physically but in his manner. He seemed slower, more haggard. Glover almost pitied him for reasons he couldn't quite fathom.

Fendelman didn't speak a word. He instead put an envelope down on the table in front of him. Glover looked at the envelope and then at Fendelman, who slowly sat down. The look on the old man's face was one of...shame? Guilt? Resignation? It was hard to tell which, or even if it might have been all three.

Glover picked the envelope up, extracting several sheets of paper from within it. He read the first one and then the next and the next, going through each one carefully and slowly. Both men were silent as Glover read. It was only when Glover read the last page that he looked at Fendelman.

"Thank you," he said quietly. Fendelman said nothing. He seemed to look past the FBI agent and at the wall behind him. "May I ask what led you to write this?"

"You wouldn't believe me..." Fendelman said before his voice trailed off. "I'm prepared to do whatever is necessary. My wife will be home later today and my children obviously are away."

"I understand." Glover put the papers back into the envelope and folded the flap back down. He started to get up, looking at Fendelman as he buttoned his suit jacket back up. "I'll need to call my superior, Mr. Fendelman. Is that alright with you?"

Fendelman nodded. Glover exited and left him alone in the silent room. Fendelman glanced at the door for a few seconds, making certain Glover wouldn't return. Satisfied, he rolled up the left sleeve of his own jacket. He rolled his arm over and reached over to unbutton the sleeve. He rolled it up and looked at his forearm.

The rash, the numbers, whatever they were, had gone. The skin was pale with not a mark upon it. Fendelman looked on sadly and rolled his sleeve back down. He buttoned it back up and rolled his jacket sleeve back down, a feeling of sadness coming over him.

Not for the first time in the past few days, a sudden feeling of exhaustion came over him. He reached up to his face with both hands, closing his eyes and put his face in their embrace. He gave out a sigh and then lowered his hands, taking a moment longer to open his eyes.

He nearly screamed. Standing in front of him, behind the same chair that Glover had been at moments before, was someone completely different. The figure was tall but bony, frail-looking in a way. Looking the man over, he realized why that was. The attire, the striped outfit complete with a round cap, called back not just across the decades but to the experiences of the past few days.

"You're him, aren't you?"

The figure nodded. Without speaking, he raised up his left arm. Using his right hand, the figure pulled up his sleeve. Fendelman knew what he was supposed to see and for a moment resisted the urge to look. He knew it would do no good, the realization dawning on him that this was what he was meant to see.

The rash he had experienced was there on this man's wrist. This, though, looked fresher, newer. Fendelman looked up at the man's face, realizing that the man was impossibly young—he couldn't have been more than twenty-five.

"I saw things through your eyes. What you felt, what it was like when you died. I ordered your death, didn't I?"

The figure nodded. He pushed his sleeve back down. Fendelman looked away and was silent for a moment. Finally he turned back to face the man he'd ordered dead more than three decades before.

"I'm sorry," he tried to say.

The figure, though, was gone, as if he had never been there at all. Fendelman sighed and sat back in his chair. He remembered what he'd said to Gorman about the wages of sin never being paid. Maybe he had paid his at last, he wondered.

His thoughts turned briefly back to Amelia. He had left her a letter at home, just in case something happened and he didn't get home. He wasn't sure if it would explain things properly but it would have to do. He wondered what would happen. Would he be deported? Would they cut off his pension? Or would it all be quietly hushed up, as it had been to begin with. For the first time in years, he simply didn't know.

He heard the door open and he turned to await his fate.

※

Day of Ascension

File name: Copernican Temple of the New Sun #578831
File type: Transcript—Radio Transmission
Frequency: KRZH 90.4 FM—Wicked and Weird
Airdate: 08/08/75—12:13 am CST

KS: Welcome back folks, my name is Kyle Sisto, and you are listening to *Wicked and Weird:* your weekly digest for the strange, the deranged, and the stuff that doesn't make it to the nightly news. Tonight we're focusing on UFOs, aliens, and all things unexplained in that big ol' sky. We're here with author Lori Taylor, expert on plane crashes and UFO phenomenon. Thanks for being here, Lori.

LT: Always a pleasure, Kyle.

KS: We've just covered a bit about your newest book, *Aerial Anomalies,* which follows phenomena relating to UFOs and flight phenomenon. Lori, I've got to ask you, what's been the most interesting case you've covered?

LT: *[laughs]* Well, I find them all fascinating.

KS: Yeah, of course, and you want us to find out more in your book! But come on, there must be a couple of stand-out cases?

LT: Well, there's one case, the case of Flight 3411, that stands out to me as one of the most mysterious.

KS: Oh yeah, that's a good one.

LT: What's interesting to me is that we don't know what happened. In so many of these cases, you know, the pilot just, uh, the pilot returns from the flight, there's an internal investigation

about what they saw, and it's closed from there. Chalked up to sleep deprivation, in most cases.

KS: True, yeah, pilots are notoriously sleepy.

LT: It just seems fishy to me.

KS: So 3411, folks, was a flight where a pilot encountered a UFO during a routine cargo flight, and then he was never heard from again. Is that the gist, Lori?

LT: Pretty much, yeah.

KS: Well, I guess that's the show!

[both laugh]

KS: But seriously, Lori, care to expand?

LT: Jeffrey Collis, the pilot of Flight 3411, was flying overnight to drop off a cargo shipment to Los Angeles. The transcript of the flight shows nothing out of the ordinary until around 3 am, when he was flying a few miles outside of a small town in Nebraska.

KS: And what happened?

LT: According to the transcript, he just came out of some cloud cover and spotted a whirling set of lights ahead of him. First, he was asking, you know, he was asking if, uh, air traffic control knew about any craft. They said there weren't.

KS: What did he seem like when he was saying this?

LT: He called the lights beautiful—I've listened to the tapes, I have a copy, he sounded almost hypnotized, and, uh, fascinated, and he started whispering—it gets indecipherable—and then he started screaming...

KS: He started screaming? Was he screaming words, or just sounds?

LT: Sounds. It wasn't pretty; it was the kind of screaming that shows real panic, real distress—

KS: And then it cut out?

LT: It cut out.

KS: Where there any sounds of impact, or anything?

LT: A few seconds later there was the sound of some scraping metal.

KS: Was the plane found? Any wreckage?

LT: No.

KS: Now, the people in the fine state of Nebraska, did they report anything?

LT: He was flying over a really rural area, several miles outside of the town of Blue Hill, so there would've been very few witnesses to something like that.

KS: Did any of the very few witnesses report anything?

LT: Well, uh, there was one call, a call to police from the area that night, but it was just background noise.

KS: Did the police investigate?

LT: They're required to investigate every call, but when they went to the property, the home was empty.

KS: No one home?

LT: Didn't look like it.

KS: So what happened to Jeffrey Collis?

LT: Well, that's the question, isn't it?

KS: Do you believe he was abducted?

LT: I can't, uh, I can't say one way or the other, really.

KS: That's a great mystery. We'll have to pause for commercials, and then we'll be back and taking your questions for Lori Taylor, author of *Aerial Anomalies*.

[12:30]

KS: Welcome back to *Wicked and Weird,* your weekly home for the strange and deranged here on 90.4 FM KRZH. I'm your host, Kyle Sisto, here with Lori Taylor, author of *Aerial Anomalies*. Tonight's show is about UFOs and flight phenomenon. We've got our first caller—Cassie, from Newton. Go ahead, Cassie.

C: Hello Kyle, Lori.

[both]: Hi, Cassie.

KS: What do you have for us today?

C: I've read a lot about the case of Jeffrey Collis and I think I know what happened to him. He and that house in Nebraska, they're connected.

LT: Why do you think that?

C: They were taken.

KS: You think the owner of the house was abducted?

C: Yes, sir. Taken. I know it, I can just tell. They were lucky.

KS: Well, now, Cassie, I don't know if I'd call that lucky.

C: It's lucky to shed your terrestrial body, Kyle. Think about it, it's the next logical step in human evolution! We come from stars, we become the stars. The aliens—they're really angels, our messengers, they're bringing us closer to the truth.

LT: That's quite the theory.

KS: Thanks for sharing with us, Cassie, we'll—

C: Jeffrey Collis was a prophet of the stars and he was taken because he was ready t—

KS: Sorry, Cassie, we're going to have to move on to the next caller. Glen in Summerville, you're on the air.

G: Jeffrey Collis was taken by the angels! He was ready for the truth.

LT: Another one...

KS: Afraid we've just covered this ground, Glen, but thanks for calling. Next caller is Sarah, also in Summerville. What do you have for us, Sarah?

S: Oh hello, it's good to be on the air. *[echoes]*

KS: Sarah, can you turn down your radio?

S: Sure thing, Kyle, sorry. Lori, I'm a big fan of your work.

LT: Thank you.

S: I think, y'know, I think Cassie and Glen might be right. This is our clearest evidence of the existence of UFOs and the aliens could be helping us. They're always the bad guys in movies and stuff but, heck, they could be bringing us closer to the truth and—

KS: Sarah? Are you still with us?

LT: Did she hang up?

S: *[muffled]*

KS: Sarah?

S: *[silence]*

KS: Uh, folks, we're having some difficulty with the phone lines right now. We'll be back to more *Wicked and Weird* after this commercial break.

❋ ❋ ❋

File name: Copernican Temple of the New Sun #578832
File type: Transcript—Radio Transmission
Frequency: KRZH 90.4 FM—News at Five
Airdate: 08/11/75, 5:05 pm CST

HS: Good evening, I'm Harold Sampson and you're listening to the News at Five. A local author has gone missing, authorities report. Lori Taylor, author of the hit series *Unexplained Experiences*, has been reported missing. She was last seen on August 9, leaving radio station KRHZ here in Silver Creek, MN, at approximately 1:00 am. She is described as a Caucasian female, aged 45, approximately 5'6" and 155 pounds, with blonde hair and brown eyes. She was wearing an orange dress, large green hat, and red leather boots. Members of the public with relevant information have been asked to contact their local authorities.

＊ ＊ ＊

File name: Copernican Temple of the New Sun #578833
File type: Transcript—Radio Transmission
Frequency: CTNS 3917 kHz
Airdate: 08/14/75—11:00 pm CST

[intro theme—instrumental]

CTNS: Brothers and sisters, thank you for joining us tonight. We are the blessed few and it's so nice that you are here with me, that we are all together. We are the Copernican Temple of the New Sun and we are brothers and sisters of the cosmos. Say it after me: I pledge myself to the truth of the New Sun, the new life that waits for us outside of our terrestrial bodies, the cosmos that nourishes us, and the celestial angels that give us this truth. Amen.

[chimes]

CTNS: My blessed friends. I have such a treat here for you tonight. We have all read the transcripts of our prophets, the pilots and air traffic control. Their words are testament to our destiny. We know this because we have had our eyes opened. The masses call our angels by the name of aliens but we know that is simple ignorance. Some of our best scientists and astronomers of the 20th century know that are not alone in the universe. The government has muzzled their brightest minds, kept them from speaking. We know that humans can handle this information. Humans are responsible enough to know their own destiny! The government thinks it knows what's best for us, the nonbelievers think they know what's best for us.

I have not forgotten your sacrifice in being here with me. Knowing the truth sometimes separates us from those who refuse to see. We cannot weep for them, but only rejoice in what lies ahead for us. These beings have promised us new life, better life, in our new cosmic bodies. Amen.

[chimes]

CTNS: The Transcript of Flight 3411 is our clearest evidence of this truth, as experienced by pilot Jeffrey Abraham Collis during the cargo flight 3411. We have read the transcript, felt its truth deep within us, in the centre of our hearts and minds—the parts of our body where the truth lives. We know it, as they say, by heart.

Brothers and sisters, we have read Collis' words, imagined his experience as he was subsumed by the holy light of the New Sun. We have not envied him. No, it is our shared destiny to reach his blessed state—but we have all desired the same for ourselves. It is my pleasure to announce that tonight, I have something wonderful to offer you.

I have the recording.

What you are about to hear, brothers and sisters, is not disturbing. It is not sad. We must remember that in Jeffrey's screaming is only truth, the sound of joining the cosmos, the holy sublime that is greater than ourselves. Please listen with me now.

[chimes]

JC: Lincoln, this is 3411 Tango.
LNB: Good morning, 3411 Tango, this is Lima November Bravo.
JC: I have lights at 2:00, any idea what it could be?
LNB: Uh, 3411, that's a negative, we don't know of any other craft in the area.
JC: Can you double check? They're whirling, some strobes—
LNB: Sure, uh, sure we'll check for any other info, hold tight.

[beeping]

JC: Lima November Bravo, those lights are getting closer. Any ideas?
LNB: Nobody's heard anything, 3411. Our radars are *[static]*
JC: Copy that. *[static]*
JC: Now confirming that it is a craft.
LNB: A-a craft? What is the altitude of the craft?
JC: 30,000, now at my 1:00.
LNB: 3411, we have no—*[static]*
JC: The lights *[laughing]* they're beautiful, kind of, they're so—
LNB: *[garbled]*
JC: Lima. *[laugh]* November. Bravo.
LNB: [garbled] JC: *[garbled]* so beautiful...getting brighter.
LNB: 3411 Tango, what is the size of the craft?
JC: *[open microphone for three seconds]* 100 feet—
LNB: What is the craft doing?
JC: It's—it's—*[whispering]*

LNB: 3411 Tango, please confirm.
JC: *[loud screaming]* LNB: 3411, please confirm status.
JC: *[silence]*
LNB: 3411 we are receiving a distress notification—
JC: *[sound of scraping metal]*

[chimes]

CTNS: I am so happy I could share that with you, my family. As we sit and ponder the message of our prophet, let us also remember the other person who ascended with Jeffrey Collis. I have here for you, a recording of the call made to police from below that night.
BHPS: Blue Hill Police Station, what is your emergency?
Unknown: *[static]*
BHPS: Blue Hill Police, what is your emergency?
Unknown: *[A TV in the background. Radio static. The sound of scraping metal.]*
BHPS: We've put a trace on this number and will be dispatching assistance immediately.
BHPS: Are you there?
BHPS: This is the Blue Hill Police Station, please tell us the nature of your emergency.
Unknown: *[Background noise ceases]*
BHPS: Are you still there? Unknown: *[silence]*

[chimes]

CTNS: Thank you for sharing these sounds with me tonight. Good-night, and may the New Sun rise tomorrow.

✸ ✸ ✸

File name: Copernican Temple of the New Sun #57884
File type: Transcript—Radio Transmission
Frequency: CTNS 3917 kHz
Airdate: 08/19/75—11:00 pm CST

[intro—instrumental]

CTNS: Brothers and Sisters, our blessed day has arrived. We know you have been patient with us these past few years. This virtue will be rewarded as we move forth into our new home in the cosmos. Today's message will be brief as we are busy preparing for the arrival of our angels.

[chimes]

CTNS: I wanted to thank you for sharing your terrestrial experience with me. It has been a pleasure to seek these Celestial Truths with you, to listen for the sweet voices of those that live beyond. Our Day of Ascension is here at last. We can now move forward from this prison, into the light of the New Sun. Our calls have been answered and now, for the last time, we wait.

Good night to you all. And good will be the morning.

❋ ❋ ❋

File name: Copernican Temple of the New Sun #57885
File type: Transcript—Radio
Recording Frequency: 87.1 CLCO—Strange Saturdays
Airdate: *[not aired]*

GF: Hello listeners, this is Gregory Fredericksen with *Strange Saturdays* on 87.1 CLCO. Our guest for tonight's program is author Lori Taylor, writer of the popular *Unexplained Experiences* series. Lori became a bit of a mystery herself, recently, as she was reported missing last month. Police ended up finding her all the way in the woods around Arkansas, but none of us know what she was doing down there. Lori, how are you?

LT: Greg. Thank you.

GF: We're happy to have you here with us. Frankly, I'm surprised you wanted to come on, considering...

LT: It's important for your listeners, for everybody, to know the truth.

GF: Well, thank you for coming on. So, let's begin at the beginning. What happened the night you disappeared, Lori?

LT: Have you ever heard of the Temple of the New Sun?

GF: Can't say that I have.

LT: They had a radio station, they used to broadcast from there. They, they trapped me, they wanted my tapes, they pumped me for information. Their whole compound was full of radio sounds, and static, that's how the aliens communicated, they said, their broadcasts were to let them know they heard them, that they understood them.

GF: I don't understand. You were taken by this Temple?

LT: Yes. Temple of the New Sun. They wanted to join the angels.

GF: There are a few organizations like that these days, I think. Aren't they usually harmless? What happened with this Temple?

LT: They took me. I sat in the dark for days and days. I lost track of time, Greg, there was no time, there. There was static everywhere, all the time, coming from, from those radios. The members were constantly changing the stations. I would hear awful sounds, scratching and humming and wailing. They were listening for the aliens.

GF: You have a bit of experience with searching for aliens, yourself. Your newest book in the Unexplained series, *Aerial*—

LT: That's why they wanted me, Greg! That's why they wanted me there. They said I knew the truth already, I deserved to be there with them for their Day of Ascension.

GF: What is the Day of Ascension?

LT: The day the aliens come. They descend, we ascend.

GF: When do they think it will happen?

LT: It already happened.

GF: It...What do you mean?

LT: They were there, I saw them.

GF: You had a close encounter?

LT: Yes.

GF: What happened?

LT: It was beautiful, Greg. There was light, everywhere light. I was locked in a room but the light went through, it went right through the walls. There was static, it was loud, my ears haven't recovered still, the wailing of the radios, it crept into my skin, I could feel the radio waves vibrating within me. I heard footsteps and yelling all around me. I started pounding on the door, I was in pain, I wanted to run away.

GF: Did someone let you out?

LT: I don't remember.

GF: What do you remember next?

LT: Light.

GF: And then what?

LT: You don't understand. The light, it, consumes you, it rips your body apart.

GF: But you're he—

LT: I know! I know! I'm here. I don't understand. *[sobbing]*

GF: Oh, please don't cry, now. Do you want to take a break? We can edit this part out when it goes to air.

LT: I'm fine. I'm fine.

GF: So the last thing you remember is light and pain?

LT: I don't know why they didn't take me. Why didn't they want me?

GF: The Temple?

LT: No. Them. The angels.

GF: I thought you said they were aliens.

LT: The aliens ARE angels. They are so beautiful. They want us to join them. I...I did see one person get taken, a small woman, the angel came up to her and held out a long metal stick and inserted it into her ear and I saw the light pour out of her eyes and nose and mouth and it consumed her and her body sank to the ground, it sank like a puddle to the ground, she left her body behind, this prison, I want to escape, Greg, they'll come for me again, they have to—

GF: *[indistinct]* get her out *[indistinct]*

LT: No no no, it's okay, I'm sorry, I'll talk about my book. Just please put this on the air: I am waiting for you. I am ready to be one with you. Please come back for me. Please send me a signal. I am ready. I choose your path. I'll be listening for you. I am ready now. Ready. I am listening now. Always.

FILE: COPERNICAN TEMPLE OF THE NEW SUN
STATUS: CLOSED POST REVIEW 04/07/1976
MOVE TO: ARCHIVES; CLASSIFIED

END FILE

※

The Night Stalker

1.

It happened in the 1970s. Then, phones were still attached to the wall, and you only stuck your finger in the rotary dial to call long distance after five p.m., when the rates were cheaper. My father, who worked at the airbase, wore paisley shirts with long collars in the ugliest colors of plum purple and burnt orange when not on duty.

After the gas dried up during the time of the second energy crisis, we stuck around our rural neighborhood, which might as well have been an island unto itself located far from the outside world. No day trips to Lake Winnipesauke or over the border of Massachusetts to Salisbury Beach. As the summer deepened, the tall pines and woods surrounding Armstrong Road seemed to press in like the dark forests from childhood fables, and the only news from the outside world came from the airbase—or the TV news, when we were lucky enough to escape rolling blackouts.

2.

Until that summer, on lazy afternoons before the grass grew too long or after the killing frost knocked it down, I would lie on the knoll in the field across the road with my doll Tillie and stare up at the sky. Often, I'd hear the purr of a plane flying somewhere up there—not a jet, no; they screamed over the woods and Corbett's Lake on approach to the airfield. These were smaller planes, some wearing their wings on top, flown by private pilots out of the civilian airport located farther up Range Road, beside the cornfields. My Grandmother Rachel made Tillie for me the Christmas I turned six. Four years later, Tillie had visited Grammy Rae's doll hospital twice for emergency surgery.

Armstrong Road was a lonely place for a young girl during a tense, hot summer, devoid of friends apart from one made of cloth with yarn hair. Even planes with their comforting purrs had abandoned me. The skies were quiet and mostly empty save for clouds and the occasional screaming jet pulling duty over our heads, but even they were fewer between, given the crisis.

Our house was a tiny two-bedroom bungalow with a screened-in porch on the back. The porch faced the lake, with the stream that ran out of the woods cutting between us on its way to the water. I was hacked off again because my favorite variety hour starring the Osmonds, who were from a faraway state called Utah, had just started when the lights went out. And I'd just managed to get the rabbit ears perfect—the signal crisp, showing all those purple sequins in glorious, glittery clarity.

I dragged Tillie to the back porch and uttered a rosary of curse words that only adults were allowed to speak, the moonless night so dark that the trees, stream, sky, and lake could barely be told apart from one another. On that night, Armstrong Road in the town of Whyndom, New Hampshire might as well have existed on another planet, at the farthest end of the universe.

Heat rose up my throat and infected my face. I felt the caustic sting of tears threaten at the corners of my eyes but willed them back, which turned out worse than if I'd let them fall. I tried in vain to swallow down the lump in my throat. Everything around me had turned bad. Looking back, the sense that the world was about to go spinning off its axis was tangible, a shadow that dogged me from every direction and one impossible to shake.

Just how bad, however, had yet to reveal itself.

That moment soon arrived low over the treetops, announced by a distant scream that whipped the hot night air into a frenzy, creating wind devils above the towering sap pines. All the oxygen seemed to vanish from my lungs, and breathing was no longer involuntary or even easy. I gulped down a sip right as the dark sky lit up. I saw the explosion before I heard it. Then, multiple trails of fire and smoke were plummeting over the lake, like fireworks gone wrong.

I must have screamed, too because the footsteps in the dark, hot house all converged on the back porch.

"Mandy?" asked Theresa, my father's girlfriend.

My father said one of those adult words I'd recently gotten away with, his in the form of a question.

"We under attack?" Theresa gasped.

"I saw it," I said. "Over the lake. A jet exploded!"

I started to tell them about the wreckage, the pieces riding fiery comets out over Corbett's Lake. But they were already navigating the house's dark interior, headed toward the phone bolted onto the kitchen wall.

* * *

They used flashlights despite that stern warning we all received in a leaflet concerning our responsibility as citizens to conserve batteries during the crisis. As search parties fanned out across the lake and shore, I carried the flashlight that had spent the summer in the kitchen's junk drawer but didn't turn it on. I didn't need to.

Even on a night when not a single star chose to shine, I knew the stream, the woods, and our side of the lake intimately. I was a bored and lonely kid whose only friends were a doll made of rags and those my imagination created.

So, as a mix of military and civilians stroked the shores of Corbett's Lake with their flashlight beams and rumors spread, I walked with my father and Theresa, knowing where to step and what parts of the ground to avoid. My sneakers never plunged into muck. No pine roots riding just above the soil tripped me.

"It wasn't one of ours," said Mister Columbus, who lived next door in the green bungalow with the black shutters. "Jackson from the base says it's a damn Soviet plane, probably powered by high-test beet juice and vodka."

I stifled a rare chuckle. Laughter had been in as short supply as energy throughout that humorless summer. And I liked Mister Columbus, who, like my father, brought in an honest paycheck working at the airfield. I'd once remarked that with a name like his, every day must have felt like a holiday, not just the Twelfth of October.

"Damn Rooskies," my father sighed. He followed the sentiment up with another, more colorful adult word despite my presence and then checked his hunting rifle.

I realized I'd become invisible and tested the theory by dropping behind, back into the folds of the darkness. The righteous patriots searching for wreckage or the ejected Soviet pilot continued on ahead, their flashlight beams jiggling frenetically as they passed over uneven ground, or whenever one of their feet tangled in a patch of grabby scrub vegetation.

I sat on the Rhino, the smaller of the two boulders in our backyard set beside the Elephant along the bank of the stream, and studied the sky for other shooting stars. Though disappointed in my lack of relevance, I had to admit how charged my cells felt at the night's unexpected adventure. At least *something* had happened, regardless as to whether it pushed us past crisis to the precipice of all out war. My heart was in a constant gallop and doing its best to jump up from my chest and into my throat. I choked it back down, considered joining the lights—now almost at the lake—but then I heard the crunch-slither of movement from the far bank of the stream.

Footfalls, coming closer.

I resisted the urge to turn on the flashlight, which I caught myself twirling like a baton, and held my breath. The walker behind those steps moved without a flashlight, and with a kind of stealth that my young mind recognized as purposeful. We'd never seen a bear at the lake, despite the acres of surrounding woods. A lynx? One grey autumn morning, a bobcat had raced up the tallest oak in the backyard, which had both thrilled and terrified me in the same breath. On that day, I imagined the animal as part house pet, half saber-toothed beast from a bygone era.

Perhaps the lynx was back, a nocturnal predator on the prowl for its next meal. Only whatever was striding toward the stream walked on two feet, not four. My ears knew the difference. Was it the Soviet pilot that had everyone so incensed? I thought about switching on the beam, but my eyes had grown accustomed to seeing in the dark. I was part lynx. Someone tall made it to the edge of the stream. I sensed them hesitate before navigating down into the running current.

Two feet plunked into the stream, the sounds distinct. Then all the other flashlights returned, with my father calling my name.

"Mandy!"

I was no longer invisible—to them or that other presence cutting across the water. I slid off the Rhino, darted around the Elephant, and met the search party along the stream.

"There's someone in the water!"

I pointed downstream. The flashlights tracked the direction I'd indicated. Not someone, no, but a some*thing*.

The beams zeroed in right as the creature emerged from the water. Faun-brown, with short hair and a giant head, a barrel for a chest, strong forearms and legs, huge paws, it was the biggest dog I'd ever seen.

"But—?" I started.

The sentence went unfinished. What I didn't tell them was that I was sure that the dog had been walking upright, on two legs.

3.

On the surface, a dog seemed the ideal solution to one of the smaller wars being fought that summer.

"A new friend," my father said, counter to Theresa's protests at having a dog—let alone one so beastly—in our small home near the lake.

And on the surface, I feigned happiness. All summer long, as the walls of trees pressed in around us, I'd bemoaned my lack of friends close enough to play with under the auspices of the travel restrictions imposed by the energy crisis. Underneath, my guts twisted into knots as the dog stood there, wet but not shaking himself off like a normal dog should. He allowed Mister Columbus to examine him.

"No collar."

"Don't the Hissocks have a big dog?"

"You mean Charlie? Put him down last year."

"Must be a stray," my father reasoned. "But stray no more."

I looked into the dog's eyes, which were glassy in the glow from the flashlights. He panted like a dog, looked like one, but my instincts told me not to trust appearances.

"I don't know," Theresa said. "It's so big. It'll eat us out of house and home. And it could be dangerous."

"It's not an *it,*" Mister Columbus said. "If you don't want him, I'll gladly—"

And then in a moment of rare generosity, my father said, "No, he's Mandy's dog now."

4.

The dog plunked down on the braided oval rug beside my bed. As the search continued well past the first murky light of the new day, I tried to sleep but couldn't. I heard the constant panting of the dog's breaths, smelled its wet dog smell, and realized my unwanted new companion felt more like an invader than a friend.

All the while, my mind recycled my first impression: that the dog now walking about on four legs had arrived upright on two.

Another voice in my head, the one forced to view the world through an adult perspective, told me I was crazy. Worse, ungrateful—what kid wouldn't want a dog of her very own? Hell, I should have been happy with an aquarium filled with sea monkeys ordered from inside one of the lame comic books my father was always bringing home from the airbase.

A dog, yes.

Just not *this* dog.

At a point just before the sun rose, I drifted into a state that wasn't asleep nor awake but somewhere in between. I sensed the dog standing at the side of the bed, staring at me with its wild, golden-green eyes. When I forced my slitted eyes to open wider, the dog was gone.

❋ ❋ ❋

So, too, was my father. Called in early to work under the base's emergency protocol, I wondered if he'd gotten any sleep following the night's adventure. Theresa was passed out in their room, I saw, which reeked from the last cigarette she'd smoked. The house was eerily quiet.

I poured myself a cup of milk—a small one, given that world events meant fewer trips to the grocery store. We'd even grown our own garden to have fresh vegetables, though the cucumbers ripened sour as the summer wore on. The temptation to refill my glass sent me reaching for the milk carton. Then I felt the humid breeze, warm and scented of the outside, and turned to see the front door standing open.

The dog was gone.

❋ ❋ ❋

The joke—at least it sounded funny in my mind—was that I would call my beast of a dog Uri, or Sergei, or Boris, like the spy on one of my cartoons. Something Russian, which I thought would be poetic and appropriate, given the story of how he came to be mine. But it was beginning to look as though I needn't have bothered being clever, given the dog's disappearing act.

There hadn't been much to laugh about over that summer. The world had forgotten how to smile. As I traipsed down the flagstone walkway my father built, past the post-and-beam fence in our front yard and across Armstrong Road, whose tired asphalt had been blanched by the sun to the color of comfortable denim, I tried to remember what life was like before the crisis. Unhappiness seemed ready to stay.

So, I figured that the dog had found a way out of the house. That maybe my father hadn't properly shut the front door—though he was a stickler for locking it after two Puerto Rican men came walking right into our house the previous summer while Theresa and I were eating supper in front of the TV. We figured they were from Massachusetts, had gone to the lake's public beach, were robbing houses and didn't realize we were home until Theresa began to shriek, causing them to run.

Since then, he always locked the doors.

I wandered into the smaller of the two meadows set before the big woods. I decided I should at least make an effort at finding my new friend, Rooskie—that was a good name for a gigantic dog, I agreed. Finding my new friend, Rooskie.

The hot, green veldt towered over me. I cut past the wood line, where it wasn't uncommon to see tangles of garden snakes sunning themselves, and beneath the shadows of the outlying trees. I knew those woods in the same intimate manner as the shore of Corbett's Lake and instantly sensed the wrongness creeping in an undercurrent from their depths. This was different than the encounter with the lynx; there'd been window and walls between us then. As I drifted farther, I cast a glance up at the Austrian pines and the patches of overcast sky visible between their scaly boughs. The trees were as tall as skyscrapers, I swore. Vertigo and gravity conspired to drop me to the ground. The scent of pine needles mixed with decaying leaves, all of it cooked up by the summer's heat, grew narcotic. Something buzzed past my ear. Sweat flowed.

Yes, there was a malevolent presence in my woods that hadn't been there before the previous night, and shouldn't be now but was.

Heat lay thick and oppressive around me. My flesh crawled and sweated. A lump formed in my throat.

"Rooskie," I called, my voice almost not there.

A low, creaking sound tumbled down from the trees. The towering conifers often groaned as they swayed in the wind, only this was different, *other,* part of the wrongness I'd sensed from the start of my arrival. Goosebumps ignited across my arms. I found myself again gazing up and slowly turning around. The trees and sky spun over my head.

I saw the man and, at first, mistook him for a life-sized puppet attached to marionette strings tangled in the upper branches. My turning about ceased. The puppet's face and throat were burned. One of his eyeballs was missing. No, not gone—that was it hanging out of its socket by a thin cable of flesh. The creaking sound resumed, its source the weight of the corpse pulling against those puppet master's strings as it swayed in the balmy breeze.

I screamed.

And screamed.

5.

I was seated on my bed. The red lights of the emergency vehicles dispensed by the airbase, some presently parked in our yard, teased my vision at the periphery, reminding me of blood.

People were speaking outside my bedroom door, their voices reaching me even when whispered. It was a very small house.

"It's the Rooskie pilot, all right," one of the men from the airbase said. "That explains one, but that jet was a two-seater, so where's the other?"

"How's your daughter," another man asked.

"She's fine," my father said.

Like he knew. Like things hadn't been bad enough before I'd gone into the woods in search of my missing dog, which I hadn't even wanted.

I slid off the bed and padded to the door. If they were so concerned about me, why hadn't a single adult checked in for what had seemed an eternity? Eyes looked down, acknowledging my arrival. Theresa detached from the small crowd gathered among our furniture and started toward me.

And as she did, I noticed the dog was back, its body plunked down in the living room before the impotent TV. Right before our glances connected, I had the impression that its eyes and ears were absorbing all being said and acted out.

※ ※ ※

We ate ham and cheese sandwiches from the food Theresa had moved from the fridge to the cooler following the last blackout. The meat had a funky taste at the edges, as though this was possibly the last hour that it would remain edible. I picked around my sandwich and caught Theresa's disapproval in her next exhale, made loud enough for me to hear. But she didn't scold me. Hard to justify, I supposed, when my father was feeding his dinner to the dog.

"I'm putting in a request at the airbase for some kind of reward or compensation," he said, turning back to the small, round table that accommodated four but had only ever seated three. "Fuel rations, food, cash. After all, we found that dead Soviet pilot."

Rage bubbled up from my guts. The temperature in that corner of the house skyrocketed. *"I* found him," I blurted out before I could censor the words.

My father scowled. "I know you did, but it benefits the entire family. If we could—"

I pushed away from the table hard enough to jiggle glasses and spill tepid water.

"Mandy," my father barked.

I ignored him and stormed through the porch and out the back door. Tears powered past my defenses. By the time I reached the Elephant and the Rhino, I was sobbing. I'd never felt so alone. Soon after the emotion embraced me, however, I wasn't.

The dog crept past the barrier formed by the Elephant's mica-flecked hide, a vast shadow beyond the veil of my tears. I tensed, swiped at my eyes. The shadow was staring at me.

Mustering the last of my courage, I said, "What do you want?"

For a second, part of me actually expected Rooskie to answer.

"Huh, dog? What are you doing here?"

The giant lowered his head. Golden-green eyes studied me. A chill sliced through the heat encasing my body, because I swore the dog was smiling.

My father called my name. I backed away, between the two boulders deposited thousands of years earlier by receding glaciers. The dog stepped forward, and I was again reminded of the size of his paws. A voice in my head sounded an alarm—*if he wants to, he could eat you!*

"Mandy," my father shouted. "Mandy, you get in here *right now!"*

The dog turned toward the sound of my father's angry voice. I took that moment to run up from the stream's bank, through the backyard, and away from what I now believe would have been my certain death.

❋ ❋ ❋

I heard the dog nosing around the house and imagined him walking upright, opening doors with front paws that were really hands. Fear paralyzed my body. What could Rooskie be searching for? Food? My mind flashed back to the miserable dinner, which had culminated with me receiving a stern warning about my attitude. Before that particular humiliation, Theresa had opened a can of beef stew—decent enough food for humans during this crisis, but gourmet faire for a dog in any situation. Rooskie had snubbed his nose at the offer.

Time slipped off the normal track of seconds and minutes, transforming one into the other. I heard the front door open. Footsteps sounded outside my bedroom windows, steady and secretive, and again the pattern sounded to my ears as though it was made of two feet, not four. I held my breath. My consciousness slipped into that fugue state as my mind raced.

It's possible that I only dreamed the screaming sounds that came from the direction of Mister Columbus's house.

6.

My father knocked, paced, and knocked again, receiving the same result: no answer.

"If he doesn't hustle soon, we're gonna be late," he said.

I waited beside his bicycle, which had become that summer's only reliable method of transportation around the lake other than legs.

"Daddy," I said, my face hot, my stomach tied in knots.

He shot a look in my direction.

"I think something bad happened to Mister Columbus. Last night, I heard..."

"You heard what?"

My father tested our neighbor's doorknob. It was locked.

Mustering courage, I said, "Daddy, I think the dog hurt Mister Columbus."

"The dog?"

"I don't think it's really a dog. Remember Laika?" My voice hitched with a sob. "She was the first one they sent up into space. On Sputnik 2. They launched her into orbit around the Earth."

Confusion swept across my father's face, along with an obvious note of frustration. "Mandy, what the hell are you babbling on about?"

"The Soviets, experimenting on dogs. That man from the airbase said there were *two* pilots in the jet. I think the dog's the other one. Only it isn't a dog."

My father sighed, tromped over to where I stood guarding his ride into work, and yanked the bike out of my grasp.

"You know, Mandy, I'm starting to worry about that overactive imagination of yours."

Shaking his head, he rode away, saying nothing more.

7.

The dog was gone, and nobody but I noticed. They were all so focused on the bigger mystery and crises that they were oblivious to the smaller, no less deadly one taking place around us.

I was right about the dog, or so my gut instinct told me. But I needed proof.

I waded across the stream at its thinnest point and cut through the sedge between Corbett's Lake and the backend of our tiny neighborhood, knowing the muddy traps to avoid. Soon, I'd reached the area where the dog had first appeared. It hadn't rained for a couple of days, and I prayed to whatever god was listening that the evidence I suspected would still be there. To my relief, it was—in the form of a dozen footprints etched into a patch of ground between hillocks. How long I stared, I couldn't be certain. Long enough to attract a swarm of thirsty mosquitoes.

The large prints were staggered in twos, not fours, definitely in the shape of a man's sole. I blinked myself out of the trance and turned toward my house, only to suffer a rush of dizziness. When the world around me again stabilized, I saw the dog standing outside the back porch, staring at me across the distance.

Our eyes connected. The dog blinked, and then he started running toward me.

❋ ❋ ❋

As stated, being alone and lonely had given me license to explore the lush green realm that surrounded my home, and I was intimately acquainted with my remote world. In his haste to reach me, the dog sprinted toward the stream where it ran at its thickest. I raced back in the direction of the spot where it was narrowest. This put me nearer to Mister Columbus's rear door than my own house and, given no option, I ran as fast as I could. I ran for my life.

Water splashed. The pounding of footsteps followed in counterpoint to my desperate sips for breath. It was chasing me, and close. It suddenly dawned on me that the back door to Mister Columbus's house might be locked, like the front. Mercifully, it wasn't. I turned the knob, flew into our neighbor's house uninvited, and slammed the door behind me. Turning the lock seemed to take forever because seconds dragged on with the weight of minutes.

Mister Columbus's bungalow was identical to ours apart from the lack of a back porch, which my father had added on, and the complete absence of a woman's touch. The air smelled stale, like a mixture of mold and sweaty socks, and another odor I couldn't place, not at first. The house would have been gloomy with the summer sun shining through the windows and the lights turned on. I backed away from the door, into the throat of the short hallway connecting bedrooms and bathroom to a similar though dirtier version of our kitchen/living room combo.

"Mister Columbus?" I called out in vain.

In the back bedroom, the one that was mine in our house, I spied an odd collection of things: men's clothes stacked on a work table beside guns—my father's hunting rifle among them, a map roughly drawn and showing the lake, airbase, and our neighborhood, and what my imagination identified as a radio cobbled together from a bunch of spare parts. I realized what the dog that wasn't really a dog had been up to at night.

I reached for my father's hunting rifle, going on automatic. Several times that unhappy summer, we'd dined on pheasants hunted out of season. I hated the texture of the butchered meat, swore I could taste the burn from the bullets. The phantom bitterness ignited on my tongue. I raised the rifle and backed out of the room.

My next instinct was to hide. I entered the bigger of the house's two bedrooms, my wet sneakers sloshing across the floor, leaving an accidental roadmap. I found Mister Columbus beside the bed. His throat had been ripped out.

8.

Poor Laika, left in orbit around the Earth. Her desiccated corpse was still up there, circling our energy-thirsty globe until some future expedition brought her back or a decaying trajectory and the planet's gravity did the same on a fiery pyre. Sputnik was only a couple of years before my birth, the story still fresh, and the cruelty forced on Laika had gotten into my young psyche and would always be there in my private thoughts.

I had no idea of the relationship between that poor canine soul and the monster throwing its mass at the locked back door to Mister Columbus's house, but assumed the latter was a Soviet spy sent to infiltrate the airbase. Our neighbor was dead, murdered, his blood the source of that other rank smell I hadn't been able to identify until my arrival to the big bedroom. My blood might soon join his.

I'd fired the gun a few times at the start of the crisis on my father's demand that I be prepared should Soviet soldiers begin dropping out of the sky. I'd laughed at him then, to his considerable annoyance. I wasn't laughing now.

The door burst open and the dog charged in. Dog? I knew it wasn't a dog, not really. The gun lacked silver bullets. I silently prayed conventional ammo would be enough.

The nightmare turned the corner growling, the claws of its big feet scrabbling across the floor. It saw me and, again, I swore it was smiling. Then its wide, gold-green eyes recorded the gun. It moved to spring at me. I fired. Thunder rocked the world.

At such close range, my aim was perfect. The abomination spilled inelegantly across the floor, hatred clear in its gaze as it labored for breath. The dog exhaled one final time and then, as screams powered past my lips, began to alter.

Before me was the body of a naked man with military-short, fawn-colored hair and golden-green eyes.

※

Decrepitude

It hit him unexpectedly as he turned the corner, slamming bodily into him and cutting deep into his flesh. With an annoyed grunt, Dino spun around, turning his face away from the brisk November wind. He'd read in a discarded newspaper that there was a cold front moving in over the city tonight from the north, but it had since slipped his mind. That was odd; usually he had a good memory for weather. It was an important skill to develop when one slept outdoors more often than not.

Dino hobbled around the street corner, trying to keep his back to the wind. Rubbing his hands together for heat, he glanced around, trying to position himself. He didn't immediately recognize his surroundings, which also surprised him. After having spent the better part of two years on the streets of Chasm City, navigation had become unconscious for him, his feet steadily directing him towards food and shelter even if he were thinking about something else.

Dino turned around, momentarily braving the chilly, blustery wind to read the street signs on the corner of the intersection: Inglemann Road and Everett Drive. Mentally recalling a map of the city, he reasoned that was somewhere in the East 'Shrooms. Dino scowled: he knew perfectly well that the 'Shrooms had no homeless shelters where he could crash for the night. The people who lived in the cramped, stacked apartments that hid the night sky overhead were too busy trying to pay their own way through life to worry about hobos on the streets. What few parks could be found in the area probably wouldn't be patrolled—the borough didn't have the budget for that—but it was far too cold to spend the night on a bench.

Dino decided was he was officially having a bad night. First he'd forgotten to plan for the cold, and then he'd gotten lost in his thoughts and wandered out of his usual territory. And, just to add insult to injury, he couldn't even remember what he had been thinking about so intently.

A voice, young and childish, from the back of his mind: *Hey mister, you lost?*

"Shut up, Billy," Dino muttered. He didn't like hearing from Billy, especially not in public. When people see a hobo talking to himself, they assume he's psychotic and dangerous. As if *they* had never told themselves off for doing something stupid.

Moving out of the wind once again, Dino scanned the street. There were still a few snowdrifts left in the street from an unseasonable storm late in October. Most of it, however, had melted away and created quite a messy sludge on the streets and sidewalks, left where it fell since the city workers were on strike for what seemed like the tenth time this year alone. On the other side of the street, a largish woman in a grey overcoat was waddling pass the rows of doors and staircases with grocery bags in her hands, intently ignoring the tramp as most people did. He didn't think the metal staircases leading to the upper flats would make good shelter, and he was certain he wouldn't be welcome if someone should find him there.

With a resigned grumble, Dino started walking back the way he'd come. He'd have to leg it back to the Old Town and Chasm Core if he wanted to find a place for the night. By the time he got there, of course, half the night would be gone. Still, when the temperature dropped this low, it was best to keep walking—all night long if you had to—rather than settling for a spot on the ground. Otherwise, you could wind up freezing to death in your sleep. Dino knew guys who had gone out that way; he'd even seen Candyman's body after the poor junkie had taken his last ride on the Needle-Track Express. After a night spent out on the streets in the dead of winter, his shaggy hair and his eyelids had been frozen stiff; his skin, brittle to the touch.

As he was crossing the first intersection back downtown, he spotted his salvation: the glowing neon-yellow "M" sign that denoted the city's metro system. Dino felt a surge of hope. There were many stations throughout the outer ring of the city that operated only during the day, when they were needed for commuting to work and back. At night, the trains would bypass them entirely and the stations should be deserted. Dino doubted that there would be a guard, since the Chasm Transport Authority usually didn't bother with such niceties in low-income neighbourhoods.

It might be locked, though.

Dino reached the station's height and hesitated. The name above the swinging doors read Arthur S. Adams Memorial Station.

He had heard of this place before: it had a bad reputation amongst the transient population in the city ever since a tramp had been found beaten to death there one morning. The city investigated under public pressure, but Dino didn't recall hearing that the police had ever found the culprits. One vagrant had said that it had been members of the Viper Kings out on a thrill kill. Dino had never actually met this vagrant, but Pops Duncan said it was true, and so it must be.

Shaking off his misgivings, Dino pushed against the door and it gave, inching open. Dino pushed it all the way open and walked inside the station's vestibule. Bad rep or not, he wasn't about to pass up a warm place for the night, provided it was safe.

And the best way to determine that was to read the writing on the wall.

Graffiti, trademark of the contemporary urban environment, considered by some to be the pre-eminent symptom of urban decay, was to others a means of underground communication. The veteran tramps taught this to those new arrivals who showed potential for survival, pointing out what symbols would denote a gang's territory, how to interpret the letters and numbers spray-painted onto a wall to avoid getting caught in the crossfire of their turf wars. The Viper Kings used a four-pointed crown, with the two centre spikes taller than the other two, as their emblem.

So, scanning the walls, Dino descended the first flight of stairs. There was nothing there beyond the usual tags and the odd phone numbers promising prospective callers a good time. At the bottom, on the concourse, he passed by the empty and barred windows of the convenience store. Looking at the rows of chips and other junk food inside briefly reminded him of the empty pangs of his stomach, but he quickly quelled them again. On the streets, one eventually learned to ignore all but the worst physical side effects of the minimalist diet to which one was constrained. He'd already had his meal for the day, a hot dog at a sympathetic stand.

Moving away from the window, Dino continued examining the concourse. There was nothing remarkable in terms of graffiti. An empty security booth stood at the end of a line of tourniquets. Dino slowly climbed over one of the chrome bars. Before, he could have easily leapt over the apparatus, but he was a lot weaker now. He had a cold pretty much all the time, even in the summer, and knew he was malnourished. He couldn't afford taking a bad spill and breaking something.

He examined a few pieces of paper that had been left lying about, but found nothing interesting, so he climbed down the left-hand staircase towards the boarding platform. Dino was left-handed, and he found that he had better luck when he went to the left.

The Arthur S. Adams Memorial Station was oddly designed. Whereas most subway stations in the city had either one platform wedged between two tracks, or two platforms on either side of a central track accommodating both directions, Adams Memorial had a separate track and platform for each direction. The platforms were on the outside, but there was a large cinderblock divide between the two tracks.

There were three benches along the platform wall, which was a definite factor in favour of spending the night here. No matter how cold or hard the material, benches were always more comfortable than sleeping on the ground. Dino wasn't sure why. Maybe it was simply psychological, in that sleeping on something raised reminded him of his childhood bed, the upper bunk of a double-decker bed. His parents had always wanted another child, which was why they had bought the two-person bed, but it had never panned out for them. Too bad, Dino mused bitterly, since the first proved to be such a disappointment.

There was a lot of graffiti here, much of it painted over older drawings. Clearly the Transport Authority had no interest in spending money to "beautify" this station, as it had in the more affluent areas. The works here were almost exclusively taggers, although he did spot a large swastika down towards the end of the platform, and a huge anarchist "A" inside its circle, painted in black against the cinderblock divide. Dino regarded this particular piece with incredulity, since the author would have had to walk across the tracks to paint it. Even leaving aside for a moment the near-continuous stream of metro trains running through the tunnel, there was enough voltage coursing through those tracks to carbonize anybody stupid enough to touch them.

After his inspection of the walls didn't turn up any evidence that the station was part of the territory of the Viper Kings or any other gang, Dino decided that it was as good a place as any to crash. He set his mental alarm clock for around six o'clock, aware that he should leave the station before the morning commuters began to really pour in. While Dino obviously didn't own a timepiece, having long ago hawked everything he owned but the clothes on his back for cash, he could infallibly wake himself up at whatever time he wanted. It was an ability envied by many transients who had awakened to the looming face of a scowling security guard.

He settled himself on a bench, lying on his right side so that his left hand was unhindered in case he needed to defend himself quickly. He never carried a blade, as Paulie had been wont to do, because that was a sure-fire way of spending time behind bars if a cop found it on you, but he'd gotten quite good at bare-knuckle fighting.

For a moment, there was only the simply joy of lying down. He spent most of his day on his feet, walking from one sweet spot to another, his worn-out Chasm City Crusaders cap in hand to catch change and small bills. It felt great to slouch there, the cozy sensation of vertebrae cracking into place. The rich might be able to sleep on plush-duvet beds rather than a cold slab of metal in a grungy subway, but the basic joy of sleep, the sheer content of being able to rest after a long day, knows no class.

One could say, thought Dino, that being able to lie down was a great leveller. He let out a wheeze of laughter. Laughter was good for the soul, he'd heard, and he knew this was true. Like sleep, laughing was free and let you be happy again, if only for a second. And there was nothing Dino liked more than bawdy jokes and bad puns. Leveller, ha!

Then there was a noise, a distant rumbling sound like thunder on the horizon. It grew in volume without becoming more distinct, before finally erupting into the rhythmic sound of the metro train rushing past. As the green-and-grey transport sped by, he could hear the displacement of the air between two cars, punctuating the general din of the speeding engine: *chuk-chuk-chuk-chuk-chuk-chuk-chuk-chuk.* Then, with an aspired sound, it was gone, rushing onwards through the tunnel, the screeching of the train on its tracks receding into the distance.

Dino hadn't even bothered to open his eyes. Although the trains wouldn't stop at a minor station in the East 'Shrooms this late at night, the metro ran all night long in this city, seven days a week. The trains that ran this late at night were expresses, shuttling people between the centre of the city and major satellite stations in the sur-rounding boroughs and suburbs, from which the intrepid commuters would have to make their own way to wherever they wanted to go. The sound didn't bother him at all. He was used to sleeping through the honking of cars and the cries of late-night revellers. One learned to block it all out quickly enough, otherwise one should expect many sleepless nights.

But he couldn't sleep. He'd always been able to fall asleep practically as soon as his head hit the ground, or rock, or metal, another skill that was the subject of envy amongst vagabonds who found their rest bothered by all kinds of ills. But tonight, for some reason, sleep refused to take him. He shifted on his bench, tried to hum a lullaby to himself, even tried counting sheep, but to no avail. During this time, a few more trains passed by, and the sound of screeching metal and cars thumping against the track grated him.

Finally, with pent-up exasperation, Dino rose from his bench. He paced the ground in front of the bench in a tight circle, hoping to exhaust himself, but quickly realized that it would be fruitless. He already *was* tired; he just couldn't seem to make that jump into oblivion.

Dino decided that he would try reading. Maybe it was a leftover of his previous life, the one before his boozy descent, when he'd still been anticipating going into language studies, but he found that reading helped to calm him down when he felt flustered. He always collected whatever newspapers people tossed away, always took the leaflets being handed out at the downtown campuses. He imagined he knew more about current affairs than did many of the so-called contributing members of society. Reading helped take him away, gave him something to focus on other than the problems that afflicted him.

Unfortunately, there wasn't much too read down here. He didn't have anything on him to read, and he already knew that there was nothing interesting in the discarded papers on the floor of the upstairs concourse, having examined those earlier. So he decided to read the graffiti on the wall in closer detail. From messages interspaced amongst the florid tags, Dino learned that a variety of personages had been here over a wide range of years; many different people were in love with other people, usually 4ever; and that another, rather substantial group of individuals were to be considered gay, stupid or fuckers, variously.

He eventually made his way down to the swastika. It had none of the artistic fancy that characterized most of the other pieces "decorating" the wall of the metro station; just eight ugly, metallic-grey lines. There was also an equal sign next to it, clearly pointing to plaque incised into the wall next to it. Dino had to squint to read it. The metal might have been bronze at one time, or more probably something cheaper painted bronze, but it had since faded to a dark green colour.

The larger letters at the top of the plaque announced "In Memory of Arthur S. Adams", and right below that "Honourable Mayor of Chasm City, 1931–39".

Most of the letters below were smaller and were greatly corroded, difficult to read even where it wasn't covered with part of some tag or another. Basically, it went on to describe all the wonderful things the memorialized mayor had done for the city, fighting the Great Depression. What Dino couldn't read, he could easily supplement with what he'd learned from the retrospective articles that the city's papers would occasionally run. He also knew the reason for the large swastika next to the plaque. According to some of the leaflets he'd get from around campus, Adams had fought the Depression in part by blaming the city's minorities for stealing all the jobs. The pamphlets had said that he was a rabid anti-Semite and had links to the northern branches of the Klan.

Dino turned away from the plaque and the accusatory graffiti. "It's too 'depressing' for me", he said. Chuckling at his second bad pun of the evening, he strolled over to the edge of the platform, standing once again across from the final masterpiece in this peculiar little museum of grunginess, the giant anarchist "A" above the tracks.

He once again marvelled at the sheer hubris of the piece and at the recklessness of the author. What kind of fool would risk his life for such a thing, when there's plenty of wall to paint on throughout the station? Dino shook his head. He often thought that affluent people did all kinds of stupid, dangerous things. It was as though they'd never come face-to-face with death before, so they thought they were immortal. *He* had seen plenty of death since he'd woken up on the street one morning with a killer hangover and the knowledge that he could never go home again. Some, like Vornsky and Candyman, had been good friends of his.

The piece had to be pretty fresh, too, since tiny steams of red paint still dribbled from the top of the circle and the edges of the "A". Dino cocked his head, momentarily puzzled. It was strange, but for some reason, when he had first came down here, he had thought the graffiti was black.

There was a high-pitched sound from somewhere to his left, and Dino took a step back from the platform as another metro train went roaring past, his wild hair flailing in the wind in time with the *chug-chug-chug* of the train. From this distance he could see into the windows of the speeding train and the warmly dressed people inside. There were businessmen in suits, students with school bags, well-dressed ladies examining themselves with pocket mirrors. None of them looked particularly happy. In fact, they were a drab and lifeless lot, but Dino supposed that was to be expected from anybody forced to commute at this late an hour.

For a moment, he wondered if the people flashing by were able to see him standing on the platform. Were they evaluating him as he had them, judging him, leaning over to their neighbour to point out the dirty hobo sleeping in the subway station? It happened all the time in the streets, passersby muttering comments under their breath, others not bothering to be so circumspect, telling him to get a job, to get cleaned up. Some, offended by his mere presence in their clean and comfortable world, would try and chastise him even as they determinedly walked by without looking. Human garbage, waste of flesh, drunkard....

Well, they were right about that last one. Dino was a man who had been born at the bottom of a bottle. The irony was that he was sober more often now than he had been before he washed out of school and life both, since he often had no money to buy booze with. He might have a weak spot for the sauce, but he knew his priorities had to be food and warm clothes. You can't get drunk if you're dead, and Dino was a survivor. The last, enduring member of the Ratty Pack.

There was a metallic scream from the tunnel to his left and the twin orbs of headlights floated into view. Dino frowned at it. Were these trains actually getting faster? It seemed like the last one had just passed by. Soon the green-and-grey beast was speeding by him, wind blowing across the platform. To Dino, it seemed as if the thin-looking people inside were actually staring right at him, resentful eyes hurrying past. As if to reflect his train of thought, the motion of air between the cars sounded as if it were taunting him: *chump-chump-chump-chump.*

Hey, mister, you're imagining things.

"Ah, put a lid on it, Billy," Dino said as he scowled and turned away from the tracks. He ambled back to his bench and let himself drop down onto it heavily, not feeling anymore tired than before, but significantly more disgruntled. He usually didn't let this kind of thing get to him, not even Billy. He had learned to build a shield against the judgment of others.

Billy was the hardest to ignore, though, because that came from within him. More than that, it was Dino himself. Billy-Boy, the child he had once been, looking out at him from that part of the mind where youthful memories are stored, feeling perfectly entitled to comment on their present situation with the innocence and straight-forwardness of a child.

Hey, mister, why are you sleeping on the floor? Hey, mister, you smell funny.

Little snot.

Dino had ceased to be Billy once he started to live on the streets. He might have still been called that for a while, but as far as he was concerned, Billy was a past life, Dino his present existence, with a blurry, drunken curtain separating the two.

It had been old Pops Duncan who had knighted the vagrant-former-ly-known-as-Billy with the moniker "Dino". Good old Pops Duncan, the wise man of Fairbrook Park, the tribal elder of all tramps and hobos from Chasm Core to the Old Town. With the exception of those transients who were violent or so mentally ill as to be com-pletely unsociable, most vagrants in the area were part of an informal communication network, passing along warnings of police raids or gang activity, or news of a particularly good shelter and where to find sympathetic vendors. And at the centre of it all, the hub where all this information would eventually flow, was Pops Duncan.

The high-pitched clarion of the metro train reverberated through the tunnel, but Dino closed his eyes and shifted on his bench to face the platform wall. He tried to ignore the huffing of the passing engine as best he could, hoping to lose himself in his recollections and, from there, into the sweet territory of slumber.

Pops Duncan was a hoary old veteran of the streets who seemed to have held court in Fairbrook Park longer than anybody could re-member. He was, in many ways, a kind of information broker. You would stand with him around a garbage can fire and tell him what you knew, and he, in turn, would tell you where to get food at a good price, where some of the best sweet spots for begging were, how you could get your hands on booze, nose-candy or needles, if that was your thing. Shortly after hitting the streets, Dino had been able to track down the old man through word-of-mouth, and Pops had taught him a lot of the things you needed to know in order to survive without home and hearth, in exchange for hearing his story. Well, Billy's story.

The ancient tramp had also been a matchmaker of sorts, and he'd often set up different transients together. He had been aware of every-one's background and seemed to know who would hit it off as friends, who could help each other out. When Pops Duncan made a point of introducing you to someone, it was best to pay close attention. It was through Pops Duncan that the Ratty Pack was created.

Another train passed by, the whine of its wheels on the track and the chuffing of the air between its cars creating a stark contrast to the music in Dino's head. They had been pretty good together, for a troupe made up of the penniless, the addicted and the unstable. Vornsky, a jovial ex-librarian, played the violin. It was his most prized possession, and he refused to part with it even though the old wooden thing was probably worth several hundred dollars. Paranoid Paulie had this uncanny ability to strike a bunch of sticks and bricks together into something quite like a rhythm. They would joke that Paulie was on the drums, like in a real band. And then there was their very own Candyman, the White-Nosed Wonder, who would dance a crazy little jig in time with the music.

Dino was the singer of the four. Despite the boozing and the less-than-ideal living conditions, he never lost the signing voice that had earned him a place in the church choir back home. They played on street corners and in the larger and significantly nicer metro stations downtown, splitting the money they received four ways afterwards. Pops Duncan had called them the Ratty Pack, like the Rat Pack out of Vegas. Pops certainly looked old enough to remember them in their prime.

"Well, I guess that makes me Frank Sinatra," Dino had joked then.

Pops Duncan had looked him over with his wizened eyes and said, "Naw, that won't work. Frankie had blue eyes, Billy, an' you doan. Your eyes be brown. You can be Dean Martin—Dino." Vornsky had then alighted on the idea that Dino could be made to rhyme with "wino" and the name had stuck ever since.

The great yawning sound of the metro train filled the station again, and Dino rose from his bench in irritation, moving towards the edge of the platform. He knew it was irrational, but he was frustrated and needed to vent. As the metal worm glided past, Dino shook his fist and threw some choice invectives against its speeding flank. He didn't care if the people inside looked out and saw him, thinking, perhaps, that he was just another crazy hobo ranting at spectres only he could see.

Besides, it wasn't as if they looked all that great either. Under the fluorescents of the station and of the metro car itself, their skin had a pallid, greenish tint to it. The trickery of light also made their faces seem gaunt, as if the flesh was emaciated and pulled too tightly over their skulls. The stream of passing people, flashing by fast enough so that individual faces blurred into the next, seemed like a kind of sickly pageant, insensate victims of some plague or pox being carted away into the black chasm.

Then the train was past, yellow taillights gradually receding into the darkness of the subway tunnel. Dino was left standing on the platform, facing the dribbling anarchist graffiti, feeling an odd, liquid chill towards the bottom of his spine. He tried to exorcise the unwelcome thoughts of death from his psyche, but the topic clung tenaciously to the walls of his mind. Even the dripping red paint of the anarchist graffiti reminded him of blood, as though whoever had authored the work had used a knife against a fleshy wall rather than a spray-paint can against a concrete slab.

Dino stood on the platform, ramrod-stiff, as his thoughts continued to gallop onward of their own accord, perhaps inevitably turning to thoughts of departed comrades. Candyman had been the first to go, victim of an overdose. Paranoid Paulie, who would confide to just about anyone he met that he was being pursued by men in black fedoras, decided one day that that he had spent too much time in Chasm and that "They" would find him if he didn't stay on the move.

For a time, it had been just Vornsky and Dino, a two-man act. Then, one morning, they found Vornsky's body smashed against the rocks a short distance downriver from the Columbus Bridge. Autopsy found an elevated blood-alcohol level and concluded the death was accidental: the hobo must have simply walked off the bridge in a drunken stupor. Dino knew better. Having drunk with the jocular man on many occasions, Dino had remarked with some resentment that the ex-librarian could imbibe for hours without even getting tipsy. Even more flagrant, Vornsky had left his violin behind that night. It was pawned off and the money distributed amongst his friends.

That blasted roar resonated through the tunnel again, barely a few minutes after the last one. The interval between the trains really was getting shorter, Dino concluded. He turned towards the left side of the platform, facing the glowing eyes and the grinning metal grill of the onrushing train. He took a step back and braced himself to suffer the looks of those inside, reminding himself that trying to punch the train as it passed by wouldn't be at all productive.

The train reached his height, and Dino stared into the flashing windows, the haggard people inside staring back out. Dino had to blink and look again, but no, he wasn't imagining things: they were actually looking right at him. They crowded at the doors and windows, palms pressed against the glass, emaciated fingers rapping against the windowpane. In every car the people inside where pressed against its side, their cadaverous faces watching him desolately. They were so close to him that he could see the forlorn look in their sunken eyes, despite the speed of the train.

With a final flick of its tail, the metro train was gone, speeding off into the abyss, gleefully carrying its damned passengers to their final destination. Dino reeled away from the edge of the platform, his movements unsure as if he were drunk but without the pleasant buzz.

Hey, mister, this place is creeping me out.

"Yeah, you and me both, Billy-Boy," Dino muttered. His back eventually hit the wall, and he started creeping along it, feeling his way with splayed out hands. He was moving towards the left, but he wasn't sure if that was because he was naturally inclined to go towards the left or because he was trying to get away from the train. If so—a detached and aloof portion of his mind advised—he was going in the wrong direction because that's where the next train was going to emerge from.

Dino felt adrift in his own mind. He watched, as if from outside it all, as the logical part of his brain tried to justify what he had just seen as a trick of the light or the imaginings of a tired mind. A lower, older portion responded that it didn't care, that it wanted to get away, but agreed with the logical part that they were going in the wrong direction. His body, meanwhile, ignored both halves of his mind and kept creeping along the wall, moving away from where he'd last seen the metro train. From his cerebral perch, Dino marvelled at how disconnected he was.

Then there was a sharp pain in his left hand, and his mind was brutally snapped back into unity. Still feeling a little disoriented, he took his left hand in his right and brought it up to his face. There was a thin but nasty-looking cut in his palm, starting towards the edge of his heart line on one side and continuing all the way around the edge of his hand ending just below the knuckle of his little finger on the back. Blood was already seeping out of the gash in his flesh and trickling down his hand. He could tell, gently pressing against the wound, that the cut didn't just go *around* the side of his hand, but *through* it. Had it occurred a centimetre or so higher, he might well have lost the finger.

Finally, it occurred to him to look down at the wall and see what had injured him so. His eyes, scrunched in pain, suddenly opened wide. He had walked along the wall until he had reached the plaque and the swastika. Only he hadn't cut his hand on the plaque, but on the swastika, bulging impossibly from the wall onto which it had been spray-painted. It had a grey metallic look to it, every branch rising to a sharp point like a series of interconnecting triangular prisms. Light from the above fluorescents glinted off the top part of these prisms, and the nearest branch had a thin red line running along its apex where he'd sliced open his hand.

Dino stared at the newly three-dimensional piece for a few more bewildered seconds, and then said, "Okay—I'm going to leave now." He spoke to no one in particular, and his breathing was quick and ragged. He took a few steps towards the stairs at the centre of the platform before realizing that he was still clutching his injured hand. He stopped and let go of the wound in order to fish for something in his coat pockets that he could tie around the gash.

He finally found some pieces of unused facial tissue and began twisting them together, tying them around his hand as best he could using his right hand. As he was doing so, he heard the scream of the beast echoing through the tunnel again, a high-pitched herald of horror. He felt the urge to run, but found he couldn't move. The piercing sound seemed to slice into his being, replacing the very marrow in his bones with ice water. First those ugly, low-set yellow eyes swam into view, then the horrible metal teeth beneath. Its high forehead was semi-transparent, and Dino thought he could see the shape of its foul brain beneath the translucent surface.

The creature slithered passed him, undulating through the tunnel by the platform. Its hoary, scaly hide—green but greying with age—was also clear in places, giving Dino a good view into its stomach. Within the belly of the beast, he could see the unfortunate commuters, their flesh burned away by the thing's digestive acids until little more remained but gleaming bones. They pressed against the side of the fiend's gullet, still impossibly alive, hoping to claw their way out but finding the monster's thick hide to be impenetrable. So their empty sockets screamed balefully out at Dino, who could only stand frozen under their accusatory glares.

Then the beast was past, still worming its way through the earth at unnatural speeds. The spell that had fallen over Dino burst like a dam, and he scrambled madly for the stairs, tissue still streaming from his incomplete dressing. He stumbled as he hit the stairs but did not stop, using his good hand to climb the staircase like a ladder. The heavy, breathy sound of the retreating creature continued to chase him up the stairs. Finally, the flight of stairs ended. He was unprepared; his good right hand flailed against empty air and he went crashing to the floor of the concourse. He kicked with his feet, old boots finding some traction against the ground and bodily pushing him across the floor and away from the staircase. After a metre or so of dragging himself in this fashion, he braced himself with his remaining hand and flipped over onto his back.

The concourse was empty and silent. The papers lying on the floor, usually tossing about, caught up in the wind blasting up the stairwells from the trains passing through the tunnels, were deathly still. The fluorescents that lined the ceiling hummed quietly, casting a constant white light across the deserted concourse. The abandoned guard booth stood forlornly at the end of the row of tourniquets. Beyond that, the closed convenience store slumped behind the bars that had dropped above its facade at closing time. Dirty, shabby walls rose all around him, despondently holding up the roof. The roof itself stretched across Dino's field of vision, cobwebbed arches looking down at him with reprimand.

Dino began to laugh. It was a wheezy, breathless laugh after his sprint up the stairs, but it felt good nonetheless, like a weight was being lifted off his chest. It echoed throughout the empty concourse. Dino thought it sounded strange, and that made him laugh all the harder. Bleeding graffiti! Creatures in the metro! How ridiculous it all seemed in the still silence of the concourse. These phantasms were no more real than Paulie's men in black fedoras. Still laughing at his own foolishness, Dino concluded that he was simply tired, and that his exhausted mind was playing tricks on him.

Besides, he didn't need the benches. There's no real reason to go down to the platform. He could sleep just as well right here on the concourse floor. He certainly felt tired enough.

The overhead fluorescents flickered, losing intensity and momentarily plunging the station into darkness before snapping back on again. Dino stopped laughing. Some of the lights were still sputtering, and Dino thought that even the stable ones didn't seem as bright as they were before. But that wasn't a problem, Dino reasoned. Flickering lights happened all the time. There had probably been a power surge in the local network. It wasn't as if one should expect quality municipal services in this part of the city. Nonetheless, Dino eyed the lights from his supine position on the floor, on guard for any treacherous shift in intensity.

A familiar whistling sound reached his ears. For a moment he hoped that it might be coming from the right-hand platform, but a moment later was forced to admit that it was coming from the left-handed one, drifting up the stairway at his feet. He tried to tell himself that it was normal, that trains ran all night long through this station, but his breath caught in his throat and made a lump there. Dino raised his head, but he couldn't see the tracks from where he was lying, and so dropped his head back down, closed his eyes and focused on ignoring the sound. It was hard, considering how high-pitched and incisive it was. It cut through the mental barriers he'd erected, ringing in his head. The sound of the air chuffing between the cars, perfectly audible even from the concourse, seemed to be calling out to him: *hey-hey-hey-hey-hey-hey-hey.*

Hey, Diiiiiiiiiiiiiiiinoooo.

His eyes snapped open. This was a new sound. Or rather, a familiar sound, but one he hadn't heard tonight, and with just reason. It was the grating screech of metal wheels rubbing against metal tracks as a metro train slowed to a stop, the exhalation of pressurized hydraulics as the doors opened, ready to discharge its cargo and take on new passengers. But Dino knew that there weren't supposed to be any stops at this station this late at night. The trains were supposed to bypass all minor hubs such as Adams Memorial and proceed uninterrupted to the major distribution centres.

Dino suddenly had a mental picture, stunning in its clarity, of the great, scaly beast he had seen before arcing its back as it slithers out of the dark tunnel and into the station, black talons jutting out from underneath its slime-coated sides like a thorny centipede. The creature drops its body against the tracks, the claws stabbing into the rails. Released electricity crackles across the worm-thing's body, the talons sparking as they carve a great furrow in the grey metal and slow the monster's frantic pace through the tunnels, finally bringing it to a halt altogether.

"No!" Dino screamed, blinking quickly to dispel the image. He brought his hands to his face, and then howled in pain as his injured left hand struck the side of his nose. Turning on his side, he clutched his left wrist in his right hand and stared and the side of his hand, the botched dressing over the wound red and heavy with blood. Some of it had seeped out, running along the furrows of his palm and down onto his wrist.

It was like a revelation. *That* was real, unquestionably. If he could believe in nothing else tonight, he could believe in the pain. And if he believed the pain, he believed he could be hurt. And if he could be hurt by whatever-the-hell it was down there....

Wasting no more time, Dino scrambled to his feet, ignoring the scream of protest from his left hand as he used it to brace himself against the floor. He didn't look towards the staircase, didn't want to see what might be there, didn't want to see what ghouls and shades might have come pouring out of the belly of the train-beast.

He ran for the exit, quickly gaining speed. He leapt bodily over the row of tourniquets, using his good right hand as a brace. Earlier, he had needed to climb over the tourniquets, but he now felt more energized than he had in years. He ran past the closed convenience store and turned onto the flight of stairs that would lead him back to the streets.

Back home.

He went up the left side of the staircase, using the ramp in the middle as support and to pull himself up faster with his right arm. He slowed only slightly as he reached the top of the stairs, turning to present his right shoulder to better absorb the shock of the impact. He slammed into the revolving doors, and then bounced back. Caught off his guard, he lost his balance and toppled backwards. His left hand burned as, out of reflex, he slammed his hands downwards to brace his fall.

Shaking his head to clear the last wisps of disorientation, Dino sprung to his feet and, more cautiously this time, pushed against the door. It didn't budge, so he tried pushing on the other side, but with no more luck. He moved to the next two doors and pushed against them as well, but they didn't shift so much as a centimetre. Dino pressed his head against the narrow, oval-shaped windows in the door, trying to see outside.

The doors were locked. He was trapped.

It couldn't be, just couldn't be. The doors had been unlocked when he had come in, a mere two or three hours ago. He had seen plenty of locked metro doors before, but never from this side. Maybe there was a way to get them open from the inside. Dino moved laterally along the line of three doors, frantically pushing, pulling, prodding, poking. He looked and felt across the doors in the hopes of finding some sort of mechanism that would release the locks. When all that failed, he began to bang on the doors, howling in frustration and fear.

Kicking and screaming, he turned his attention to the windows. Striking it with fists, feet and elbows, Dino tried to break the glass, but to no avail. In a neighbourhood such as this one, even the Transit Authority would know to buy unbreakable glass. And even if the glass had broken, he never could have fit through the narrow oval windows.

The desperate rage began draining away from him, like body heat being leeched away by freezing waters. He started to sink, pressed against the door and giving it some last, meek jabs. His knees buckled, his legs failed him, and soon he was curled up on the floor against the door. He could feel the cold seeping through the edges of the door; see the frosted cityscape of the deep November night outside.

Finally, because he couldn't bear not knowing, he turned to look at the staircase behind him. It was empty for now, but Dino knew that it wouldn't stay that way for long. The beast had stopped at the station, and it wouldn't have done so unless it was planning on releasing its passengers. And why not? They were dead already, even though they didn't seem to have noticed yet. They would march up the staircases, through the concourse, past the store, going about with the business of their former lives.

Dino could see them now, in his mind's eye, turning the corner and up this flight of stairs. There would be skeletons with briefcases, skeletons with schoolbags and purses. Skeletons in suits and shirts and skirts. Skeletons in hats and shoes, and maybe some of them will have bundled up their bones warmly against the chill of the wintry night outside. Maybe some skeletons with broader pelvises would have blush colouring their pearly-white skulls, eyeliner around empty sockets, lipstick on their lipless faces. Maybe one wasted spectre would bring his bony wrist to his face, trying to see his watch without eyes, wondering if he's late for an appointment and not realizing that, oh yes, he's all too late, indeed.

Dino waited for them to come, rapidly shifting between despondency and nervous fear. Every flash in the corner of his eyes was the light glinting off the skull of the leader of the damned cohort. Every second was the second just before they would turn the corner and begin climbing up the stairs. And while most people usually ignore the hobos slumped into the corner of a metro station's entryway, Dino knew that this drudge host wouldn't do so. For one thing, the doors were locked, so where would they go? They would cluster around him, swamp him, bony fingers digging into his clothes and flesh, the one with the wristwatch trying to pry his eyes out of their orbits and socket them into his own skull.

The seconds crumbled by, coarse sand in the hourglass. Seconds stretched into minutes, and still nothing came from below. Dino couldn't hear a single sound coming from the bottom of the stairwell, let alone a horde of skeletons. Hope began to flow through his veins again, and he cursed it. He had thought everything would work out when lying on his back in the concourse, and see what had happened there. He didn't dare to hope for a happy resolution to all this matter, lest he be cast down even deeper into the chasm next time. Better to end it now. With a groan of pain, he pushed himself off the floor. All the aches and sores he had accumulated in his mad flight away from the concourse and his fight with the doors were making their presence known, but they were drowned out by the constant scream coming from his left hand. Dino stared at it again. The dressing had come away completely, and a coating of old blood had crusted over the wound and the side of his hand, turning a dark, syrupy brown colour. Fresh blood still seeped from the wound and over the scab. He hadn't forgotten about the hand this time around. It was hard to forget since the throbbing appendage clamoured for his attention with every beat of his heart.

A tiny, timid thought crept out from the back of his mind. Wasn't it more logical to believe that he had cut his hand on a piece of broken bottle or on a jagged edge from the memorial plaque? It certainly made more sense than thinking he'd sliced open his hand on a magical bit of swastika graffiti.

Dino sighed, feeling a great weight fall on him, because he knew in that instant that he would have to go back down into the station. He couldn't pass the evening cowering in the corner of the vestibule. He didn't think he had any dignity left to his name after two years on the streets, but everything human in him rebelled at the thought of being treated in such a fashion. He had lost his home and his belongings, what few possessions he had were dingy, dirty things, and his body was in ill health, home to colonies of germs. His mind was truly the last thing that was still his, and he refused to let anything fuck with it. For his own sake, he had to go back down to the platform and confirm the situation either way. He had to know.

End it now, he thought again. *End it here.*

Slowly, cautiously, he made his way down the stairs. He used the other side this time, so that he could brace his descent with his good right hand. He peered around the edge of the stairwell as he reached the bottom, but the concourse was deserted. The closed-up convenience store looked as stolid as usual. Nothing seemed to have changed down here; as far as he could tell, even the discarded papers were in the same spot they were before. But he found no relief in the still silence of the concourse. Whereas before it had been a comforting oasis of reality, now a sense of foreboding hung over the entire station like humidity, building up unseen before unleashing a sudden tempest. Dino could feel the hairs of his skin prickle, as if he was standing above an electrical conduit.

There was something ominous about the deserted metro station that hadn't been there earlier. He felt like the last survivor of some great cataclysm, walking through the ruins of a fallen civilization. Just to keep himself company, Dino asked, "What do you think of this, Billy-Boy? Not a great idea, huh?"

Billy did not answer. Dino figured that the little boy had gotten his metaphorical ass in gear and skedaddled.

"Chickenshit," Dino cursed, as he approached the left-side staircase. He slowed as he reached its height, all but tiptoeing. Finally, he stopped just before the stairwell, and inched his head forward. He was braced to turn tail and run away again should he find anything aberrant down there, although, with the only doors leading outside locked, he had no idea where he would flee to. With a mental shrug, he peered down the stairs.

And saw nothing.

No skeletons, no metro train, nothing.

The place looked as deserted as it had been when he had first arrived.

Slowly, taking care not to use his left hand, making sure he was ready to turn and bolt back up the stairs, Dino began to climb down to the platform. As he was coming down, he caught a glimpse of the anarchist graffiti that had been painted onto the concrete division. The dripping red paint had now completely filled in the circle, obscuring the "A" and making the piece look like nothing more than a barbed red spot on the wall.

Dino stopped when he saw this. Wasn't this the confirmation he was looking for? Sure, maybe there was some kind of defect in the spray paint that had caused it to dribble like this, but in a perfect circle? Dino couldn't conceive of it.

So, if he had the explanation, or rather lack thereof, that he had been looking for, why was he still walking down the stairs? Dino asked himself this as he reached the last few stairs before the platform. He should stop now, turn around, and go back to the doors, where he would wait out the morning and gladly face the ire of the security guard who would unlock the station.

Still thinking this, Dino walked out onto the platform proper and found himself turning to his left. He knew where he was going: the memorial plaque. He had to see what was there that had eviscerated his left hand. It would be his litmus test. As he walked closer to the plaque, he saw the unmistakable glint of light on a metal surface. Stepping forward, he saw the impossible, three-dimensional shape of the swastika graffiti. From this angle, with the light reflecting off the top of each arm's axis, it looked even thinner and sharper, like a coldly gleaming knife. Slowly closing the distance, Dino scanned the nearest branch of the perverted symbol. There, practically imperceptible against the dark, metallic grey, was the thin red stripe of blood.

Nodding solemnly, Dino turned away and began to hobble towards the staircase. The pain in his hand accentuated a limp he'd picked up running up to the exit earlier. He proceeded with speed but without hurry, walking forward with the determination of an airplane crash survivor plodding through snow or jungle to reach civilization. He had reached the staircase leading up to the concourse when he felt or heard (he couldn't be sure) something like a breath on his shoulders. There were no words to it, but Dino thought he sensed both despair and familiarity.

Turning around with a distinct lack of enthusiasm, Dino faced the gory spot on the wall from which the felt/heard projection was clearly emanating. The red circle seemed to be pulsating, stretching out of its cinderblock abode with each noiseless beat of the station's foul heart. Pockmarked and glistening wet, it expanded outward like the thin film of a bubble, drops of something red splattering onto the track below.

Dino walked over the edge of the platform, his gaze fixed on the bloody circle, his chin slightly raised as if asking the inflated thing why it had called out to him. A shape formed under the elastic barrier of the erstwhile anarchist graffiti, pressing against the slimy skin. It was the shape of a visage, the nose, chin, cheekbones and forehead of a face, empty eye pits staring out blindly, mouth open in a soundless wail. It was easy for Dino to recognize the features of his old friend Vornsky.

Another shape bulged out from under the sinew of the red semi-sphere, and this time Dino was able to make out the narrow face of the Candyman. Then a third face appeared, and Dino was un-surprised to see that it was old Paranoid Paulie. Any why not? The pathways of an itinerant's life are fraught with dangers. Maybe the men with the black fedoras finally caught up to him. It was impossible to hear what they were saying, mouths opening and closing beneath the crimson veil like fish gasping for air, but he could *feel* their meaning clearly enough. It was time for the fourth member of the group to join them, time for one last reunion tour of the Ratty Pack.

Slowly, nursing his injured hand and weak leg, Dino sat on the edge of the platform, letting his legs dangle for a moment before letting himself drop fully into the depression. He walked over to the cinderblock divide, taking care to avoid the electrified rails and step only on the rubber-coated segments. He felt strange, walking on the bottom of the chasm he had looked down upon so often. He resisted the urge to look behind him, up at the ledge that he had abandoned. Standing before the bulging red sac, he reached out with his good right hand, brushing the improbable thing with his fingers. Something wet and sticky, burgundy in colour, came away from it, staining the edges of his fingers.

And then he heard the high-pitched scream of the onrushing creature, turning his head to the left just fast enough to see the monstrous fiend speeding towards him, yellow eyes shining malevolently, the black silhouette of a corrupt brain behind the translucent forehead, scales of green tinged with grey, the narrow teeth of the grill spread in a rictus, the black gaping maw opening to swallow him whole and add him to its collection of the dead and damned, trapped for eternity within the belly of the worm burrowing its way through the bowels of the earth.

✳

The Sweet Dark

"In nature, nothing exists alone."
—*Rachel Carson,* Silent Spring

1.

In February of 2016 I returned to Canada after many years abroad.

I never thought I would once more tread carefully on sidewalks frosted with a treacherous glaze of ice while breathing air so painfully sharp it was like inhaling swarms of razor blades.

I had to buy a parka, gloves, and warm boots, as I no longer owned any of those things. I rented a car in Toronto, and drove northeast. Under a lowering sky like a canted and weathered tombstone, I saw trees that looked as if they would never bloom again, unforgiving granite, and relentless snow; Ontario in the dead heart of winter.

I coughed up blood a couple of times during the latter part of the drive, spitting into a McDonald's coffee cup I'd emptied earlier. I would have preferred to pull over on the shoulder of the road and spit out the car door instead of looking at a vessel containing proof of my imminent dissolution, but I was afraid the car would get stuck there. I'd grown up in this part of the country but I had no idea how to drive on snow and ice.

I was headed for Kitchissippi, where I was born. The town was 100 miles northwest of Ottawa, not far from where the Ottawa River formed a natural border between the Provinces of Ontario and Quebec.

In the little town of Arbor, I met a fellow named David Rensch, who gave guided tours through what was left of my home town. I knew from reading Rensch's website that part of the Kitchissippi Ghost Town Tours itinerary was a visit to an abandoned building called Cruickshank's Sugar Shack, visiting the place where Terry Cruickshank's last entrepreneurial endeavor caused so many deaths, thirty-eight years ago.

I knew Terry Cruickshank; his son Jeffrey was my best friend, the only real friend I've ever had.

Rensch tried to engage me in conversation as he drove us to Kitchissippi, his big four-wheel drive truck crossing snow-swept black ice that would have killed me. I sat in the passenger seat. I didn't feel like saying much, and after a while he got it.

"You're from the Kitch, aren't you?"

I nodded. Cold was seeping through the window to my right. I hated the cold.

"Me, too," Rensch said. "Not too many of us around these days. The few I see are people like you, returning for a look at the old—"

"Shut the fuck up," I said. "I'm paying you to drive me to Kitchissippi, not to be my friend."

"Not an unexpected response." Rensch said this as if speaking to himself, and didn't say much after that aside from asking if there was anything specific I wanted to see.

"Cruickshank's," I said.

Twenty minutes later I was walking along a familiar path behind the remains of my best friend's home. It was getting colder, and night was coming fast. Rensch called out, asking if I wanted a guide, or at least a flashlight.

"No," I said. "I'm good. In fact, you can leave me here tonight and pick me up in the morning."

"What," Rensch asked, "Are you nuts?"

"I can spend the night in the house," I said, referring to the half-burned shell of the Cruickshank home that—like the rest of Kitchissippi's ruins—had never been rebuilt.

Rensch tried to argue with me, but I eventually persuaded him to leave me alone. He was a responsible guy, a business owner, so I knew he would be back soon, likely with the Ontario Provincial Police.

I was pretty sure I would have time to do what I came here to do, before anyone found me.

I went deeper into the woods, moving under the stark light of a moon the color of weathered bone.

As I walked I recalled what happened to my friend and his father in 1978, when I tried to destroy the Sweet Dark.

2.

A few weeks before Christmas, Jeffrey said, "My dad bought a sugar bush."

Jeffrey lived on what was once a family farm beyond the west end of Kitchissippi. When we were little kids we spent our summers playing in the corn, building forts on the edge of the woods, or going deeper into the heavy growth of maples behind the Cruickshank home, where we chased frogs around the placid black oval of Villeneuve's Hole.

When Jeff mentioned a sugar bush, I thought he was talking about a potted plant.

We were farting around in my room, hoping to find something good on TV. It was just after eight o'clock on a Saturday night. Downstairs, my dad was watching *Hockey Night in Canada* in the TV room. My sister was with him. She was 14 and a girl and a hockey freak. It was weird.

"It's about five hundred acres."

I wondered if I had missed something. "What is five hundred acres?"

"The sugar bush my dad bought." Jeff said this as if he was speaking to an imbecile.

I lived in a little house at the corner on Ypres and Doncaster streets, near the old water tower that once stood on the edge of the woods. Jeff and I spent many twilight hours catching fireflies in the woods as the water tower's saucer-shaped tank loomed over us like one of H.G. Wells' Fighting Machines.

Jeff came over to my place as often as he could. We'd watch TV and eat chocolate bars and caramel cakes and ketchup-flavored chips.

"What the fuck is a sugar bush?" I had just started using the word *fuck,* even though I'd been hearing it forever. It made me feel grown up to say *fuck,* although I'd never say it around my dad. If he heard me say that he'd go out of his tree, even though he was always swearing in cool ways, like telling people to go pound salt up their ass or go fuck their hat.

Jeff rolled his eyes. "It's land that was owned by one of our neighbors, but the old guy died and his son is selling it. My dad thinks he can turn it into a maple syrup farm"

"Your dad is gonna try to make maple syrup?"

My skepticism must have been clear in my voice.

"He could do it, you know!" Jeff's tone was angry and defensive.

"Yeah man, I know he could." I said that to make Jeff feel better. Everyone knew Jeff's dad Terry was kind of a loser and a weirdo.

My dad was a mechanic. He owned McCormick's Golden Eagle Gas & Auto Repair on Laurier Street. He was a bit of a dick until my mom died, and then he eased up and became a nice guy to me and Paul and Abigail.

My dad was always doubtful of my friendship with Jeff, saying things like, "I hope that kid isn't as much of a fuckup as his old man." According to my dad, Terry Cruickshank *couldn't piss into a pot without making a goddamned mess even if you sat him down on the fucking thing.* They had gone to school together at Clouthier High, just like Jeffrey and I did now, and my dad said guys like Terry were born to lose.

Terry's wife left him when Jeff was five. That was something Jeff and I had in common when we met as little kids: neither of us had a mom.

Terry said he was a farmer, but it seemed like every kid in town knew he was actually growing pot. That enterprise had taken ages to get going. His first crop was eaten by deer that leaped over a fence. When Terry raised the fence and started a second crop, it was eaten by rabbits. He lowered the fence again and had success for a while, until bored kids climbed over the fence and destroyed the whole operation.

Terry was always throwing money away on something foolish.

In the summer of 1973, he invested in a store just a block away from the Golden Eagle on Laurier Street, opening a shop that sold nothing but clogs for men and women, ridiculous shoes with stiff soles and platform heels. That didn't go over well, especially after Patsy Paquette stepped out of Aline's Hair Salon on three inch heels, lost her balance on the curb and fell into the street, shattering one ankle and screaming loud enough that most of Kitchissippi heard her. In a small town that's the kind of thing people talk about.

Patsy was in a cast and on crutches for a long time after that, and whenever my dad saw her he would quietly express his relief that she was no longer *bleating like a lamb.* Patsy had nice legs, and she wore miniskirts that made all the guys stop and stare whenever she passed by. Her attractiveness was not diminished by the cast; in fact, it made her even hotter. After her accident, a kid named Todd Ryerson said the reason he jumped the curb and crashed his bike into old Rene Lacombe outside Gendre's Variety Store was because Patsy's miniskirt was caught by her crutches and it rode up so high Todd could see her panties.

By the winter of 1977, Patsy only had a year left to live, thanks to Terry and his maple syrup.

Terry also bought a bunch of mopeds and tried to convince my dad to help him sell them at the Golden Eagle. My dad told Terry that he didn't want any *goddamned candy-colored arsehole bicycles* in front of his station and that Terry should *peddle them somewhere else, like Europe.* Terry rented a lot and tried to move the mopeds on his own, with no luck, eventually selling the mopeds to another dealer at a loss. And now he was going to make maple syrup?

"Does he know how to do it?"

Jeff nodded. "He bought a book on it. You just collect the sap and boil off the water until you have the pure sugar."

There had to be a lot more to it than that, but I didn't say anything.

"He says it's important to take care of the environment, to get back to nature" Jeff said. "My dad thinks that we're ruining everything, that we are poisoning our water supplies, polluting the air, and taking catastrophic risks with nuclear reactors."

I didn't want to say that Terry had been complaining about things as long as I'd known him. The last few times I'd been over to Jeff's house Terry had been raving about Trudeau *shoving French down our schoolchildren's throats* and *the new metric system that our Prime Minister can shove a meter up his ass.*

Things were changing fast in those days, and men like Terry were afraid of change.

I had no problems with trying to learn French. Quebec was a short way away by car, half the kids in Kitchissippi were French-Canadian, and I watched a lot of TV that was broadcast from Montréal.

It didn't hurt that my French teacher at school looked like the actress, Carole Laure; she had a shag haircut like Joan Jett from The Runaways, eyes as dark as a moonless night in winter, and if honey could speak, it would have sounded like her. Her name was Angelle Delacroix, which means Angel of the Cross, and she wore a big crucifix every day. French Canada was probably hit the hardest by the revolutionary changes of the sixties and seventies, but there were still hordes of devout Catholics back then, despite the tumult of the sexual revolution. However, neither Christ on the Cross nor Mademoiselle Delacroix's faith could stop me from getting a raging boner in class almost every time she talked to me, like the time she saw me chewing a wad of spearmint Freshen Up, leaned close, and whispered in my ear, *"Monsieur, jette ton gum, s'il vous plaît."* How could you complain about a language that made *spit out your gum* sound so goddamned hot?

Mlle Delacroix didn't like sweets. That may have saved her life, when so many of her students died.

"Anyhow," Jeff said, "My dad says that if you want a job, you know, something to do after school, he'll pay you to help out. He needs to get organized so he can start tapping trees in the spring. We have to hang buckets on every tree after we tap them."

"Buckets?" I got up and changed the channel on the little black and white TV on the corner of my dresser, finding a new *Bionic Woman* episode. I had a crush on Lindsay Wagner, even though she was really skinny.

"Yeah," Jeff said. "We tap the trees and when the weather is right, all that sap pours into buckets to be boiled down to syrup."

Jeff had obviously been reading up on this. He absorbed the information in how-to books the way I read sci-fi and horror paperbacks and comic books. It was his one saving grace with my dad; Jeff read auto repair manuals for kicks, and could discuss the intricacies of engines on a level that was beyond me. This is why he thought shows like *The Six Million Dollar Man* and *The Bionic Woman* were retarded.

"Jaime Sommers has a robotic arm and legs, but the rest of her skeletal system is completely human," Jeff once said. "If she tried to pick up a car her arm would just tear right off of her body, and then she'd probably bleed to death."

"Let me get this straight," I said. "We stab sharp taps into the trees, and drain them of their sap?"

"Yeah," Jeff said.

"So, we're tree vampires, eh?"

"Look, I'm serious," Jeff said.

"I'm *see*-rious," I replied.

"You're being a dork," he said.

"*You're* being a dork," I said.

Jeff picked up a book and threw it at my head.

"Jeez, take it easy," I said.

I realized it was time I got a job, a real job, even if it was part time. I loved my dad, but there was no way I could work for him at the Golden Eagle. That would be too weird.

In winter, we always left our snow boots inside the front door and walked around the house in sock feet. This gave me the opportunity to pull off one of my socks and throw it in Jeff's face, shouting, "Stench attack!"

Jeff made gagging noises, fell flat on his back, and began thrashing about on the hardwood floor, something he would never do at home. He was a really uptight kid whose dad could be amusing when he wasn't carried away by rage the way drunks went on benders, so cutting loose like this would never happen in the Cruickshank home.

"Vincent, there's two kinds of crazy in the world," my dad once said. "There's sunny crazy, like your mom was before she died, and there's dark crazy, like Terry Cruickshank. If you're gonna hang out with Jeffrey, and I know what kids are like when fathers say no, then hang out with him in your room or down in the TV room, not out at Cruickshank's farm. I'd rather have you influencing him, than him influencing you. Maybe if he hangs around with you long enough, it'll suppress his apeshit gene."

After a pause he had said, "You're not the greatest role model, but you'll do." He gave me a little wink when he said that. My dad was too old-fashioned to ever say he loved me until late in life, but that familiar little wink always said it all.

Jeff was lying on floor with his tongue hanging out of his mouth, playing dead.

"That tree-bleeding job sounds cool," I said at last.

3.

Terry eventually gave up growing pot because the laws regulating it were so strict.

Despite Prime Minister Trudeau saying he didn't think a single joint was a big deal, he played to both sides by insisting that dealing was a serious crime. Earlier in the year Trudeau said, "If you have a joint and you're smoking it for your private pleasure, you shouldn't be hassled," yet he still insisted that trafficking was a criminal offense. The government wanted to decriminalize the private possession of weed, but they would still nail you if you sold it, which was a screw-job for the people who grew marijuana, since a lot of people didn't have the time, patience or skill to grow their own.

I got most of this information from my older brother Paul, who smoked a lot of reefer grown by Jeff's dad. Paul was always warning us that 1984 was right around the corner and talking about Big Brother and government corruption and intrusive laws. "The reason Canadians aren't out in the streets protesting this silent takeover is because we're too docile," Paul said once.

My dad liked to stretch out on the chesterfield and watch *The CBS Evening News* at supper time—he thought Walter Cronkite was the only honest man in America—and then *The National* on CBC, before bed. When I asked my dad why Canadians didn't riot in the streets like the Americans did, my dad said, "Because we're lucky that we've got it pretty good here. And because we're not fucking idiots."

Paul had a friend in up in Petawawa who was marched straight off to prison after he tried selling a handful of joints to undercover cops, not the brightest move. And Paul knew another guy got two years in Millhaven Penitentiary for importing hashish from Afghanistan. For such a smart guy, my brother had some really stupid friends. I would never say that, though, because Paul had a mind-blowing record collection and he let me listen to his albums, when he was in a good mood.

I tried smoking weed once and it made me so dizzy I puked, which was just as well, since I was only sixteen. My dad would have killed me if he knew I was smoking pot, which is part of the reason he wasn't too keen on me hanging out with Jeffrey.

It was a bit easier to move weed outside of cities like Ottawa and Toronto, where the local cops and RCMP were carrying out street-level enforcement under pressure from a Federal Government that did not want Canadian municipalities going the route of U.S. cities, but you still had to deal with the Ontario Provincial Police in small towns like Kitchissippi and Miramichi, and the Sûreté du Québec over the river in Brûléville and Des Loups.

By the end of 1977 Terry was done with marijuana and fully invested in the maple syrup business. He put all of his money into 500 acres of thickly forested land, most of it maple trees.

I wanted to help my friend, but I hated the taste of maple syrup.

I know that seems impossible; I'm Canadian, so hating maple syrup is like hating ice skating, but it's true. Something about maple syrup just made me want to puke. I could handle the smell well enough, but something in that sugary mapleness just gagged me. Otherwise, I had a sweet tooth like any other kid.

I guess it ran in the family. My dad could not eat a bite of chicken, he really couldn't stand it, and my brother had an equally strong aversion to cheese. My little sister thought this was further evidence that all boys were weird no matter how old they were.

In the end I helped Jeff and his dad. I had to. He was my friend and he needed me.

4.

I was about to knock on Jeff's front door when I heard his dad yelling inside the house.

It was the middle of March, 1978. The nights were still cold, but temperatures were rising enough during the day that the spring thaw had begun, and that was perfect weather to get the sap flowing.

Every weekend since Christmas, Jeffrey and I had gone out into the woods with Terry, helping him select and mark trees, since the sap of sugar maples and black maples had a higher sugar content than red or silver maples, and then drill holes and insert spiles, which were stainless steel taps with hooks that would hold buckets. We had to be careful to choose trees that got a lot of sun, trees that were undamaged, and trees that were more than twelve inches thick.

It was a discipline, a science, and it was no surprise that analytical Jeff really seemed get off on it. I just liked hanging out with my friend.

It would only occur to me afterward that when they were in the woods together, lost in work, Jeff and his dad liked hanging out with each other, a rare thing. Usually Terry was either ignoring Jeffrey, or shouting at him, as he was doing now.

Jeffrey's dad was so loud I swear the front door rattled in its frame.

"You think your father's an arsehole, eh?"

I snorted laughter, glad that I was out on the front step. Terry would have knocked my block off if he'd heard me laughing, but it was impossible not to. When he was angry, Terry's Canadian accent extended the long A in some words to such lengths that it almost sounded like he was singing.

Even Jeff said he had to fight not to laugh, because there were times when his dad's rage was serious business no matter how comical it sounded.

I knocked on the door. Terry opened it and saw me standing there. He was furious.

"Are you taking notes, Mr. Eavesdropper?" He asked harshly. "There'll be a test later!"

"Dad!" Jeffrey sounded embarrassed. "Vince is here to help!"

"Maybe you and your little friend can prance out into the woods and pick the nits off of the tree roots," Terry said, turning and walking down the hall to the washroom. "Pick-pick-pick-pick," Terry said, making odd little plucking motions with his fingers.

I stepped inside and closed the door behind me, taking off my parka and tuque and boots. I went into the living room, where Jeff had library books spread out on the floor in front of the TV. I saw photos and drawings of odd-looking bugs.

"What's all this?"

Jeff made a face. "Some of the trees deep into the lot have insects on the roots."

"Remember when we climbed that tree that was crawling with ants?" I asked.

That had happened when we were in elementary school, and the memory was still vivid. Being thirty feet in the air and realizing you and the tree you were clinging to was covered with ants was a good way to break your neck, because your first instinct was to run. I got lucky. I had Jeff climbing right below me, and just before I launched myself into space I heard him calmly point out that these ants didn't usually bite.

"That's what is so weird," Jeff said. "These insects are only on and around the roots of the trees. They aren't climbing up the trunks. We aren't sure if it's some kind of contamination, or if it's harmless."

"Will the trees still produce sap?"

"Yeah, as long as they aren't diseased, or weakened by the insects." Jeff said. He handed me a Bick's Pickle jar. A hunched-over insect circled the walls of its glass prison. It looked like an old man stooped with age and wearing a brown overcoat.

"I must have made a dozen phone calls to universities and libraries, asking about these things. I've never seen anything like them, I can't find them in my books, and no one I talked to could identify them based on my descriptions, aside from saying they had to be some kind of beetle."

The toilet flushed. Terry came back down the hall and said to me, "The prick who sold me these trees deked me out with his fancy footwork and misleading bullshit, eh? I've been scammed!"

"That's too bad," I said, hoping a more adult response would make Terry realize he was acting like a petulant child.

"Too bad?" He seemed angrier than ever. "Too bad? Big Industry is poisoning the planet and paying off elected officials who let it happen! We have acid rain in the air and pesticides in our water and toxic runoff in our soil, all of which can weaken sugar maples and make them susceptible to blight or infestation. The whole world is polluted and irradiated and we're all going to be eradicated, and I'm so damned infuriated that now I'm constipated."

I tried my best to stay cool. Part of me wanted to bray laughter and part of me wanted to run like hell. Terry was really going off the deep end. His eyes were as wide and shiny as new nickels, and he kept grinning in a really creepy way.

"Dad!"

Terry quailed under Jeffrey's cry, and for a moment it was as if their roles had been reversed.

"Sit on the couch and calm down. Just because these bugs are on the tree roots doesn't mean they are harming the trees. Vince and I will go out and mark any of the maples that look unhealthy. I don't think there will be that many. If we have to, we can cut them down and sell them for firewood. Then we can get back to work on the maple syrup."

Terry sat down and sulked like a child.

"Let's go," Jeff said to me, "before he goes off again."

I got back into my coat and boots and when we were outside I asked Jeff what was up with his dad.

"He put all of our money into buying those maple trees," Jeff said. "If we don't make back any money, we may have to sell our house."

I couldn't imagine that happening. Jeff had lived here all his life.

We got into Terry's old pickup truck. Jeff drove; he got his driver's license years before I did. When we reached the far side of the lot, we got out and Jeff gave me a can of orange spray paint.

We made our way through the woods, past skeletal beech and birch, and ash and elm that had yet to bud, and under the closed ranks of dripping pines and spruce. Jeff led me into the deepest part of the sugar bush, where some of the maple trees did indeed have bugs on their roots.

I watched the hunched up little insects as they trundled along the partially-exposed roots of a tree. "Isn't it too cold for these things? And why do they look so weird?"

"My dad mixed his own home-made pesticides when he was growing marijuana," Jeff said. "None of them worked for long. I guess the insects developed immunities to the pesticides because his crop was always like a salad bar for darned things. I'm surprised he didn't give us cancer with all the crap he sprayed everywhere. I can't help wondering if he didn't create these bugs through mutation."

We began looking for trees to mark with the orange spray paint.

After a while I asked, "Would you think I was a dick if I said your dad was acting kind of scary?"

Jeff considered this and then shook his head. He seemed sad when he admitted, "He scares me, too."

I was glad that Jeff didn't read the same kind of fiction I did, most notably what he referred to as stupid horror books.

I had spent much of February 1978 reading *The Amityville Horror* and then *The Shining* late at night, by flashlight, enthralled and terrified. Those stories about fathers going right off the rails scared the shit out of me, and afterward, whenever I was at Jeffrey's house and his dad was raving about something that pissed him off, I always expected Terry to appear in a doorway holding a shotgun or an axe, his eyes gleaming with insanity.

As nutty as Terry could be, he could also be really funny, intentionally funny, and that was something I only saw once in a while in my dad, or Jeff for that matter. Jeff and my dad had great senses of humor, but they rarely made me bust a gut laughing.

It was sad to see that funny side of Terry being eclipsed by a darker, more contemptible side.

We examined a couple of trees with buckets already hanging from their spiles, part of a test to see if the trees would actually produce any sap. They did. Jeff took one of the buckets with him.

We were in the woods for a couple of hours when Jeff said, "Screw this, let's go home."

"Language," I said with a laugh. Jeff never swore.

We hadn't found any diseased trees. All we saw was those odd old-man bugs trundling across roots in their hunched-over way.

When we got back to Jeff's place he and I and Terry took a good look the sap in the bucket.

It looked good, with just a few flecks of debris, plant matter that had fallen into the bucket.

Jeff and Terry tasted it and said that what they called *maple water* tasted fine.

Terry decided to go ahead with production after all, saying, "Maybe I got lucky."

Terry *never* got lucky.

5.

In the last week of March, Terry boiled off his first big batch of syrup, and I was there to lend a hand. It was a long weekend with the Easter holiday, so that gave us three full days to work.

We collected a lot of watery sap, filtered it though fine steel mesh filters, and then poured it into big flat pans set over a cinderblock fire pit outside the big shed he was now calling his sugar shack. We couldn't let the sap sit too long. The sooner you started boiling it, the less the chances that bacterial growth would taint the sap. It was hot work, despite the coolness of early spring.

Terry could be a loon, but when it came to his maple syrup he was dead serious. I could see where Jeff got his studious side. Terry now had a huge stack of books on collecting sap and making syrup, books written in English, French and one in German, and he could read all of them.

He told Jeff and me to watch the pans for char, overcooked sugar solids on the sides of the pans that could fall into the boiled down syrup and affect the flavor. When char began forming we had to filter the syrup a second time, through coffee filters.

We would filter out any dark solids from the finished syrup, but white solids with a feathered texture were left in place; this sediment is called sugar sand, and some syrup makers refuse to remove it, as it enhances the flavor.

After that all we had to do was pour the thick maple syrup into canning jars and seal them. We were producing Grade A Medium Amber syrup, the most common color and flavor strength, and Terry was quite pleased when he saw the sealed mason jars.

That didn't last long.

The following Friday I stopped by Jeff's house and heard Terry in the kitchen, cursing a blue streak.

Snow had given way to rain, April showers that washed away all the dirt and dog turds accumulating in dwindling snowbanks.

Inside the Cruickshank home, the air smelled of maple. It was gross.

"My dad's going nuts," Jeff said, his nose buried in another book. "The syrup turned dark."

"What does that mean?" I took my raincoat off and sat beside him on the sofa. There was a coffee table in front of us piled high with books. Closer to me on the table were a ring of keys, a stack of Canadian Tire money, and a passbook from the Toronto-Dominion Bank in Kitchissippi. The passbook was open and I could see handwritten entries showing deposits and withdrawals.

"It means we may have made Grade B syrup," Jeff said. "It's okay for cooking, but you wouldn't want it on your pancakes. And it's hard to sell for a decent price."

Jeff showed me a jar. The syrup was a dark amber color, and I could see black flecks suspended in the thick liquid.

"What is that stuff? I thought we filtered this syrup?"

"We did, and I don't know what it is. My dad and I looked at it with a magnifying glass and it almost looks like pollen. Anyhow, we tasted it—"

"You *what?*"

"Relax, man," Jeff said. "We boiled the heck out of it, remember? And it's actually really sweet, with a strong maple flavor. The problem is that it would be difficult to sell syrup that looks like this, like crap. Not to mention the fact that it may be actual crap."

"What are you talking about?"

"The dark specks in the syrup could be frass," Jeff said, "otherwise known as insect poop. It could have been deposited in the roots or trunks of the trees by burrowing insects."

"Are you kidding me?"

"Jeez, relax, Vince," Jeff said. "Did you know that the first meal a young termite gets is feces fresh from the anus of an adult? It provides them with essential gut bacteria." He laughed at the look of disgust that was twisting my face. "Besides, it's harmless. It was boiled forever. It's just inert matter now."

"Yeah, but are you gonna add *bug poop* to the list of ingredients on the label?"

"It does present some marketing difficulties," Jeff said, and we both cracked up.

Terry came into the room looking deranged, and for a moment I thought, this is it, the cops are going to find pieces of us in mason jars a year from now, and then he smiled.

"I did it," Terry said. "I just solved our problem."

Outside, the rainclouds parted and a ray of sunshine came through one window.

Terry held up a tray like a muffin pan, but the cups were tiny, and each one was shaped like a maple leaf. Each of the cups or cavities appeared to be holding that dark maple syrup.

"Boys, you are looking at our salvation. Hard maple candy made entirely from maple syrup. I tried some and it is mind-blowing. I haven't tasted candy this good since I was a child, and I'm sure the children of Kitchissippi won't be able to get enough of it."

Terry pried a piece of out of the tray and held it up. It was almost black, but when the sun struck the candy the light revealed a lurid vermilion heart.

"I call it the Sweet Dark," Terry said.

I thought *that is what my death will look like,* and then I shivered as if this were the deepest part of winter and not a warming spring day.

"Why is it so dark?"

Terry and Jeff looked at me as if I had said something bad, as if I were about to jinx them.

"Why does it matter?" I could see Terry struggling to maintain his good will. "The taste is indescribably delicious."

"Seriously, Vince," Jeff said, "it's a part of the cooking process. As more water is cooked off, the remaining matter becomes darker."

"Okay," I said, not wanting to start a fight. "It's just that I've seen that kind of candy at Gendre's Variety Store and it's usually lighter than that."

"What do you know?" Jeff said. "You don't even like maple syrup."

"True," I said. "Can you sell it without a permit though? I mean, doesn't food have to be inspected by the government before it is old?"

"The *government?*" Terry sounded as if he was referring to something revolting. "The government instituted the War Measures Act and put soldiers on Canadian soil in response to the valiant freedom fighters of the FLQ. Screw the government. Do you want to live in a police state, where soldiers inspect the goods at every bake sale and potluck?"

I had learned about October Crisis through TV documentaries; they certainly didn't talk about the fall and winter of 1970 in school. After the separatist group *Front de libération du Québec* kidnapped and murdered a politician, Prime Minister Trudeau authorized the use of troops in Quebec and Ontario, and gave the police the authority to arrest people without a warrant. That was exactly the kind of incendiary subject matter that would set Terry off.

Jeff tried to calm his dad by taking a piece of candy. "Oh, man," he said, "this really is good. It's intense."

I didn't want any candy, and I didn't want anyone else having any either. I don't know why, maybe it was just the macabre nature of the blood-red heart I'd seen in that single piece of the Sweet Dark.

The TD bank passbook caught my eye again. I knew it was a book for a savings account because my dad had one just like it. In the *balance* column someone had written $3,300.

It would be years before I understood the significance of that number, before I realized that a man with no job, a son to raise, and only three grand in the bank could be under a lot of stress.

Terry swooped forward like a bird and snatched the passbook up off the table, whispering, "What a fucking nosey parker, eh?"

Jeff frowned at me like I had done something wrong.

Terry and Jeff were standing close together, and each gave me a look as if to ask why I was still in their home. After all the help I had given them, I was dismissed, apparently.

I pulled on my raincoat, feeling incredibly uncomfortable. "I'll guess I'll see you around," I said to Jeff, and then I went home.

6.

I didn't see much of Jeff for a while after that. I was able to lose myself in school, getting ready for end of the year exams, and when summer rolled around again I ended up helping my dad at the Golden Eagle after all, which gave me a lot of money to see movies and buy books.

The Maitland Playhouse showed a great run of science-fiction and horror flicks, including real gems like *Dawn of the Dead,* and *Martin,* both from George Romero, but that would be the last summer of steady business for the Playhouse. On the last weekend of 1978, during a screening of *Invasion of the Body Snatchers*—the one with Donald Sutherland—some kid would find rat poop in his popcorn and that would be the death knell for Kitchissppi's only movie theater. Pete Maitland would shut the place down a year later.

In the middle of August I was in Gendre's Variety Store looking at the latest issue of *Detective Comics* when I saw a display beside the cash register.

Terry's leaf-shaped candies were in a fancy plastic case, each piece of *Sweet Dark 100% Pure Maple Syrup Candy—Canadian Candy for Canadian Children* wrapped in clear cellophane. If that stuff would sell anywhere, it would sell here. Gendre's was just down the street from the Maitland Playhouse, in the center of town. There were more little kids from Victoria Elementary and Bonnechere Middle School in the store than kids my age, and the place was always busy.

It saddened me that Jeff had not told me about this. Since I had last seen him he had not come over to my place, and whenever I tried to talk to him at school he looked at me like I was a pile of shit.

I missed my friend.

I went into Gendre's a few days later and the container was almost empty.

A few days after that there were two containers of Sweet Dark near the cash register.

The candy was selling like crazy.

The seeds of chaos had been sown, and soon they would take root and bloom.

7.

One of Canada's most revered and long-lived television programs is *The Nature of Things,* a weekly hour that looks at all aspects of life through the eyes of scientists.

The show was on the air when I was a kid, and it is still on today, which means it will outlive me.

In February of 1980, host David Suzuki introduced an episode called *The Pied Piper of Kitchissippi,* an investigation into the work of a frightening figure, a monster of a man who "designed and kicked into high gear a biological engine of destruction that led to the utter ruination of a generation of schoolchildren."

That man was Terrence Cruickshank.

Terry is no longer with us. Neither is his son.

I saw to that.

8.

Early in September 1978, I was waiting for the school bus when I saw a little kid down the street trying to set fire to a pile of leaves. The kid looked old enough to be on his way to Victoria Elementary, but instead he was messing around on the edge of his yard.

I watched him make a pile of leaves, and then stand in the center of it. It looked like he was trying to strike a match. I ran closer and sure enough, the kid had a matchbook and he was trying to light a match, but the matchheads were damp, so they just left smears on the strike strip.

I said, "What are you doing, kid?" When he looked at me I could see he was messed up. He had dark circles under his eyes and his lips were bleeding as if he had been chewing on them, but he was smiling.

The boy's mother came out the front door and shouted, "Can I help you?"

I saw my bus coming and ran for it, calling back, "You better keep an eye on your kid!"

* * *

In the middle of that month I was on the school bus filled with students from Bonnechere Middle School and Clouthier High School, when I noticed a younger kid scratching his head. The kid was really digging in, and as he got off the bus at Bonnechere I saw that the tips of his fingers were bloody. When he noticed his fingers he laughed out loud.

* * *

By the second week of October, it was chilly enough to wear heavier clothing. I was looking at comics in Gendre's again when I saw a little girl standing at the cash register with her mom. The mom was paying for something—and grabbing a handful of Sweet Dark from the display case—and then she looked down at her daughter.

"Stop doing that, sweetie," the mom said. "It's disgusting."

The little girl was chewing on one of her mittens. What the mom must not have seen, and what I saw as they passed by me, was that the little girl was chewing and swallowing a strand of powder blue wool from one knitted mitten, the strand disappearing into her mouth as she chewed and swallowed. Most of her small hand was exposed by unraveled, eaten wool.

* * *

Not long before Halloween, I was in my little sister's room helping her put up a poster she'd gotten in an issue of *Tiger Beat;* it showed Shaun Cassidy and Parker Stevenson as the Hardy Boys. Abby wanted to tape it over her bed. She had asked my older brother for help, but Paul said if he got too close to it he'd puke on it. I was helping Abby when I saw a handful of Sweet Dark candies on the corner of her dressing table. Once the poster was on the wall to her satisfaction, I left her to her daydreams of teen heartthrobs, scooping up the candy as I left her room. I threw it in the trash.

A few hours later, Abby threw a fit looking for her candy. I'm not talking about the usual tween girl histrionics; my little sister went apeshit. She was like a junkie looking for a fix in a bad movie. My dad read Paul and me the riot act for stealing her candy, but I didn't say a thing about it. I didn't want my little sister anywhere near that stuff.

* * *

Things were getting weird in Kitchissippi.

* * *

Halloween came on a Tuesday that year. I was old enough by then that trick-or-treating no longer meant anything to me, but I could see good and bad in it for younger kids this year. The bad was that Halloween was on a school night. The good was that there wasn't much snow and it wasn't so cold that kids had to be bundled up under their costumes.

On Friday night, just a few days before Halloween, I went to the Maitland Playhouse and saw a new film called *Halloween,* by a guy named John Carpenter. It scared the crap out of me, which was wonderful.

I was in a good mood Tuesday morning as I walked from the school bus to Clouthier High.

I heard one kid whisper to another, "There's a fight," and followed them to the track and the football field behind the school. I could see a cluster of older kids by the bleachers. They were kicking at another kid who was on his back.

I had known Jeff all my life; I didn't have to see his face to know that it was him on the ground.

One of the kids kicking at Jeff shouted, "Give us some candy, you cocksucking faggot!"

"Hey!" My outrage overruled my common sense. These guys could have cleaned my clock. "Leave him alone!"

Jeff raised a hand, holding up a ziplocked baggie. You'd think it was weed or cocaine, the way it was snatched out of his hand. The older kids wandered off, divvying up the Sweet Dark.

I helped Jeff to his feet. The small crowd that was gathering broke up. Jeff had a cut lip and his legs and arms would be bruised later, but otherwise he was okay.

"What the fuck was that all about?"

"It's the Sweet Dark," Jeff said. "Those guys threatened to beat the crap out of me if I didn't get more of it for them. People are becoming addicted to it, and I think there might be something wrong with it."

"Have you told your dad?"

"I tried," Jeff said. "He said I was being nonsensical and told me to shut up."

I could tell there was more. I waited.

The homeroom bell rang, and we both ignored it.

"My dad has been making lots of Sweet Dark," Jeff said. "Loads of it. He got a distributor interested in it, a company that wants to sell it in Ottawa and Montreal, and maybe even down in the States."

I couldn't see what the problem was. "Wouldn't they test it to make sure it is safe?"

Jeff nodded. Yeah, but those tests may not show what's going on. I think the candy contains a toxin that has an aggregate effect after a certain accumulation point has been reached—"

I held up a hand. "Whoa, man. You're losing me."

Jeff was frustrated with my ignorance, and not for the first time.

"Meet me in the science lab at lunch," he said.

✳ ✳ ✳

I nearly lost my mind waiting for the lunch bell, and I ran to the science lab. There were a few kids like Jeff in the room, total dorks working on projects while their PB & J sandwiches sat ignored in ziplock bags beside Bunsen burners and stacks of chemistry textbooks.

Jeff had a microscope set up at a table near the back of the room, and he asked me to take a look as he set up a slide.

"Did you hear about what happened at Victoria Elementary yesterday?"

I shook my head and looked through the eyepiece.

"Everybody is saying a little kid went nuts," Jeff said. "He stabbed three other kids in the eyes with pencils before any teachers could restrain him. And while that was going on, a little girl drowned herself in a toilet bowl. She just stuck her head in and held it there, man."

"Are you serious?" In the microscope I saw a sea of liquid with the slightest golden hue; floating in it were tiny white spheres.

"What am I looking at?"

"That's filtered maple sap," he said. "This is what we typically collected in the buckets and filtered before cooking it down into syrup."

"What are those white balls?"

I looked at Jeff and he had a terrible expression on his face. I had read about despair in people under duress, but I never thought I'd see it on the face of a kid my own age.

"I think they are eggs," Jeff said, "Eggs small enough to pass through the initial filtering stage. He put another slide under the microscope.

I looked through the eyepiece again. This time I saw dark flecks trapped in amber.

"What—"

And then I saw it. The black flecks were pieces of some kind of worm or grub.

"You're looking at boiled maple syrup before it was baked in the oven to make Sweet Dark," Jeff said. "Have you ever heard of psychoactive insects?"

I didn't have a clue what he was talking about. "What the hell, man?"

"I'm talking about hallucinogens in bugs, instead of LSD or magic mushrooms. I think that's what we have here. Psychoactive larvae. And I'm afraid they could make people dangerously insane."

I began thinking of all the odd behavior I'd seen recently in kids all over town, even as I tried to argue with Jeff.

"That's impossible. We filtered the sap before and after boiling the hell out of it."

"I know," Jeff said, "but remember the sugar sand, that white stuff we left in place because it's supposed to add flavor to maple syrup? I think the white-shelled larvae eggs were hidden in that, and I think that the boiling process weakened the shells, shells that may have become super-resistant to any other harm thanks to my dad and his homemade pesticides. When the boiled shells finally broke up they revealed the dark flecks we saw in the syrup, and when those flecks of dead larvae were baked in the oven the hallucinogens remained."

"Jesus," I said. A couple of kids stared at me and I said, "What are you clowns looking at?"

In a quiet voice I asked, "How could a person get stoned off of bugs?"

Jeff shrugged. "Who knows? I called an entomologist at Carlton University down in Ottawa, and he said there actually are a few historical records of psychoactive compounds in insect larvae. They are dubious, but they exist."

This made me smile, despite the grim circumstances. Jeff was still Jeff, casting nets far and wide for information.

"Whatever is affecting people could be something the insects ate, or it could be part of a biochemical defense mechanism."

He looked at me a moment, and I could tell he was trying to find the courage to tell me more.

"One more thing," he said, putting a third slide under the microscope.

I looked through the eyepiece and saw raw sap again, eggs floating in pale golden liquid, and—

Something moved, something ten times bigger than the eggs, something with a translucent bloated body and dark internal organs.

"That's raw, unfiltered sap," Jeff said. "One sip of that maple water and I think you'd go off the deep end. And I think the sugar bush is infested with these things."

"Wait," I said, "why aren't you and your dad sick? You both ate that syrup."

"I don't know," Jeff said. "I'm guessing it is affecting children because they have faster metabolisms or because they are eating a lot of it. My dad and I only ate a bit of syrup that had been filtered twice and boiled down. We never drank any raw, unrefined sap. Maybe the active compounds in the dead larvae have to build up in the body over time. All I know is that the Sweet Dark is dangerous, and...my dad is planning on giving away a whole bunch of candy to trick or treating kids tonight."

9.

I went home with Jeff after school. As we rode the bus home together we sat in silence while kids all around us made the usual racket. I envied those other kids and wished Jeff and I could be farting around instead of being weighed down by such an unsettling business.

We were seated near the front of the bus. I had an aisle seat. I don't know what made me look at the road ahead, but I did.

Two little girls in matching yellow peacoats held hands as they ran in front of the school bus. They were skipping, with dreamy smiles on their faces. The bus hit the children and they were sent spinning down Doncaster Street like smooth stones skipped across a pond. Kids on the bus began to scream. I saw blood, way too much blood. It seemed cherry red on the girls' peacoats and as black as Sweet Dark candy where it pooled around them on the road.

We got off the bus and Jeff looked like he was going to throw up, but he held it together. We didn't want to wait for the police to show up, so we walked down Doncaster, past my house and around the woods to the Cruickshank home.

Jeff was quiet as we walked, his face as white as paste, his lips pressed together.

I had to ask. "Do you think they ate any Sweet Dark?"

He shook his head in denial, but he looked like a little kid who was afraid to go to sleep because he knew nightmares were waiting for him.

When we got to the house Terry was in the driveway, putting a big cardboard box in the trunk of his Chevy.

Jeff sounded anxious when he asked, "What are you doing, dad?"

"I'm heading out to the Hall," he said. "Gonna hand out Sweet Dark to all the kids that stop by."

The Hall was the Kitchissippi Community Hall, directly across the street from Saint Bartholomew, the Presbyterian Church downtown. People handed out candy in the hall on Halloween, relying on donations from local businesses and residents. October 31st had always been a big day for the town hall, and for Kitchissippi.

"Dad, you can't give out that candy," Jeff said. "It's dangerous."

"We're not having this conversation again," Terry said. "This candy is our future."

I reached into the car and raised one flap of the box, seeing bags of individually wrapped Sweet Dark candy that now had labels on them saying the candy was a product of Cruickshank's Sugar Shack. There was also a logo, a creepy-looking man in the moon smiling and winking as he floated in a dark sky.

"This stuff is making children sick," I said. "I've seen it happen."

Terry didn't say anything for a moment. His mouth was crimped as tight as a balloon knot. Then he gave me a shove, away from the car.

I backpedaled like a cartoon character, slipping and falling with one arm behind me to cushion my fall. The Cruickshank's driveway was bordered with big pieces of stone, like a miniature wall. That's what I fell on. I heard a cracking sound like dry sticks being broken over someone's knee, and then things went black for a moment.

The next thing I knew, Terry and the car were gone. When Jeff tried to help me to my feet, I screamed. My right arm was twisted behind me, and it felt as if it had been tied in ragged knots.

I felt the back of my head with my left hand, and saw blood on my fingers.

"You idiot," Jeff said, "You could have fractured your skull."

"Your dad's crazy," I said. It came out *yer da scray-zee.* I felt weird.

Jeff looked at me like he was studying a bug. "Don't even think about moving," he said. "We need to get you to a hospital."

I waved him off and tried to sit up. The world rolled and I fell onto my side and puked.

The next thing I knew Jeff was easing me into the passenger seat of the old truck and begging me not to say that his dad had pushed me.

Things became hazy after that.

I remembered seeing my dad and Abby on the doorstep of our home. My dad was worried and cursing and Abby was crying. Under my coat, my shirt felt warn and wet. I remember my dad rushing me to the hospital in Miramichi, and holding my hand. I remember being in a hospital room, smelling antiseptic, squinting against bright lights, and having nurses lift me up so they could slide bedpans under me. Those goddamned bedpans were always ice cold.

It was as if my life was nothing but cuttings from an editing room floor, and the main feature didn't pick up again until I opened my eyes and saw my older brother Paul sitting in a chair beside my hospital bed and reading a copy of *Penthouse.*

"Dad will kick your ass so hard you'll be wearing it like a hat if he sees you reading that," I said. My voice was a dry croak.

Paul tucked the skin mag into an issue of a magazine called *OMNI,* came over to me, and touched my forehead. He'd never done anything like that before.

"Welcome back," he said.

"Back?" I asked. "Back from where?"

Paul shook his head and said, "You nearly died, you dickhead."

10.

I ended up spending much of the next two months in and out of the hospital. I had not only broken my arm in two places and suffered a serious concussion when I fell, but I had cut the back of my head open on a rock. My tuque had been sopping wet when I got home, and when they saw all that blood my family thought I'd really had the biscuit. I had the back of my head shaved, and I got a dozen stitches that itched like crazy. I also had seizures for three days after my accident. The seizures scared the hell out of my family, and I don't remember any of them.

The first week after my accident I was in a hospital bed, my arm immobilized in a heavy cast and my head bandaged. When I was finally allowed to go home, I was told I had to stay home from school and make regular visits to Miramichi Regional Hospital to check my progress. I would have to wear a cast on my arm for ten weeks.

As I was leaving my hospital room after that first strange week, I passed a table filled with cards wishing me well. My dad gathered everything up for me. Besides sympathy cards there were free passes to the Maitland Playhouse, a $10 gift card for the W.H. Smith bookstore in Miramichi, and a large bag of Hostess Roast Chicken Flavor potato chips, probably from Jeff, who always said I had breath like a circus geek after eating them.

I asked my dad if Jeff had come to see me. I couldn't remember a whole lot.

"Every day after school," my dad said. "He said he'd pick up your homework and drop off school assignments once you're settled in at home. I guess he's a good kid after all."

Someone had also left me a little cellophane bag of Sweet Dark.

"You can throw that in the garbage," I said.

My dad was surprised. "You don't want it? I though Terry Cruickshank finally had a winner on his hands with this candy."

"It gives kids the runs," I said, saying the first thing that came to mind. "I'd keep it away from Abby, too."

Abby frowned at this.

"Just as well," Paul said, as he threw the candy into a wastebasket. "I heard Patsy Paquette had one of these in her hand when she took a header off the roof of St. Bart's."

"What's a header?" Abby asked.

My dad put his hands over Abby's ear like earmuffs and gave Paul a nasty look. "Watch what you say around her."

I whispered to Paul. "Patsy fell off the roof of the church?"

Paul shook his head. "She jumped. And I heard that she was grinning like a kid diving off the old raft at Boyd's Pond."

"That's enough out of you two," my dad said.

※ ※ ※

On a follow-up visit with my doctor in November, a custodian was cleaning up some broken glass near our usual entrance to the hospital, so my dad led me into the building through the emergency room.

It wasn't until we were leaving that I glanced into the Emergency Room waiting area. The room was filled with parents and their children.

"There are a lot of kids here," I said.

My dad nodded. "It's been a strange couple of weeks. There have been lots of accidents around town involving children. A couple of them have been killed. That's why I feel so grateful to have my boy back." He put one big hand on the back of my neck and kissed the top of my head. He may have had calluses, and grease under his fingernails, but it felt wonderful.

I looked back into the Emergency Room. The parents waiting there looked sick with worry and fright. The children looked happy and content, and had the same dazed expressions I'd seen on other kids, like the twins who had run in front of the bus. They looked like Paul did when he was stoned. The shared look on their faces was one of bliss.

That was when I decided to burn down Terry Cruickshank's sugar shack.

11.

Darkness comes early in December, and by five o'clock on the Wednesday before Christmas the sun was below a horizon the color of spilled ink. My dad had called earlier and said he was working late. Paul was out with his buddies, and Abby was at school doing something with the Girl Guides. I finally had the house to myself. If I was going to do anything, I had to do it *now.*

When I left the house I had one of my dad's lighters in one pocket of my jeans. My dad had quit smoking years ago, but still kept a few Bic lighters in a kitchen drawer. I was wearing an oversized sweater over a sweatshirt, and a military surplus poncho. I couldn't wear my old parka with the cast on my arm.

The moon was three quarters full and the stars shone with crisp winter brightness as I walked past the silent woods on my way to Jeff's house. It was cold, and a brisk wind made it colder.

Walking was tricky because the bulky cast threw off my balance, and I had to focus on my feet as I trudged through the snow and not become distracted by the beauty around me; the hard white forest floor glowed like polished marble.

I went up to the Cruickshank's front door and listened for a moment. I could hear the muffled sound of a radio playing inside.

Walking as carefully as I could, I went around the side of the house to the old shed that had become the sugar shack.

I didn't have a detailed plan in mind. The shed was locked, but the door and frame were very old. When then wind rose up and howled in the eaves of the house, I hit the door with my shoulder, nearly losing my balance, and it popped open.

The wind was blowing in the direction of the sugar bush, that thick stand of corrupted maple trees.

I went into the shed looking for something flammable, and saw stacks of old newspapers tied up with twine. I tossed yellowing copies of *The Ottawa Citizen* across the shed, loose pages settling against the wooden walls. I flicked the lighter and started a fire. It was as simple as that.

I walked out of the shed, heading for the path and home, and that was when Terry's Chevy came up the road and pulled into the driveway, the headlights blinding me and making me feel like an escaping convict in an old movie.

Terry was out of the car in an instant, slipping and sliding on snow and ice as he ran to me, his teeth bared in what I took to be a mad grin. I snorted nervous laughter at his approach, and that enraged him.

I tried to stay cool, and said, "Mr. Cruickshank, you can't—"

"You can't, you can't, *you CAN'T,*" Terry said, almost singing. His rage emanated from him in waves, like heat from the fire pit by the sugar shack.

He reached out and grabbed the cast on my injured arm.

"I hope you told anyone who would listen that this was just an accident," Terry said. He twisted my arm and the whole world went white with pain. "Otherwise I won't be angry with you. I'll be angry with Jeff. I've hurt him before, and I'll hurt him again."

I wondered what that meant and what Jeff had been hiding from me, remembering that when I had said Terry was acting scary, Jeff had replied, *he scares me, too.*

He leaned close and hissed, "Distribution of the Sweet Dark is going nationwide next year and *nothing* is going to stop me."

The front door opened and Jeff came outside, pulling on a coat. Terry let go of me and took a few steps back.

"What are you doing, Dad?"

Terry smiled a genuine smile this time, not his lunatic grin.

"Your friend and I are just having a cordial chat, eh, Vince?"

For a moment we stood breathing in cold air and watching each other in a silent standoff. Inside the house, the radio was playing a Gordon Lightfoot tune.

From the shed behind us, something made a sound like a pine knot popping in a campfire. The wind shifted toward the Cruickshank home and I smelled smoke.

Fuck, I thought.

Terry bared his teeth again and reached for me, screaming, "What have you done?"

I ran for the woods, for the sugar bush.

When I think back to that chase now, it seemed to go on forever.

Jeff's father was right on my heels as I ran between pines encrusted with ice and skeletal deciduous trees reaching into the night with branches like extended fingers, Terry shrieking profanity every time he ran into a low branch in the dark and was stabbed by blunt spears.

When I reached the clearing around Villeneuve's Hole, where Jeff and I used to try and catch frogs as kids, I realized I was moving too fast, and I prayed that the ice on the pond would hold me. Kids skated on the pond, but never this early in the year.

I stumbled at the edge of the pond and fell forward, hitting that black ice in a belly flop that saved my life, sliding fast with the wind knocked out of me and my balls painfully slammed, the brittle sound of fracturing ice following in my wake. The ice cracked, but did not give way, because my weight was spread over a wide surface area. I had almost made it across the pond when I slowed to a stop. From there I carefully wiggled over the slick surface like a worm, reaching solid ground on the far side.

Terry reached the pond at full tilt, took three huge strides across the ice, his grin as bright and white as the moon, and that was when his weight drove one foot and then the other through the weakened ice like nails through plywood, and he dropped out of sight.

As I got to my feet I saw Jeff standing on the other side of the pond. He looked at me, and then down at the circle of sloshing black water with a border of shattered ice.

As kids we had once measured Villeneuve's Hole. It was thirty feet deep.

"No, man," I said.

"He's my dad," Jeff said.

I've never heard so much bitterness and anguish as I heard in Jeff's voice.

He walked out onto the ice, got down on his knees, and peered into that black hole. He reached out, and a white hand grabbed his, the fingernails on that hand turning blue.

Terry's head broke the surface of the water. He gasped, "Jeffrey," and then pulled my best friend into the pond with him.

They would stay down in the cold, dark water until a special dive team with the Ontario Provincial Police pulled them out around noon the next day.

I smelled burning wood as I walked back to the house. My arm ached; I was pretty sure I had fractured the bones again.

When I got to the Cruickshank home, fire was raging on the edge of the sugar bush. It had consumed the shed and half of the house, and now it was leaping from tree to tree. The night may have been cold, but it was also dry, and the trees were burning like kindling, the snow-covered floor of the forest glowing golden-red.

The side of the house that held Jeffrey's room collapsed. Sparks spiraled up into the night as if freed from some terrible fate.

Somewhere in the Cruickshank home the radio still played, and a song drifted out into the night. It was Chris Rea's "Fool If You Think It's Over." I started to laugh.

12.

Firefighters and police arrived at the Cruickshank home after I left. When the fire was put out, they looked for bodies. When they didn't find Jeff or Terry, they began searching the property, and found the tracks in the snow that led them to Villeneuve's Hole.

My dad never said a thing about the Cruickshank's demise, and he accompanied me to their funeral. It was said that Terry and Jeff died by misadventure on that cold December night, which was true.

I mourned my friend and let him go, and when I was old enough, I left Kitchissippi for good.

13.

And now I am back.

I have cancer. My body is riddled with it. I am going to die soon, and it is not going to be pleasant.

I coughed, and spat on snow that shone like fresh linen under the stark light of the moon. A wad of bloody tissue lay on that blanket of white crystals, a dying piece of me as dark as night, save for a lurid vermilion heart.

I wandered among the burned stumps of trees, part of Terry's sugar bush that had never grown back. I found a half-constructed chain-link fence and entered an old-growth stand of maple trees.

I brushed snow away from the roots of one tree and found the desiccated bodies of dead insects. They looked like old men stooped with age, wearing brown overcoats.

I had a hammer with me, and a spile. I drove the spile as deep into the tree as I could, pausing to cough and hack and spit, and then waited.

One glimmering drop of raw maple sap formed on the end of the spile, and then another. I took off my gloves and caught those drops on one finger, and slipped my finger into my mouth.

I tasted the corrupted sap of the old maple tree. It was watery, with just the slightest hint of maple sugar.

After a time warmth enveloped me. I sat down, and then lay down in the snow, realizing only now that I was on the edge of Villeneuve's Hole. I sank into the cold of the bitter white as I drifted into the warmth of the sweet dark, my pain forgotten.

I wanted to die, and it was good...so good that I laughed when the last thing I saw was a sign on the half-completed fence:

Coming Soon—Finnegan's Pure Maple Water
Made from Raw Maple Sap

Health is not a fad, it's a lifestyle!
Enjoy the healthiest drink nature has to offer!

✳

Sacred Death

I. Den of the Seal

Irons felt warm legs untwine from his own and he opened his eyes. Violet slipped a peasant dress over her willowy form and pushed hands through her waist-long black hair.

"Wakey-wakey, time to bakey." She smiled at him and slipped out of the room.

He rose and dressed. For too long, he'd lounged around the Pine Street flat, a guest of the man called the Seal. The Seal shared the apartment with three beautiful women. Irons didn't mind a bit that the women catered to him as well. He could still smell the rose and patchouli scent of Violet on the pillow. Irons looked out the window.

While the flower of the Haight-Ashbury had faded, a few hippies still occupied the area, and it felt a little like a homecoming to Irons. He'd been in San Francisco for more than three weeks, the early October days hot and dry. All the residents of the flat were Heads, and he began to fatten up on junk food stockpiled in the place.

Irons had no idea why the Seal was putting him up. The man was a pharmaceutical chemist with a respectable research position at Cal. Heinrich Seilenbacher was a few years younger than Irons, born in Germany as what the papers called a Thalidomide baby. Seilenbacher's hands and feet ended in flippers, giving him a moniker Irons found distasteful. But Seilenbacher embraced the name, much as he embraced the industry that had caused his disfigurement. The Seal was the biggest dealer in the City, selling illegal prescription meds and a lot of weed. Irons thought it was Seilenbacher's way of getting back at society. That didn't bother Irons. He merely waited to see what the Seal wanted.

It was Saturday morning, usually a lazier day than most. In the living room, Violet reclined on a set of pillows on the floor. "Wanna hit, big man?"

She offered Irons a cigar-sized joint. He only smiled and refused. "Psychoactives aren't my bag."

"Bad trip?" Violet, smiled and took a big hit.

Irons nodded. "Something like that."

Another of the roomies, a blonde named Darla, wheeled Seilenbacher into the living room. The Seal, a fat joint clutched in the two fingers of his right flipper, nodded sleepily at the biker. "Teddy, I know you're wondering why I'm giving you the royal treatment. I got a job for you, man."

Nobody called Irons "Teddy" except the Seal. "Yeah, I figured, Henry. Lay it on me."

The Seal took a hit, blew the smoke out his nose. "See, I need you on a run. Like, my regular couriers aren't suitable, you dig?"

Seilenbacher's regular couriers were Hells Angels. "You know plenty of big dudes on bikes."

Henry smiled a lazy smile, squinting bloodshot eyes at Irons. "I'm working on some new product. Processing is up near Shasta. And, frankly, the dudes on the project have been making some weird noises."

"Weird how?"

"Like they're seeing things," Henry said. "Now, I know the product is potent stuff, but it isn't *that* potent, baby. I'm getting some real weird vibes from them."

Irons shrugged. "I still don't get it."

"Teddy Roosevelt Irons, you don't dig that you are the weirdest of the weird? I mean, people talk about you hanging out with monsters and wizards and magical whatevers. I just think you're the man for this. All you gotta do is run the product down from Siskiyou County and deliver it here. You won't have any trouble with John Law, so don't get uptight."

"I got no kick about the pigs." Irons sat on a low couch, folding his long legs in front of him. "What's the product?"

"Lila, baby," Henry called. "Show Mr. Irons the new dope."

The third roomie, a voluptuous redhead in a tie-dyed dress that just reached her thighs and hair that reached longer sauntered in from the back bedroom. She handed Irons a sheet of paper. It looked like heavy art paper, with a ragged weave, yellow-green in color, the size of typing paper.

"Blotter acid?" he guessed.

"Not even close, man." The Seal leaned back in his wheelchair. "That's what I call 'Hurdy-Gurdy.' The paper is made from the fibers of the hurd of a *Cannabis sativa* stalk. Not much THC in the paper.

But kief is pressed into the weave—concentrated stuff. You can roll it up and smoke it, you can soak it, evaporate the water and press it into hash or make butter or whatever. Takes care of all the leftovers." Irons handed it back to Lila. "Sounds like a lot of trouble, Henry."

"Well, dig this: my fields got raided by the Man at the last harvest. I had no new bud to sell, and pounds of leftover clippings and what-not. I could've had the trichromes extracted and pressed into bricks. But hash is as illegal as weed and my customers don't like it. This way, it'll take the pigs years to figure out what Hurdy-Gurdy is, and in the meanwhile, I'll be able to sow green fields again." Henry took another hit of the joint. "You in?"

"Price of gas is over four bits, you know." Irons frowned. "Oil crisis, and today's Saturday." Nearly all gas stations voluntarily closed on the weekends to maintain the supply of gas.

"Don't sweat the gas."

Irons had nothing better to do. "For old time's sake, yeah, I'm in."

"Old time's sake my ass, brother. I replaced that POS hog you rode in on with a new shovelhead. I don't want any mechanical failures messing this up. Once you deal with the weirdness and bring my stuff back to San Francisco, keep the wheels, and I give you twenty percent."

"And leave all this comfort behind?" Irons smiled at Violet, who returned a goofy grin. His eyes roved over her figure, her long, tanned legs. She put the bomber to her cupid bow lips and blew smoke through her nose. Blue eyes gazed at him from heavy lids. It was easy to get lost in Violet's eyes, and getting easier with each passing day. In truth, he was getting edgy to get the hell back on the road. As much as the Seal's place offered, he was beginning to feel claustrophobic.

"I'm already gone, man."

II: Welcome

Autumn wind in his hair, Irons powered up the highway on the new hog. Irons opened the throttle and listened with pleasure as the big-V sang.

His hair was still pretty short from his last encounter with Big Brother, so other than his size, he didn't stand out much. Three California Highway Patrol cars had passed him by without so much as a dirty look. By late afternoon he rode toward the watchful silhouette of Mount Shasta.

He cut east on 89, heading for the tiny town the Seal specified, Trace Run, which sheltered between the shoulders of the mountain and the surrounding national park. Practically a ghost town since the logging and paper industry died, Trace Run was beyond remote, and he missed the turn-off twice, finally landing in the tiny downtown near sunset.

The only other vehicles on the street were a new Super Beetle and a dusty gold Toronado. Irons pulled the saddlebags off the Harley and headed for an inn, one of four structures on the right side of the street.

He pushed through a set of batwing doors, feeling like he was starring in a western. The bar was empty, but a sign pointed the way to the front desk. Irons' boots echoed as he passed through a short hallway. A man in a white velour leisure suit, Panama hat and pencil-thin mustache smiled up at him from behind the desk.

"You must be Señor Irons." The man had a heavy Spanish accent. He gestured Irons forward with his fingers. "*Bienvenidos.* Welcome to Trace Run. I am Miguel."

Miguel pushed a ledger and a pen across the desk at the biker. "How do you know who I am?"

"We have so few guests." The man continued to smile.

Irons leaned over to sign the guest book.

"I have a message for *La Foca.*"

Irons looked up, and found himself facing the business end of a machete. He froze.

"*La Foca,* how do you say—the Seal." The smile didn't leave Miguel's face. "I have bales of perfectly fine marijuana in a San Francisco warehouse. Yet even with his little plantation closed down, he refuses to sell it for me."

When Irons swallowed, his Adam's apple met the point of the machete. "That isn't a message."

"Tell him that I will shut him down the same way I shut down his fields." The man bent his neck, making it crack. "I hope you aren't one who talks a lot with his hands."

Miguel raised the blade. Irons leapt backward, freeing the double length of drive chain he wore as a belt. The man was already atop the desk, chopping down. Irons swung the chain hard, the links slamming Miguel's legs out from under him.

Panama hat flying, the man managed to land on his feet. Blade held before him, Miguel closed with Irons, limping slightly. From the way the smile stayed beneath the mustache, Irons recognized his opponent as a professional killer.

They danced across the lobby, Miguel moving like a fencer. Irons wasn't a fencer; he was a brawler. The mustached man lunged, bending at the knee, extending the machete with lightning speed.

Irons turned his upper body. He felt a chill slicing through his shirt, his skin, rattling over his ribs. But Irons wasn't focused on the blade. He smashed the chain into Miguel's upper arm, blood and bone jutting from the impact. Irons followed with a roundhouse left. Miguel's jaw snapped shut, head spinning, enamel and blood flying.

The blow turned Irons slightly toward the bar. He glimpsed another white-suited man step through the doorway, a submachine gun leveled. Army training told Irons that the recoil would lift the barrel up. At the first crack, he hit the ground, sliding in his own blood, scrambling around the desk. An instant later, another burst chattered from the gun.

Crablike, Irons scurried to a door behind the desk, crawled inside, and slammed the door with his foot. Bullet holes stitched light into the small office.

In a crouch, he searched for something to help him. As he met the blue eyes of a man in the corner, his heart skipped several beats. The old geezer lay next to a desk, a gag in his mouth, hands and feet bound with bailing wire. Though he was secured from knuckles to elbows, his hands gripped a big revolver.

Irons held his hands up. "You think I could borrow that?"

Another line of bullet holes blasted the office. Big-eyed, the man nodded, gesturing with the gun. Irons took it. With a quick peek through a bullet hole, he saw the gunman leaning over the fallen Miguel. He quietly opened the door and shot the gunman in the ass.

Irons ducked back around the frame, hearing the man howl. When he didn't return fire, Irons moved out. Miguel was conscious again, half-dragging the gunman out the door. The gunman babbled in Spanish, and when he saw Irons, he brought the gun around. Irons hit the deck as bullets chattered deafeningly in the lobby. He returned fire without looking; then jumped up to see the two fleeing out the door.

Irons drew a bead and fired, but the batwing door caught his bullet. Miguel wrestled the submachine gun away from the other man and aimed it at Irons one-handed. Irons flung himself sideways. A short rattle of gunfire followed, stopped short, the submachine gun had clicked dry. He made the swinging doors, only to see the two hunkered behind the Olds. His shot blew the windshield out of the car.

Seconds later, the men piled into the Toronado and caromed a way with a squeal of rubber.

Breathing hard, Irons put a hand to his ribs. It came away red.

III: Las Centinelas

Irons figured he lost a full pint of blood before he could untangle the old timer, but the man got right to work, digging up a first aid kit and bandaging Irons' wound.

"Ain't much more than a deep scratch, Mister. Don't think you need stitching."

"My shirt sure does." He stuck a hand out. "Irons."

The old man had to shake some feeling into his fingers before gripping. "Sloat."

He handed the gun back to the old timer. "Sorry, haven't done much shooting lately."

"Son, I don't know what I woulda done if you hadn't come along. Them Mexicans were probably gonna cut out my tongue so I wouldn't talk. You know who they were?"

Irons shook his head. "Enforcers of some kind." He suspected they were from a drug cartel, but he didn't let on. "Do you have a reservation in my name?"

"Nope. Haven't had a guest in three months. Hell, everyone up and left town when all the weirdness started." Sloat dumped the shells from the gun, reloaded from the desk drawer. "That why you're here? The weirdness?"

Sagacious blue eyes examined Irons' face. He decided to level with the old man. "Yeah, pretty much."

"Hope you're better with weirdness than you are with a pistol." For a moment, Sloat gave Irons a serious look. Then, his face squeezed into a million wrinkles and he laughed out loud. "Easy, kid, I'm just joshin' you."

Sloat tried to reward Irons with a free room, but given the state of business, Irons insisted he pay, and settled on a free drink instead. He wanted to hear the old timer's version of the "weirdness" anyway. In the room, he unpacked his saddle bags, which contained a single change of clothes. Space was needed to move the Seal's Hurdy-Gurdy back to San Francisco. But to his surprise, he pulled out something he hadn't put in.

Irons gazed at the object for a full minute before deciding what it was—a fetish charm. An eagle's skull was pierced by a bent, rusty nail. Leather thongs looped the head-end of the nail, braided together around several feathers and a single brownish gemstone, and lashed the whole to a bird's talon. Irons hadn't seen this kind of magic before, but he understood the sympathetic meaning—it was how the enforcers had located him.

He shoved it in his vest pocket—the enforcers already knew where he was—and went down to the bar. Sloat saw him and poured two shots from an unlabeled bottle.

"Here's mud in your eye."

Irons downed the shot, the mescal smooth. Sloat refilled his glass, but the biker needed to keep a level head, and left it on the bar. "So, what's the weirdness?"

"Can't rightly put a name to it." Sloat knocked another one back. "But people've seen it in the sky, seen it in the woods, but mostly smelled it. Smells like a pile of fish gone over. Some say it's a giant bird, some a snake or a fish. The things come into town at night, just...looking. Searching.

"They got big eyes, blue like a gas flame." Sloat indicated the size, circling his thumb and forefinger as if palming a knuckleball.

"You've seen it?" Irons sipped the liquor.

Sloat shrugged. "Once in a while, I'll smell that fishy rot, comes on an unnatural breeze, sometimes inside the hotel, and I'll see a slinky, shadowy thing out of the corner of my eye. It's damned creepy, but it ain't enough to chase me off."

The biker twirled the shot glass in his fingers, gazing into the clear liquid. "Anybody been hurt by these things?"

"Nah." Sloat poured himself a third. "But some have gone missing. Maybe they up and split, but maybe not. That help you any?"

"I'm not sure." Irons had seen things, strange and terrible things that most people would never believe. But he hadn't heard of any kind of hoodoo like this. Unnerved, he finished his drink. "I'll do what I can."

Thanking the innkeeper, Irons left the hotel. Early evening stars blazed above, air balmy from the day. Other than directing him to Trace Run, the Seal hadn't given him any more information about the Hurdy-Gurdy operation. The answer was painted on the side of a general store the size of a barn. Trace Run Paper Works, the sign said in bright red and yellow letters, with an arrow pointing to the right above the legend: 5 Mi.

The main drag intersected a narrow road past the four buildings of downtown, and Irons figured he knew where to go. As far as he could tell, Trace Run consisted of the motel, a Catholic church, the big mercantile, and a low brick building housing a barber, beauty salon, drug store and city offices.

A chill breeze shot through him like an icicle, and he was engulfed in a terrible odor of rotting offal, heavy enough to smother him. He jumped back, freeing himself from an invisible grasp. Eyes everywhere, Irons spotted it against the moon. Barely more substantial than a cloud, a form wriggled in the air, great wings or fins spread out from a long, narrow body. It neither looked like it was flying, nor quite floating, but rather seemed detached from the physical world. Blazing blue eyes locked on Irons, and the smoky creature descended rapidly.

Irons tore down the street. He couldn't judge the size or speed of the creature, so he moved in a sprint toward the nearest building—the church.

Again the air turned fetid, making breathing a sickening burden. Irons didn't allow himself to slow. A second later, he was struck, the blow almost imperceptible save the damp, heavy feeling on his shoulders, a frigid rubber band around his legs. Nearly toppling, he kept running, overbalanced but fighting on. A line of welts formed on his arms, becoming long, shallow scratches. He felt the wound across his abdomen forced open.

Flesh rippling in repulsion at the thing's unnatural touch, Irons batted at it, desperate to shrug it off. He felt nothing more than air. He continued his run in lurching steps, the chill, nearly intangible mass coating him like a froth of slime.

He barreled into the wide double doors of the church at full charge, putting his shoulder down like a linebacker. They flew open, unlocked, and Irons sprawled across the floor.

Yet even across the threshold of the sanctified building, the half-seen creature continued its assault. Irons caught a glimpse of a tubular body ending in a lacy tail, a head of a fish with fiery eyes, the mouth the beak of a falcon, long, delicate fins hooked with single talons. When a talon raked him, he felt nothing, yet blood welled at their touch.

Irons rolled to the doorway. He took the fetish-charm from his vest pocket and dunked it in the holy water font on the wall. Immediately, the thing fell into pieces. Turning, he saw his attacker disintegrating into glistening particles, scattered by the wind.

Irons folded his arms around his knees, his back to the wall. It took a long time to catch his breath. When he looked up, he started at the sight of four men standing over him.

"It's worse than I thought." The man speaking was short and round, balding, wearing round spectacles and the garb of a priest. He bent down and picked up the rotting thong that had bound the talisman. "The enforcers seem to have the power to summon *Las Centinelas*."

Another one, a skinny kid with acne scars and long, unwashed hair, shook his head. "Don't tell me you're the guy the Seal sent. I thought you'd be more...enlightened."

Irons' eyes went from one face to another. Other than the pudgy priest, the other three were young, shaggy-haired. Two were skinny, Acne Scars and a guy with Elvis-sized mutton chops, the third was burly. All were dressed in bell-bottoms and sandals, and either a college T-shirt or tie dye.

"You must be the Hurdy-Gurdy men." Irons stood up, legs shaking. He jumped slightly as the holy water font shattered, a foul-smelling brown muck leaking down the wall. "Sorry, Padre."

The priest shrugged. "We all make sacrifices in the battle against evil. You better let me get some iodine on those scratches. God only knows what *Las Centinelas* might carry."

Irons fell in behind the priest, the three hippies following him.

"If you're the guy the Seal sent, and you ran in here with the rest of us, I think we're in real deep shit." The kid with the acne scars made a face. "Sorry, Father John. It's like we're stuck in some kind of Bermuda Triangle or something."

The priest waved him away and led the way back to a rectory. He sat Irons down and returned with a bottle of iodine.

"I've never seen a *Centinela* so solidly before," Father John dabbed Iron's scratches.

Irons didn't feel the iodine any more than he felt the wounds. "What're *Las Centinelas?*"

"*Centinelas*—sentinels, some kind of watchful creatures sent by the enforcers, no doubt." The priest shrugged. "I have very little idea what they are, other than pure evil."

"That one had my scent," Irons said. "Someone stuffed that charm in my saddle bag. How do you know about the enforcers?"

Behind Father John, the hippies went a little pale.

"They confessed what they were doing in the old paper plant when the sentinels started appearing, and I granted them sanctuary." Father John finished his work and capped the iodine. "A few days ago, three gentlemen from south of the border started asking around about these boys. I put two and two together when I saw the machine guns in their car. Fortunately, *Las Centinelas* had scared just about everyone out of town before they got here. There was no one to question."

Irons began to form a picture. The cartel wanted the Seal to distribute product for them. When he refused, they closed down his pot fields and now were trying to shut down the Hurdy-Gurdy plant. But not until they figured out what Sielenbacher was up to, first. The cartel used supernatural creatures as spies.

"As soon as the enforcers figure out what you're up to, they'll burn the plant to the ground," Irons mused. "That won't make the Seal happy at all."

"What's he gonna do, flipper us to death?" The acne-scarred kid scoffed.

But the burly one hit him hard in the shoulder. "Dude, shut up."

As helpless as the Seal seemed, his own enforcers were hardly gentler than the men from Mexico. If these hippies failed to produce, it wouldn't go well for them. And, it seemed, even if they did, it would not go well for them, given the proximity of the cartel's men.

"Yeah, dude, shut up," Irons agreed. "You guys better give the Seal what he wants."

"We can't, man, not with those freaky things floating around." Acne Scars frowned. "I mean, look at what just one of 'em did to a big dude like you. The CIA is into mind control, the Soviets have telekinesis, and now the drug lords have space aliens. We're doomed, man."

In the three hours Irons had been in town, he'd taken out two armed enforcers and one *La Centinela*. Apparently, the kids either weren't aware of, or were not impressed by, this track record. But maybe what he'd accomplished wasn't nearly enough to see the Seal's enterprise through.

IV: Evil for Evil's Sake

Irons pulled Father John to the side. "I don't know how much they told you, but those boys are deep in the shit, Padre."

"I guessed as much. I have no personal issues with marijuana, but it is illegal, and hard men tend to deal in illegal trades." The priest sighed. "What can be done?"

The biker pursed his lips in thought. "You seem to know about these sentinel things. What else can you tell me? What kind of hoodoo is this?"

"*Santisima Muerte,* it's called, the most sacred death. Mostly, it's a harmless kind of saint-worship, unorganized folk religion, practiced by otherwise good Catholics. But she's also the patron saint of criminals, and drug lords use it to control their workers. The way the criminal underground practices it, it's evil for evil's sake. It's a combination of witchcraft, *Santería, Palo Mayombe* with a deep-seated root of pre-Columbian ritual, especially human sacrifice." Father John rubbed his eyes. "I've never seen it this strong. They must've brought in a very powerful maestro."

Irons considered the words, wondering how to deal with magicians who worshipped death. Holy water had an effect, yet the *Santisima Muerte* also had an effect on the holy water. The sentinel had no problem trespassing on sacred ground. He'd seen demonic creatures summoned to their earthly genius loci, but these sentinels were not only summoned, but dispatched and controlled. Enormous power was at work here.

But the priest talked of three enforcers. Maybe the third was this maestro, some high priest of *Santisima Muerte*. If Irons could reach him physically, he might be able to shut down the supernatural forces at play. He couldn't see another choice. But first, he had to protect the hippies from the wrath of the Seal. "I want you to do me a favor, Padre."

Father John nodded. "If it will help these boys, I'll do it."

"I want you to come with us in the morning and bless the paper plant."

The priest blinked a few times. "Well, that's highly irregular, considering we're talking about a criminal enterprise."

"But you'll do it?" Irons prompted.

"I'll meet you there in the morning." Father John squinted at Irons for a moment. "You know, for a hard man, you don't seem like a bad man. In spite of what you're here for."

The biker held up his palms. "Things are rarely what they seem. You know a lot about an evil, pagan religion for a priest."

"Former congregation in El Paso—I got a lot of it there. You seem to be dodging my assessment of you." The father looked at him frankly. "Maybe you haven't decided for yourself."

"I've done bad things," Irons confessed. "Made mistakes, caused people pain, cost some their lives. Some that didn't deserve it. Other times, I pulled people out of a jam. It doesn't make me evil, and it doesn't make me God's strong-arm man. I just take it as it comes. I'll see you in the morning."

"Where are you going, dude?" Acne Scars called after him.

Irons paused at the front door. "That *La Centenela* thing got in here just fine. I'd rather spend the night in a soft bed than on a hard pew." Despite his bravado, he tried to look in all directions at once as he made the short walk back to the inn. Goosebumps raised his flesh at the thought of the half-visible fliers scanning the night.

The old codger, Sloat, had left him a plate of barbecue on the bar and a note that said he'd gone to bed. Irons helped himself to a beer and tucked in. He'd likely need all the strength he could muster. On his way to his room, he stumbled across Miguel's machete on the lobby floor. In the dim light, he saw the blade inscribed with symbols he didn't know on one side; the other was carved with the likeness of a hooded woman with a skull for a face: St. Death.

He took the long knife with him, hanging it from the inside knob of his door. Irons knew a ritual or two that might keep him safe. But his lack of expertise in rituals had ended disastrously in the past. He opted to take his chances, and fell into a dreamless sleep.

V. The Haunted Plant

Irons jerked awake, curtains framed in the grey of early light. He grabbed the saddle bags, and after a moment of hesitation, stuffed the machete in one of them, handle protruding from under the flap.

He caught the scent of frying bacon. His nose led him to a room behind the bar. Sloat stood in a small kitchen flipping pancakes on a griddle. He looked up at Irons. "I thought you might be getting an early start."

When Sloat brought a tray heaped with scrambled eggs, sausages, bacon and flapjacks to a card table set up in the middle of the floor, Irons laughed. "You cook a mean breakfast, Sloat."

"Hell, you should see me when the dining room's open." Sloat smiled, and fetched some plates and flatware, and the two sat down to eat. "If you need help up there, I worked at   Trace Run Paper Works 'til they closed it down."

Irons considered it, washing down a mouthful with a cup of coffee. He certainly didn't want to leave the old guy here, especially if the enforcers came calling again. At the same time—"You know they're not just making paper up there."

Sloat nodded. "I guessed it. Three longhairs like that—but hell, as long as they're not making bombs or something, I don't much care."

Irons thought it over, finishing the huge meal. He figured they needed all the help they could get. "All right. I'll meet you up there."

Outside, the VW was already gone, leaving the Harley the only vehicle parked on the street. After securing the saddle bags, he took a meandering route toward the paper plant, putting up side roads, startling a few mule deer and a flock of birds. None of the cabins seemed to be occupied, until he got to one near the top of the hill. He saw the dusty Olds parked outside and killed the bike's engine. He pulled the machete free.

Walking the last few yards, he inspected the Toronado, finding a smear of blood on the door handle, a missing windshield. He slashed three of the vehicle's tires. Then, casting glances over his shoulder, he opened the hood and cut a few hoses and belts.

He reached Trace Run Paper Plant just as the sun broke over the horizon. Light revealed a parking lot choked with weed trees. Beyond, a razor-wire-topped chain link fence surrounded a long, low building with a hundred broken windows, two crumbling smoke stacks, several old-fashioned water towers and a yawning loading dock. Irons had seen more inviting prisons.

The hippies' VW was parked near the gate, all of them still in the car. Irons parked next to them, then got off and tapped on the passenger window. It rolled down. "What are you waiting for?"

Burly Hippy pointed at the front gate. Irons saw something hanging there, vaguely pretzel shaped. The biker grabbed up the machete and moved to inspect it, but even several yards away, he could smell the rot.

The charm was made of a human spine, contorted into that profane glyph. It was hung with ornaments like an obscene Christmas tree. Irons got close enough to see that the spine had been strung with eyeballs. Swirling symbols had been drawn on each vertebra. Seven votive candles had been nailed into the bones, five red and two black. Irons felt the handle of the machete grow ice cold. Suddenly, the wicks sputtered and lit, flames guttering high. Did the dangling eyes turn to look at him?

A dented pickup truck rattled into the lot. Irons turned to see Sloat driving, Father John riding shotgun. Both men stared at the grotesque installation before getting out.

"What the hell kind of mess is this?" Sloat murmured.

Father John exited the truck with a scepter-shaped aspergillum. He shook holy water at the gate in the form of a cross, whispering a prayer. For a moment, the candles burned impossibly high. When the priest again splashed the display, it crumbled into dust.

The boys slowly got out of the Bug. "Holy crap." Acne Scars looked at the ashy pile at the foot of the fence. "Let's just do it," Burly prompted. Acne Scars fumbled a key out of his pocket. It skittered around the keyhole in his shaking hand.

"Here, I'll do it," Burly said, holding out his hand.

"I got it," Scars said through his teeth.

The grounds outside the plant were overgrown with waist-high weeds, the cracked sidewalks choked with wild vines. At the front door, the third hippy, Mutton Chops, produced another key. Inside a vestibule stood another gate, chain link, with a pushbutton combination lock. Burly punched in a code and cranked down the handle.

Inside was one long room, stretching from the door to the loading dock. Cobwebs hung from an office loft overhead, and half the space was piled high with rusting machine parts. A single machine stood to one side, a hundred feet long, made up of mismatched cylinders and exposed motors.

"It's your baby, give 'em the nickel tour." Acne Scars stood near the door, arms folded, eyes constantly moving.

Mutton Chops nodded reluctantly. "Okay, this is a pretty basic Forudrinier machine. We had to assemble it from four nonworking machines, so it looks a little rough." Chops led them to the far end. "This is the pulper, it grinds and cooks the stalks into a slurry, then dumps into the wet end. The breastbox spits slurry through the slice onto the wire, and it rotates around here, under here to the suction box. The couch picks it up, squeezes out more water, pulls the paper into the press."

Irons followed along, not particularly interested. By the door, Father John stood, eyes closed in silent prayer. Burly and Acne Scars stood close to him, apparently praying along. Sloat nudged Irons. "This thing is a piece of junk. I'll be surprised if it runs at all."

"This is the dryer, where the paper gets coated before getting squeezed again and heated. We installed a cutter at the far end of the calendar section, because we don't want a big roll." Mutton Chops stepped to the end of the calendar, past a dangerous-looking set of cutting blades, and pulled a greenish sheet of finished paper from the hopper. Irons recognized the same stuff the Seal showed him back in San Francisco.

"Lotta work to make an ugly sheet of green cardboard." Sloat shrugged. "Maybe you need more bleach in the cooker."

Something rattled in the huge mound of machinery pushed up against the far wall. The ignition of a nearby forklift clicked a few times. Overhead the lights dimmed.

"It's just rats," Mutton Chops whispered, closing his eyes.

Father John gave Irons a look, and the biker nodded. The priest lowered his head in prayer, then began walking the inside of the plant, waving the aspergillum. Slowly, procession rounded the room, progressing to the machine itself. In Irons' hand, the machete buzzed angrily, sending a shock up the biker's arm. He slid the blade through his drive chain belt and moved away from the priest. Let Father John deliver the blessing; Irons would carry the curse.

VI: Steel Sentinel

The day dragged. Irons rode Father John back to the church, returning to find nothing accomplished. Mutton Chops and Sloat argued over some malfunctioning part of the wet end while Burly and Acne Scars fiddled with the staggered rollers of the press. Sometime after noon, the machine started rolling. Irons choked on the exhaust fumes of the engines and cooker, the skunky weed smell in the air that huge fans in the ceiling couldn't pull out fast enough. The hippies shouted at each other over the roar of the Rube Goldberg Fourdrinier machine. Irons couldn't take it.

Outside, he patrolled the grounds under a hot sun. Hundreds of lizards clambered over the plant façade. Irons had seen similar sights south of the border, reptiles hanging on the shacks of drug runners, attracted to the vibe.

No breeze blew, no birds flew, no cars passed. From the top of the hill, woods rolled away eternally. In the far corner of the grounds, another pile of broken machinery sloped against an outbuilding, partially under wide blue tarps. He saw bearing housings, axles, bright yellow fencing, beams, blades, a thousand screws and bolts and rivets, cracked rollers, bales of rusty wire conveyor belts. The plant must've been something in its day, he mused.

Six hours later, the roar of the plant died, and Irons hurried inside at the sound of shouting. The hippies and Sloat were slapping each other on the back, eyes narrow and red, smiles wide. Mutton Chops reached into the hopper and grabbed up the finished paper. When he smacked the ends together, he had a stack nearly two inches thick. Again, the men howled in celebration.

Irons stared at the stack, heart sinking.

"Man, do I have the munchies. Let's drive to McCloud and get six pizzas and a bucket of chicken," Burly said.

"That sounds real good," Sloat said, "and maybe a dozen beers. I forgot how hot this work is. You in, Irons?"

The biker frowned at them. "I'm supposed to bring back two saddle bags stuffed with Hurdy-Gurdy. I'm supposed to bring them back yesterday. What do you think the Seal will do to you idiots if that's all I bring him?"

"Bust out the jackboots, Mr. Fascist, why don't you? We don't work for the Man. I say we knock off." Acne Scars moved toward him, THC putting a swagger in his walk. He stuck his chin out at the biker. "What're you gonna do about it?"

Irons considered knocking Acne Scars on his ass. When he took a step forward, the hippy shuffled back. "Eat, drink, whatever. But the three of you are back here in two hours, no excuses. Or I'll come find you and drag you back here."

"What about the old man?" Acne Scars whined.

Irons poked the hippy with a finger hard enough to knock the kid back a step. "He's a volunteer, you three are on the payroll. There's no punching out for you."

"Dude, I don't care how big you are, how mean and strong and tough you are, there's nothing you can say that's gonna make us work here at night." Acne Scars folded his arms in defiance, looking at Burly and Mutton Chops. "No freakin' way."

An hour after sunset, the plant rolled on. The hippies reluctantly returned after pigging out in McCloud, not looking at Irons as they entered the plant. Sloat returned also, smiling at the biker. "You sure got a way with kids, Irons."

"Little discipline never hurt anybody. Why are you here?"

Sloat looked toward the plant. "Brings back the old days, I reckon. Plus, the contact high is a real bonus."

"Well, then, make me some paper, old timer. I'll see you get paid."

Irons watched them all enter the plant, and soon enough, smoke from the cooker rose from the cracked smokestack. For hours, the plant growled monotonously as the biker prowled the grounds.

Night and the moonlight cast sinister shadows, the forest and the breeze stirring to life. The constant rumble of the paper machine drowned out the sound of an approaching vehicle. Irons didn't realize it was there until he rounded the corner of the building and saw headlights.

Moving through the junk trees, keeping low, he quickly approached the dusty Olds. It sat awkwardly on four different size tires. He saw no one inside. Then he heard muffled screaming.

A few hundred feet away, he saw them. Four men stood near the fence—no, three men stood, the fourth hung from the chain links. Again, the screaming started. Knives glittered, reflecting the moon. Irons drew the machete from his belt and charged forward. He saw that the fourth man was secured with baling wire, his body spread-eagled, face against the fence, held in place by his wrists and ankles. The other three plunged knives into his back, bringing forth another shriek.

Too late, Irons noticed the bright glow emanating from the machete. Two of the men shouted, and brought out guns. The biker only had time to notice that the third enforcer wore a flowing shroud of black robes before lead flew.

He crawled into a slight depression. Bullets hummed overhead, automatic bursts and single heavy shots, but Irons couldn't help but look up. The hooded man kept at his work with the knife, the victim struggling against his bonds. With a final gasp, the hanging man went limp. The robed enforcer grunted, slashed into the body again; then pulled the spine out from his victim's ragged back.

The third enforcer—the maestro—waved the spinal column around like a wand, gore raining down, a twisted parody of Father John's blessing.

At the same time, the two others spread out—Miguel, Irons realized, and the man he'd shot. The biker tried to move toward the maestro, but bullets blasted, whipping through the foliage, every time he moved. They had him pinned down.

His eyes caught the muzzle flashes, and he memorized their positions. Memories of the war flooded into the biker with adrenalin. The grounds were too flat to move across.

The maestro began a strange dance, moving around in a circle. The sorcerer struck the hanging body with the spine, the head turning unnaturally, held in place only by muscle. Irons saw Father John's blood-spattered face.

Red occluded his vision, leaving only the maestro in a tunnel of vision, fear in Irons' blood became a raging, erupting fury. Gunmen receded from his thoughts, and Irons rose on his knees. He raised the machete and hurled it with all his might. The blade whirled in the air, bounced off the ground, and buried itself in the black magician's thigh. The momentum of his own body brought Irons face-down into the weeds as bullets hissed through the leaves around him.

"*Vamanos!*" Irons heard Miguel's voice.

The maestro yanked the machete out of his leg. Irons, still in the grip of fury, cast around until he found a fist-sized rock. Sidearm, he whipped it toward the nearest muzzle flash. Rewarded with a grunt of pain, Irons dug around for a second stone.

"*Miguel, estoy herido!*"

"*Vamanos!*" In the darkness, Miguel moved, firing at Irons' position. When Irons looked up, the maestro vanished. He pulled the chain from his belt, intent on killing any of them if they got within reach. But in a moment, Irons heard car doors thud shut.

As the Oldsmobile pulled away, Irons hurried to free the dead priest. But as he reached Father John, Irons heard a rattle. The sound repeated, followed by a heavy thump he could feel in the ground.

From behind the outbuilding, a glimmering shape emerged, enormous, scuttling and insectile. It crashed into the outbuilding, nearly knocking it from the foundation. Then, tiny lights appeared, swaying toward Irons and the priest.

It came toward him on legs made of rusty rollers from the press in squealing, rusty progress, claws of cutting blades clanking together like pincers. The claws slashed through the fence on both sides of the dead priest, then hauled the body and fence alike into a maw surrounded by crushing gears. The maestro had raised a giant, metallic crustacean from the graveyard of discarded parts. Irons couldn't think of anything to do about it, except run.

VII: Temporary Sanctuary

It can't enter the plant, he thought desperately. The priest had blessed the place, quieting the noises inside. It had to be enough. Legs burning, the biker sprinted across the parking lot. The mechanical thing's screeching, clanking motion was blanketed by the sound of the running paper machine, but Irons could still feel the thunderous footsteps through his boots.

Inside, work went on uninterrupted, the hippies and Sloat too intent on the paper machine to even notice Irons' entrance. Outside, the steel sentinel paced with earthquake strides that grew in intensity.

He could only hope that the blessing would keep it at bay, that sunrise would return it to a pile of rubble. Swiping sweat from his brow, Irons began to walk around the plant, looking for something to combat the scrapheap nightmare.

The pounding continued to vibrate the plant, the junkyard horror's shadow passed by the broken windows. If the hippies remained occupied long enough—

One by one, the plant's sections began to shut down. Irons turned to see Mutton Chops stacking paper—now six reams of it—near the hopper. The wire, now empty, slowed to a stop, the wheels pressed out the last of the water and their grinding, whining motors wound down. The fly end of the paper passed through the dryer, and ten minutes later, the cutters went off-line.

Acne Scars whooped. "That's all of it! We are done, man!"

Mutton Chops slapped Sloat on the back. "You really made that machine sing, old man."

"I can still teach you kids a thing or two."

Despite the paper machine being shut down, a groaning mechanical din still vibrated through the plant. The hippies looked at each other, looked over the Fourdrinier. Ground-shaking footsteps now sounded through the building with hollow booms. All four looked a question at Irons.

"I don't think it can get inside here." Irons didn't know what else to say.

"What can't get in here?" Acne Scars turned toward the windows, and his jaw sagged. Others followed his eyes.

A vast carapace of yellow safety mesh geometrically spotted with rusty grates lumbered by, the earth shaking in time with its motion.

"Dude, I think we've been in here too long," Mutton Chops gasped.

"We'll be safe inside." Irons saw panic rising in their features and tried to stem it. "Father John blessed this place."

"How long are we safe in here? We ate all the food." Burly couldn't take his eyes from the windows.

Irons held up his hands, saw blood on them, and lowered them again. "I don't think it can live in sunlight. None of the sentinels ever appeared in the day, did they?"

The hippies and Sloat looked at each other, coming to a silent agreement that *Las Centinalas* were seen only at night. They'd been steadily working for hours, and dawn wasn't long.

A gunshot crack of concrete came from the loading dock. Dust and rubble rained down, the building swaying. The plant's walls cracked and growled. Booming blows dented the steel doors. All stood frozen as the rolling gates crashed to the ground in a cloud of disintegrating bricks. Through the obscuring miasma, a long arm reached into the building. Scissor-like claws sliced through the air, skirled together with the sound of steely death. Even if the recycled monster couldn't get in, it could reach in.

It seemed both mechanical and alive, rickety and rusty, but impossibly powerful. Lights glowed on the end of steel cables, eyestalks peering into the gloom. Shrugging, it reached deeper into the plant, crumbling half the loading dock wall. Wires, cables and pulleys acted like muscles. The blades clamped a few yards away, and the hippies backed up.

"We should make a run for it." Acne Scars shouted over the grind and wail of metal. "It doesn't move that fast."

As if in response, the pincer reached out, snapping twice with blinding speed.

"You kids get goin'. Me and Irons'll keep the thing busy." Sloat pulled the pistol from his belt. "Hell, we could probably take it apart with a big monkey wrench."

The idea was ludicrous—nothing about the living junk pile seemed to follow mechanical rules—yet at the same time, it did make a strange kind of sense. "You have tools here, for the press, right?" Irons turned and asked the hippies.

"Well, duh." Acne Scars was still backing toward the door.

Irons didn't have time to address the attitude. "Did Father John bless them?"

"Yeah, he blessed everything in here." Acne Scars held his hands out. "Can I run away now, please?"

Irons examined the walls, finding hanging tools near the pile of junk inside. He headed for them. "Run, but I won't guarantee your safety."

"Blessed tools to take apart a diabolical machine." Sloat took a big wrench from a pegboard.

Irons grabbed a pear head ratchet, and when the mechanical pincer reached in again, he flung the tool hard. It clattered harmlessly off the reaching claw. A moment later, however, the lower blade of the pincer fell to the ground. The arm waved wildly in retraction. Sloat jogged forward with the heavy pipe wrench and slammed retreating limb.

"Sloat, don't get close!" Irons cried out, but too late. A second arm reached in, knocking the old man off his feet. The biker grabbed a pry bar leaning against the wall and in a fluid motion, hurled it like a javelin. Stuck between the rails of the monster arm, the bar stopped the thing from crushing Sloat. Each time it slammed down, it drove the bar deeper, until the entire arm clanged apart.

The biker ran to Sloat's side, scooping up the three-foot pipe wrench. As he dragged the old man out of reach, he smashed the remains of the first limb aside as it tried to crush them. The force of the blow stung Irons to the shoulder.

The hippies stepped up. They grabbed every tool they could find—ratchet heads, screwdrivers, pliers—and pelted the steel lobster. Irons thought the attempt looked puny. Yet they drove the sentinel out. It took most of the loading dock with it in an avalanche of grey and brick red.

"Goddamnit, I think I busted a leg," Sloat said through his dentures.

Breathing hard, Irons pointed to the hippies. "You three, get out of here, get him to a doctor."

"What about that thing?" Burly still held a nut driver in his fist.

Irons ignored him. He unlooped the chain from his waist, clamping the end in the pipe wrench, tightening it down as hard as possible. "Just go. I'll deal with this."

Unwieldy as the weapon was, it at least gave him some reach. Irons grabbed a handful of socket heads and chucked them at the thing, getting its attention. Then he grabbed the wrench and chain, moving steadily toward the loading dock. He grabbed the pry bar along the way. He didn't give himself much of a shot, but Sloat had been nothing but kind to Irons and the hippy kids, scared as they were, finished their work for the Seal. At least he would give them a chance.

VIII: The Power of Death

The iron crustacean had more fight in it that Irons would've hoped. Despite its lack of pincers, it still attempted to batter Irons with stubby arms. With the wrench whirling dangerously around his head, the biker stuck again and again. Unbalanced as the flail was, it did its work. With the arms gone, Irons struck at the legs, slowing the impossible machine's retreat.

Barely in time, he leaped to the side as a scorpion-like tail slammed into the concrete inches away. Irons bashed at the tail, stabbed it into uselessness. A tooth-jarring blow flung the big man several yards. He looked up to see one of the steel roller legs following through, coming toward him.

In the distance, the Bug's four-cylinder engine chirped to life. It distracted the sentinel for an instant, and Irons rolled to his feet.

The chain and pry bar grew slippery with his sweat. He managed to dart in and smash the glowing lights. For his trouble, he was kicked again, and tumbled halfway across the parking lot. He smarted from road rash, muscles bruised and strained, but he got up.

Maybe this creature was tougher than the other sentinels, made stronger by the death of a priest. He'd torn it apart, and yet the junkyard creature moved away with its awful, earth-shaking pace. Oil, grease, and hydraulic fluids leaked like blood, and the smell of burnt oil hung in the air. Irons saw that it was headed back to the refuse pile that birthed it.

It burrowed in, like a crab into sand. A few shuffling shifting moments later, it emerged again with new claws, new eyes, new legs.

"Aw, shit." Irons whirled, his attack frenzied, his thoughts on the dead priest, on the injured old man. Vengeance lit him afire, his blood boiling, his sight dim and red. He hit and hit and hit. *"Die!"*

Opponents staggered apart. Lungs burning, face aflame, sweat dripping from every pour, Irons hefted the five-foot pry bar. The crab machine limped backward, sparking and smoking, heading for the last of the discarded parts.

"No you don't!" With a few running steps, he jumped, diving forward, leading with the bar. All of his weight was behind it as he reached the thing's rearmost leg. It punched through the metal, punched through to the blacktop below and stuck deep. With a few quick blows, he drove the bar deeper into the pavement.

It whirled on Irons, a leg bashing him away. As he lay gasping for breath, the sentinel turned. And turned. It could not free itself from the blessed pry bar. It staggered in a circle, Irons out of its reach. Above, the sky paled with first light. The creature fell apart, a piece at a time, once again a loose pile of junk.

Whether it was from his efforts, or the effects of the dawn, Irons didn't care. He felt like a collection of contusions, lacerations and abrasions; exhaustion rolled over him like a wave. He wrapped the chain around his waist and stuck the wrench through it.

Still, a white-hot ember of anger burned in the back of his brain. He limped to the half-shattered building, grabbed the bundles of Hurdy-Gurdy, and stuffed them in his saddle bags. Then, he rode off, letting the wind and the road revive him. Too quickly, he made the enforcers' cabin.

"Miguel!" he screamed, then bashed the knob off with the pipe wrench and kicked the door open. It looked like a makeshift hospital inside. Miguel in his cast, the other enforcer with bandages over seeping bullet wounds, the maestro in flowing robes spun to face him.

"Must I show you the power of death myself?" the maestro's words hissed in the bikers' brain.

Irons stood in shock as the hooded figure brandished the machete, and in two quick moves, beheaded his comrades.

The machete glowed like an arc welder, searing Irons' eyes. Incredibly, the man made a twenty-foot leap, landing in front of the biker, weapon poised.

Irons had a little going for him. He was a head taller than the maestro, the pipe wrench a yard of steel to the machete's two feet, and had the reach. Irons was stoked by pure fury, while the maestro was cold and emotionless. But the maestro was energized by the frightening death magic. Grey smoke issued from the black hood. Light leaked out of shrouded pupils, and the white flame of the machete danced, taunting, licking out like a snake's tongue.

Like lightning, the machete struck. Irons barely flinched away, the blade cutting the biker below the ear. It brought the robed man in too close. Irons kneed him in the balls with all the force he could muster. But the maestro only laughed and danced back.

The robed maestro took on a fencer's pose, knees flexed, body turned sideways. Irons took on a batter's stance, choking up on the pipe wrench. "Come on, you sick bastard, I'm tired of playing games."

"No game, Señor Irons. I take your death very seriously. How many men I have sacrificed, how many I have murdered? None of them are half the opponent you were. Your death will give me unbelievable power." Glowing eyes took in Irons' pose. The robed man gestured with slender fingers. *"Come, take your best shot. Then I kill you."*

"Cool." Irons swung, but not at the hood. Instead, he brought the wrench down as hard as he could on the machete. With a blast of light like a thousand flashbulbs, it shattered. The maestro screamed a high-pitched banshee's scream, falling to his knees. Irons smiled and kicked him in the head.

The scream seemed to go on, echoing in the highlands. The robes shriveled, a whisper issued from the deflating hood. *"This is not the end, Señor Irons. The eye of Santa Muerte is upon you."*

With that, the robes fell into tatters and dust. Irons now stood in an abattoir, headless corpses and lakes of blood on the cabin floor.

But he knew the maestro was right. It was not the end.

IX: The End

He allowed himself the luxury of three hours' sleep before mounting the hog and pointing it back toward San Francisco. Darkness fell as he took I-580 from 5, heading west from Tracey to Oakland and

across the Bay Bridge. He took the Embarcadero off-ramp and drove
to the dark panhandle of Golden Gate Park, finding a spot for the hog
outside the Seal's pad. Irons hefted the saddlebags over his shoulder.
The door to the stairs was unlocked—no one, not even the most
desperate junkie or speed freak—would dare rob the Seal. Unan-
nounced, he entered the living room. The nurses lolled in their usual
places; the Seal sat in his wheelchair, wide paisley tie loose around
his neck.

"Hey, Teddy, I wasn't expecting you back so soon," the Seal
opened his arms, a joint clutched in one of his flippers. "Jesus, you
look like hell."

Irons forgot how busted up he must look. He gazed at the Seal and
his nurses. "Sorry to crash the party."

"Sit down, take a load off, Teddy." The Seal waved him to a seat.
"Is that the stuff?"

Irons saw him eyeing the saddlebags, and he dropped them next to
the wheelchair. "That's the stuff."

"I knew those losers just needed a kick in the pants. Let me see it,
Lila." Seilenbacher anxiously looked on while Lila pulled the reams
of yellow-green paper from one of the bags. Irons had his attention
focused on Violet.

"Welcome back, big man." Violet's eyes were innocent, yet she
had hardly showed him an eager welcome. Her eyes narrowed at the
green paper.

"Oh, beautiful, beautiful! A little brick of hash in every sheet. One
two three—six reams, times five hundred is three thousand sheets,
times fifty bucks is a hundred fifty grand." The Seal chuckled. "And I
thought I was gonna lose money when the feds got wise to my fields."

"About that, Henry." Irons took a few sheets of the thick paper.
There was nothing about them that indicated they held a potent drug.
"The Man didn't bust your fields without help. Why didn't you tell me
about the cartel?"

The Seal's eyebrows came together. "The Mexicans who want a
cut of my business? What do they have to do with anything?"

"They don't wanna be cut in, Henry, they wanna cut you out.
When your fields got raided, they offered weed for you to distribute."
Irons found a lighter on an end table.

The Seal pounded a flipper on the arm of his chair. "The Seal
works for nobody. I told 'em to take their weed and shove it."

"So the cartel needed to put more pressure on, to shut down more
of your operations. They found out about the Hurdy-Gurdy." Irons

took a sheet of Hurdy-Gurdy, folded it in thirds, and rolled it tight. He thumbed open the Zippo and lit the little tube. He handed it to the Seal.

"No way." Seilenbacher took a hit of the joint, blowing through his nose. "Only me, those hippy dudes, and you knew about it."

"Except the enforcers knew I was coming. I think the cartel wants to take over your distribution, force you to move their product by destroying yours. They gave the location of your fields to the feds, gave the location of the Hurdy-Gurdy operation to the enforcers—"

"I have my phones checked for taps, my place swept for bugs, my deals are all face-to-face." As Henry passed the Hurdy-Gurdy to Lila, his handsome face turned dark and ugly. "You saying I've got a rat?"

Irons murmured his agreement, eyes intent on Lila. "Someone on the inside."

Lila passed the paper joint to Darla.

"Someone put a gift in my saddlebags. It led the enforcers right to me." Irons let his eyes drift over to Darla, watching. "I don't think it's about drugs. I think this cartel wants your distribution for another reason."

The Seal's face grew darker by the second. "What are you saying?"

Darla passed the Hurdy-Gurdy to Violet.

"This cartel worships a goddess called *Santisima Muerte*—The Most Holy Death. I think what they want, what she wants, is followers. You have, what, a couple hundred dealers?"

Henry laughed. "Now you're just tripping me out. What are you talking about?"

"Thousands of customers?"

The nurses looked up at him as if he were crazy—all except Violet. She got to her feet, hand at her throat. She dropped the Hurdy-Gurdy joint to the floor. "What is that? What have you done?"

Henry rolled up to Violet, picking up the burning paper from the Oriental rug. "Why is she freaking out, man?"

"Get away from me!" Violet's features blurred, her hair rising as if blown by an unfelt wind. Her blue eyes went black, then the whites as well. Mouth opened wide, teeth seeming to grow. She hissed at them like a snake and raised her hands.

"The Hurdy-Gurdy's blessed!" Irons jumped up, yanking Henry's wheelchair back. "The whole place was blessed, including the paper machine, the cuttings, the water."

Violet let out a scream that shook the windows. All looked on in horror as Violet's dark face split and peeled back, revealing the skull visage of the saint of death. She raised human arms over her death's head. "I am *Santisima Muerte!*"

Red smoke poured from the top of her peasant dress, billowed from the eye sockets and open mandible. The skull-faced woman contorted, bending completely backward, her human arms outstretched and thrashing. Groaning, the evil goddess levitated in the air, pointing a shaking finger at Irons.

"This is not over, *Gringo!* No mortal can defeat the most holy death! The eye of *Santa Muerte* is upon you!"

Irons took the Hurdy-Gurdy from the Seal and stood in front of the writhing goddess. "I banish you, *Santisima Muerte.*" He made the Sign of the Cross with the burning joint. "In the name of the Father, the Son, and the Holy Ghost—"

The red smoke now boiled from Violet, obscuring the unholy vision. The joint flared like a candle in Irons' fingers. In a moment, the roiling smoke contracted, imploding inward. The Seal's pad shook, as if from an earthquake. And then *Santisima Muerte* was gone.

Epilogue

Henry gaped at the empty space. "Dude, you are the weirdest of the weird."

"Everyone all right?" Irons' voice was a croak as he took in the shocked faces.

"Whoa. That was a bummer. Could've been a much worse scene." The Seal rolled a little closer. "I owe you, man."

Irons looked at bleached, slack faces. "I better split."

"Hang on a sec. What the hell was all that?"

"Violet was possessed, Henry. Probably willingly."

"Possessed? She's been with me for years!"

"Whoever Violet was, her humanness was totally consumed by *Santisima Muerte.*"

The Seal stared at Irons, wide-eyed.

"The cartel wanted your distributors and dealers to be missionaries, converts to *Santisima Muerte.* Your people believe, and make your customers believe, and pretty soon, the cartel is the most powerful in the Bay Area. Then in California, then the U.S."

The Seal shook his head. "That's total bullshit."

"Really?" Irons headed for the door. "You don't believe what you just saw?"

Seilenbacher opened his mouth to say something; then thought twice.

"I was high as a kite, but I know what I saw," Lila whispered.

Darla traded wide-eyed looks with her. "Yeah, me, too."

The biker shrugged. "Okay, give me my bread so I can split."

Henry held up a hand. "Be cool. I'll get it."

Henry Seilenbacher rolled out of the room, retuning a few moments later with a brick of money. Irons shoved it in his vest pockets.

"I gave you a couple grand extra."

"Why, Henry?" Irons couldn't remember the Seal ever being generous. Seilenbacher scowled. "Because we're friends, man."

"Uh-huh." Irons headed for the stairs "Don't bullshit me, man."

"Wait up, wait up." The Seal tapped his two fingers on the arm of the wheelchair, lips pursed. "Okay, I got another job for you."

"No." Irons opened the door.

"Dude, you can make another seventy-five Gs, maybe more."

"Forget it, Henry."

"It'll just take a few days, Teddy." The Seal wheeled toward him, but Irons walked down. "C'mon, it's down south—your old stomping grounds. I'll make it worth your while. Hey, Teddy. Irons!"

But the biker made the street, straddled the hog. He gunned the engine, blocking out the Seal's pleading, and rode away.

※

Biographies

Daniel S. Duvall spends his creative time writing speculative feature film screenplays and short stories. His tale "A Huff Motel Halloween" appears in *Robbed of Sleep Volume 4*. His script *The Offended Ancestor* (a spooky family-friendly mystery) placed as 1 of 25 semifinalists in the 2015 Zoetrope screenwriting contest, and one of his other projects *(The Marsh Wolf)* placed in the top 50 of the 2015 Launch Pad Feature Competition. He dwells in his native Ohio once again (following a seven-year detour to California, where he studied screenwriting at UCLA and wrote dozens of articles for *Creative Screenwriting* magazine). He sat in as a guest bassist for one tune with his favorite band (Fairport Convention) on the 18th of September in 2002. He enjoys interacting with cats, swilling Irish breakfast tea at odd hours, and watching televised baseball games. He earned a bachelor's degree in psychology back in the olden days when televisions were square and VHS was the dominant home video format. He finds existence fascinating and has never been bored. In cyberspace: www.DanDuvall.com

David J. Fielding is a writer and an actor. His published works have appeared in Nevermet Press, Rebel ePublishers LLC, Source Point Press, Oak Press, Flinch! Books, and he has self-published a superhero novel—*Vigilance*. You can find a complete list of his work here: http://www.amazon.com/-/e/B00HRN1JMG. He is also the actor who originated the role and provided the voice for Zordon of Eltar, the mentor to a group of teenagers with attitude on the hit television series, *The Mighty Morphin' Power Rangers*. He is busy polishing a series of paranormal stories, working on several web-series and attending various comic and entertainment conventions.

Clare Francis is the brainchild of two Sacramento area teachers who discovered their passion for storytelling while exploring the trails of the American River. They can often be found at Starbucks swapping plot lines and stories about their children. When not grading or writing, they enjoy camping and mountain biking with their husbands and kids.

John Linwood Grant lives in Yorkshire with a pack of lurchers and a beard. He may also have a family. He has an obsession with Edwardian horror and alienation, but occasionally leaves his comfort zone for explorations of contemporary darkness. His most recent works range from madness in period Virginia to tales of the monsters we ourselves become. You can find him every week on greydogtales.com, often with his dogs.

Matthew Kresal was born and raised in North Alabama though never developed a Southern accent, weirdly enough. Since 2010 he has been the write of the Sci-Fi Review column in the North Alabama arts & entertainment magazine, *The Valley Planet* (his review of Gareth Roberts' novelization of Douglas Adams' famously largely unfilmed *Doctor Who* adventure *Shada* for that magazine is quoted in its US paperback edition). He had also contributed to online Doctor Who fanzines, *The Terrible Zodin* and *Whotopia* and has been a longtime contributor to the *Doctor Who Ratings Guide* site. His essays have been featured in books including *Outside In, Celebrate Regenerate*, and various volumes in the *You And Who* series. Since 2014 he's been a regular contributor to *Warped Factor* covering topics ranging from *Doctor Who* to *Star Trek,* cult TV and everything in between. He hosts the *Stories From The Vortex* podcast which focuses on the audio dramas based of *Doctor Who* and is a reoccurring co-host on the *20mb Doctor Who Podcast.* "Shadows Of The Past" is his first piece of published fiction.

Tiffany Morris is a writer and witch from Nova Scotia. Her horror fiction, poetry and creative nonfiction have appeared in anthologies from Nosetouch Press, Hocus Pocus & Co, and Radar Productions, as well as in magazines and online. Her current projects include *Wendigo Heart*, a horror poetry chapbook, and *Athame*, a YA novel about ghosts, punk rock and Canadian witches.

Gregory L. Norris is a full-time professional writer, with work appearing in numerous short story anthologies, national magazines, novels, the occasional TV episode, and, so far, one produced feature film. A former feature writer and columnist at *SCI FI*, the official magazine of the Sci Fi Channel (before all those ridiculous Ys invaded), he once worked as a screenwriter on two episodes of Paramount's modern classic, *Star Trek: Voyager.* Two of his paranormal novels (written under his rom-de-plume, Jo Atkinson) were published by Home Shopping Network as part of their "Escape With Romance" line—the first time HSN has offered novels to their global customer base. He judged the 2012 Lambda Awards in the SF/F/H category. In 2016, Norris won Honorable Mention in the prestigious Roswell Awards in Short SF. Three times now, his short stories have notched Honorable Mentions by Ellen Datlow, and in 2016, he won Honorable Mention in the Roswell Awards in Short SF.

Trent Roman is a Canadian writer and academic interested in speculative fiction of all sorts, currently completing a dissertation on the origins of disaster fiction. He is a recipient of the Chester Macnaghten Prize in creative writing, and his short fiction has appeared from independent press venues in Canada, the US, the UK, Australia and South Africa. You can find out about new and upcoming projects on his blog, at trentroman.wordpress.com.

John McCallum Swain wrote his first story in the sixth grade. While other children were writing about kittens and summer vacations, he wrote of the annihilation of humanity by invading aliens. Progressing from longhand to typewriters to laptops, he continues to write tales ranging from graphic horror to alternate history. Swain's stories have appeared in *4pocalypse, 4rchtypes, Weird Menace Volume 2, Spawn of the Ripper,* and *Peeling Back the Skin,* as well as numerous anthologies from Thirteen O'Clock Press. His own titles include the novel *Made in the U.S.A.,* and the horror and speculative fiction collections *My Vile Bounty* and *Califhorrornia.*

Eric Turowski haunts an abandoned military base in the San Francisco Bay Area, plotting world domination with his Fiancée, Mimi, and Tiger the Cat. His novels, *Willing Servants, Inhuman Interest* and *The Hatching* are available from Booktrope.

Copyrights

Finis

Printed in Great Britain
by Amazon